Christmas Rising

by the same author

SATURDAY OF GLORY

DAVID SERAFIN

Christmas Rising

A Superintendent Bernal novel

St. Martin's Press
New York

Library of Congress Cataloging in Publication Data

Serafin, David.
   Christmas rising.

   I. Title.
PR6069.E6C5   1983   823'.914   82-17056
ISBN 0-312-13414-2

First published in Great Britain by William Collins
Sons & Co. Ltd.

First U.S. Edition

10 9 8 7 6 5 4 3 2 1

For Walt

L'histoire n'est que le tableau des crimes et des malheurs

(Voltaire, *L'Ingénu*, ch. X)

Author's Note

All but two of the characters who appear in this novel are fictitious and do not bear any resemblance to actual persons living or dead, though the action is set in the new democratic Spain around Christmas 1981. It is my earnest hope that the two real persons who do make a brief appearance, were they ever to read this book, would not find the words and acts attributed to them too far-fetched.

Madrid, April 1982   *D.S.*

CONTENTS

ADVENT: FIRST SUNDAY (29 November)

The piercing wind blowing through the Guadarrama peaks snatched at the fur-lined hoods of the linesmen's parkas as they struggled to repair the thick electric cable, which was rimed with ice. The youngest of them, Julio Prat, shinned half way up the steel-framed pylon, his commando-soled boots and insulated gloves sticking uncomfortably to the frosted metal. There he paused to pay out some of the finer cable with which they would ultimately lift the current-bearing line once it was spliced and its casing re-welded.

Through the swirling snow he caught occasional glimpses of the whitened roof of the royal palace of La Granja far below, and the lights in the windows of the village of San Ildefonso beyond. The first mountain blizzard of the winter was still smothering the weak rays of morning light, and Prat's mind dwelled longingly on the prospect of a hot coffee laced with brandy that he knew they would seek in the village as soon as they had reconnected the supply. He shouted to the foreman after he had succeeded in threading the thin cable through the pulley he had rigged just above the main insulators: 'Haul it up now! Hurry, before it freezes on to the pulley!' The foreman waved an acknowledgement, and got the four other men to pull on the line.

After a forty-minute struggle in a temperature of eight or nine degrees below zero, they completed the repair, and Julio Prat, being the last to descend the pylon, noticed the tremendous scorch-marks on the metal-frame, and then, as the light momentarily strengthened in a gap between the heavy snow-clouds, he glimpsed further down the slope a blackened patch which the strong gale had uncovered in the powdery snow—a patch that was roughly in the form of a transverse cross. While his work-mates were piling into the jeep, slapping their arms against their chests in a vain effort to regain their body heat, Prat was suddenly seized with an urge to urinate. Moving a short distance down the slope to get into the lee of the wind, he pulled off the thick gauntlet protecting his right hand, while his colleagues shouted crude warnings: 'Watch it doesn't freeze and fall off!' 'Make us some snow-balls!'

Being near the blackened patch of snow, Prat was puzzled by something he could see protruding from the upper part of it, and, having emptied his bladder with some difficulty, he scrambled through a small snowdrift to get a better view of the mysterious object. Then he shouted to the foreman, who was revving up the engine of the jeep: 'Come and see this, *jefe*! It's a burned corpse!' Reluctantly the foreman scrambled down the slope, and they looked with amazement at a completely carbonized cadaver, lying on its back on a darker frame of what appeared to be charred wood. What surprised them most was the pugilistic posture of the body, with both fists raised as though to ward off an assailant.

At a somewhat later hour that morning, some 75 km. to the south-east in the heart of the capital, Superintendent Luis Bernal was awakened from an uneasy sleep by the lively chatter of female voices. He turned to lie in a pros-trate position, and tried to ungum his eyelids, but he was at once dazzled by brightly coloured and rapidly moving reflections cast by the strong sunlight on to the peeling wallpaper and cracked ceiling of the bedroom. He shut his eyes again and groaned, but, his curiosity alerted, he rubbed his eyes once more and peered through the crack at the hinge of the wooden shutters. Already aware that he was now the sole occupant of the lumpy, kapok-filled mattress, he thought he recognized the low-pitched voice of his wife Eugenia coming from the flat roof across the well of the deep patio.

Bernal felt for his watch on the broken chair beside the bed and saw that it was only 8.10 a.m. The sun could only just have risen. What on earth was Eugenia doing out there on the communal terrace at that hour on a Sunday morning? And was that the portress with her? As he put down his wristwatch, his clumsy early-morning hands knocked an envelope to the tiled floor. He fumbled for it and making out the blue seal on its flap that read REAL CASA and the imposing coat of arms, he remembered the surprising contents of the royal missive: '*His Majesty's private secretary would deem it a privilege if Supt Bernal could find time to visit him at the Zarzuela Palace on Sunday 29 November at 11.05 a.m.*' A telephone extension number was added in ink at which he could leave word. Luis had been much perplexed by the message since it arrived by special messenger the previous evening, when he was at the Latina Theatre. As a result he had not yet replied, but intended doing so as soon as it seemed likely the King's secretary would be out of bed. What puzzled him was the day chosen for such an unusual appointment: it was almost unheard of for official business to be conducted on a Sunday, unless it was of extreme urgency. Likewise the time proposed, 11.05 a.m. Why was it so precise, yet odd? He at least had a guess at that: Mass was usually sung at 9 or 11, so it was likely that most of the royal household would be in church at that later hour, and this suggested to him that his visit was meant to be as discreet as possible. He could still not guess, however, on what business he was required, and he had heard nothing from his own superiors in the Ministry of the Interior.

'Luis!' shouted Eugenia from across the patio, interrupting his musings, 'I can see you've got up. Do get dressed and come and give us a hand. We can't manage all these heavy things on our own.'

Luis ducked below the window-ledge out of his wife's sight, and put on his slippers. As he emerged into the icy tiled corridor, he pulled his woollen dressing-gown more tightly round his shoulders. From the bathroom window, which Eugenia had left wide open, he shivered in the frosty air and, leaning across a battered rubber plant in a plastic pot that stood in the cracked bidet, he called out: 'Give me time to shave and dress, Geñita.' He saw her head disappear again amid swirls of brocaded silk, which he realized were the source of the kaleidoscopic patterns he had seen on wakening, and he caught a glimpse of two trefoil-shaped, bamboo carpet-beaters being sturdily wielded on the enormous pieces of heavy cloth that billowed dustily across the wire clotheslines.

When he thought himself sufficiently presentable to appear before the portress at that unaccustomed hour, Bernal crossed the landing to the communal roof, which was festooned with television aerials. In the far distance, in a rugged line on the north horizon, he could see the white peaks of the Sierra del Guadarrama, blurred by flurries of snow under leaden skies that contrasted strangely with the sunny, sparkling air of the Meseta on which Madrid stood.

'What are you up to, Geñita?' and then, belatedly, '*Buenos días, señora*' to the sallow-faced spinster who usually presided over the downstairs hall as though she were the janitress of a convent.

'We promised Padre Anselmo that we would clean these vestments for him on the first fine morning, Luis.' He now noticed that both the portress and his wife had scarves tied round their heads and mufflers across their noses and mouths. 'Dry-cleaning is so expensive, Luis, and in any case the Father was afraid that some of these dalmatics and chasubles would fall apart if they were stuffed into one of those machines and soaked in benzine. Some of them are over a hundred years old, you know.

Look at the gold embroidery on this orphrey.' She ran her hand lovingly over the back of a faded chasuble. 'He'll need this one for this morning, because the colour of the vestments changes today for Advent, though I don't suppose you'll remember about that; you're too wrapped up in worldly things.' The portress listened to this jibe in respectful silence, and looked disapprovingly at Bernal. 'You must help us fold a complete set,' Eugenia continued with some firmness, 'and aid us to the church and stay for Mass.'

Luis calculated he had best give in to the first part of her demand in order not to comply with the second. 'I'll help you, of course, but I have to go on duty by nine-thirty.' He smiled at the portress. 'The criminals don't go to Mass, señora, I can assure you, unless it's to steal from the offertory box.'

'And such a terrible crime wave we're having, Don Luis,' she replied, rolling her eyes dramatically above the tightly bound muffler. 'Since the poor Caudillo was taken from us, what a mess Spain has got into!' Bernal knew that this would be the commencement of a long litany of exasperation.

'Why don't they bring the *serenos* back, Luis?' interposed his wife sharply. 'They used to keep the streets safe at night.'

'They are trying out these new *vigilantes nocturnos*, Geñita, who are younger men and armed with pistols, and there are far more patrol cars. The latest crime figures are showing a reduction—'

'Reduction, nothing!' she expostulated. 'It's just propaganda of your Ministry, Luis. Everyone knows it isn't safe to go out after dark any more. Even the policemen dress like American soldiers now!'

After helping the two ladies to carry a large wickerwork hamper along the street to the sacristy of the parish church, Bernal was out of breath. He greeted Father Anselmo with as much warmth as he could muster, uneasily remembering that he hadn't confessed for years, and as the *beatas* or devout ladies and an acolyte fussed around the celebrant, helping him into the various vestments, Bernal crept out of the sacristy and sat at the back of the ornate church to get his breath. There were no more than a dozen parishioners waiting for the 9 o'clock Mass, and he thought he would rest for a while to allow time for the coffee-bars to open and get steam up in their expresso machines.

Having listened to the introit and collects, which he noted were still said in Latin in this ultra-traditional parish, and seeing that Eugenia and the portress were safely engaged in their devotions in the front pew, he slipped out of his seat and made for the door just as the epistle was beginning: '*Nox præcessit, dies autem appropinquavit. Abjiciamus ergo opera tenebrarum, et induamur arma lucis*—The night is past, and the day is at hand. Let us therefore cast off the works of darkness, and put on the armour of light.'

Out now in the Calle de Alcalá, Bernal observed that his usual breakfast haunt, Félix Pérez's bar, was closed at that hour on a Sunday, so he strolled down towards the Puerta de la Independencia. There he was struck by the appropriateness of the words of the epistle prescribed for the day, for workmen standing on a lorry which had an extended platform were placing strings of white lightbulbs in the plane trees that lined the pavements, in readiness for the Christmas illuminations, which would, he knew from previous years, bestow a bright, frosty glow on to the Calle de Alcalá.

Stepping out more jauntily now across Cibeles Square, the chief crossroads of Madrid, Bernal began to whistle a snatch of an air from *La Violetera*, one of the nostalgic songs he had heard performed the night before by Sarita Montiel, who had been the idol of his early middle age. At first his mistress, Consuelo Lozano, hadn't particularly wanted to go, alleging that La Montiel was middle-aged when she was still a teenager (Consuelo was, after all, nearly thirty years his junior), but even she had admitted that Sarita still had *duende*—that mysterious Spanish quality that lay somewhere between dæmon and charisma. Somewhat to Consuelo's jealous annoyance, Bernal had left the Latina Theatre in a romantic daze after the artiste had thrown a blood-red carnation right into his lap as the curtain fell. He was still sporting the crumpled flower, pinned to the lapel of his dogstooth tweed overcoat, as he crossed the Calle de Alcalá to one of the public phone kiosks outside the Banco de España.

He placed three *duro*-pieces on the slide above the receiver-rest and dialled the Palace number. Only two prolonged rings sounded before one *duro* was swallowed by the machine, and a pleasant female voice cooed: '*Zarzuela. Dígame.*' 'Extension Twenty-two,' replied Bernal. He thought it best not to state his business on this open line, unless the palace operator demanded it.

The extension number was buzzed and was at once picked up. 'His Majesty's personal secretary.'

'This is Bernal. I'm sorry it was too late to call you last night.'

'Will you be able to come here at eleven-o-five?'

'Yes, of course.'

'Will you come in your own car?'

'I'm afraid not, Mr Secretary.' Bernal didn't like to admit he had never learned to drive and therefore didn't possess a car.

'It would be best, then, to come by taxi to the Somontes gate, where I'll wait for you near the sentry-box.'

Bernal agreed to this arrangement, but it increased his mystification. One thing only was clear: discretion was to be the order of the day. After stopping at a news-stand to buy *El País* with its Sunday supplement, Bernal decided to stroll further up Alcalá to the Cafetería Nebraska for a breakfast of hot croissants and good coffee.

*

The taxi-driver looked at Bernal in the driving mirror with some curiosity. Why would anyone want to go out to the Zarzuela Palace at that hour on a Sunday? Or at any time, come to that, since it was never open to the public? But his fare, a short paunchy man with a small grey moustache, didn't look or speak like a tourist. In fact he faintly resembled the late Generalísimo, the taxi-man noted with some amusement. He tried to engage Bernal in conversation. 'We still need rain badly, don't we? Those few showers the other day hardly wetted the ground, and the countryside is parched.'

Bernal debated with himself the wisdom of entering into any kind of familiarity. Some of the taxi-drivers were off-duty policemen, and he knew that others of them commonly supplied the police and security organizations with information about their clients and their destinations.

'Yes, it's been a bad year everywhere in the Peninsula, and not just on the Meseta.'

The taxi was speeding up the almost empty Calle de la Princesa, where the early Mass-goers were chatting in the sunshine.

'Which gate of the palace do you want, sir?' asked the driver.

'Oh, the Somontes entrance. I'm just going to see my brother-in-law, who works in the gardens there. It's his birthday, and my wife insisted I go to take him a small present.' Bernal hoped that would satisfy the driver's curiosity about his mission.

'Will you want me to wait for you?'

'No, that won't be necessary. He'll probably invite me to the staff quarters for a *copa*.'

At the palace gate, Bernal paid off the taxi, and one of the two royal guards saluted him as he went up to the sentry-box. Inside the gate Bernal could see a small white Fiat parked at the foot of the drive.

'The King's secretary is expecting me, Sergeant.'

'Yes, sir, he's coming over now. May I see your *carnet*, sir?'

Bernal produced his official badge surmounted by the imperial eagle, and the guard saluted him once more and opened the side gate.

As the official drove him past the long white railings to the side entrance of the old palace, which had been built as a royal hunting lodge in the seventeenth century, he apologized for dragging Bernal out on a Sunday morning. 'The situation is unusual, Superintendent, and calls for unusual measures to be taken.'

They met no one as they entered the side door of the Zarzuela, and the secretary led Bernal to his private office that overlooked the rising parkland with a view of the white Guadarrama peaks beyond.

'Do sit down, Superintendent. I'll come straight to the point. His Majesty wishes particularly to have your assistance, and has arranged matters with your Minister to release you and your regular team from your ordinary duties in the Brigada Criminal for as long as will be necessary. You are, of course, free to decline this secondment, but the King, who recalls a brief meeting with you five years ago, hopes very much you will agree to enter the royal service for this most secret and urgent matter.'

Bernal was both intrigued and alarmed by this statement. 'Before I commit myself, Mr Secretary, can you tell me if it is a political matter? I realize that His Majesty does me a great honour, but I have almost always been a catcher of vulgar criminals, and have tried to keep out of affairs of state.'

'This may become an affair of state, Superintendent, but to us at present it seems no more than a criminal matter, although it has a political guise.'

'Would I still report in the usual way through my Ministry during the proposed investigation?' asked Bernal, feeling his way.

'No, you would report directly to me, or to the King in person. We'll obtain for you a special warrant, with extraordinary and plenary powers to investigate anything and anybody you think necessary.'

'What about my team? Without, of course, knowing the details of the problem as yet, it's likely I should require the assistance of my five inspectors and some access to technical and forensic aid.'

'Your warrant will extend to those you consider essential for the task, but you should make it plain at the outset that their participation would be voluntary, and very secret. Once they agreed, there'd be no backing out. Can you trust them politically, Comisario?'

'In the sense that they support the 1978 Constitution and the restored monarchy? You can never get inside people's minds, Mr Secretary, but they've always been loyal to me, even when an investigation has strayed into politics, and I'm sure there are no extremists among them.'

'Given all these guarantees, will you become the King's detective *pro tem.*, Bernal?'

'What a question for an old Republican!' joked Bernal. 'I'm sure you could find someone brighter and younger. You realize I am nearly sixty-two, and even now could apply to be passed to the *A* Reserve List?' Bernal had been thinking of retirement for some months past, if you could apply the word to the Spanish system, which simply made you *de pasivo* instead of *de activo*; no one ever actually left his profession in the eyes of the State.

'The King asked for your file, and is fully cognizant of your age and former political views. Indeed—' the official hesitated—'I think your age was a crucial factor in his choice.'

'You mean that if I make a mess of it, I could be quietly passed to the reserve?' observed Bernal.

'It's not quite that,' the secretary replied smoothly. 'He thought your age and experience would give you a natural authority among those you may have to investigate.'

Bernal lit a Kaiser and drew on it as he gazed into the park. 'Very well. Subject to my group's agreement, I'll take it on.'

The official appeared to be relieved. 'I'm so glad. His Majesty will be most pleased. He's at Mass at present, but would like to greet you when he comes out. In the meantime you may care to glance at this folder.'

The red-covered ring-file contained less than a dozen sheets on to which had been gummed a number of press-cuttings, with the date and source of each written in above.

The first cutting was dated 14 November and was annotated in red ink as being an extract from the personal column of the right-wing daily *La Corneta*. Among the other, seemingly quite normal, personal announcements of rich, retired widowers seeking hardworking, kindly and virtuous young women, and financially embarrassed but honourable ladies of a certain age advertising for discreet benefactors, the red felt pen had ringed the following item: 'Magos *Purple A.1. San Ildefonso*'. The next four sheets in the file contained a photocopy of two fairly inflammatory articles by serving officers that had appeared in the last two numbers of *El Toque*, a military weekly journal that circulated throughout all the garrisons of the armed forces. Though he had not read them, Bernal had heard about their publication, because there had been much comment and speculation about them in the ordinary newspapers. The gist of both articles was that in the six years that had passed since General Franco's death in November 1975, the attempt to turn Spain into a democratic monarchy had led to disaster on all fronts—social, political and economic—and the only solution covertly advocated was seizure of power by the military.

Glancing at the secretary, who sat looking pensively at the distant sierra, Bernal flicked over these pages without reading them in their entirety. The following page contained another clipping from the personal column published in *La Corneta* on 20 November: 'MAGOS *Blue A.1. El Pardo*'; and the next a further entry in the same journal in its issue of 27 November, only three days ago, Bernal noted: 'MAGOS *Pink A.1. Segovia*'. The rest of the file was blank.

The secretary turned back towards Bernal expectantly. 'What do you make of it, Comisario?'

'Is that all there is? Hasn't the Segunda Bis looked into it?'

'That's what is worrying us, Bernal. As I expect you know, the intelligence services have been reorganized a number of times in recent years. The SIM, the old Segunda Bis, of each of the armed forces were unified into one new joint service, the CESID, under Adolfo Suárez's second administration in 1977. It now comes under the Ministry of Defence and reports to the president and the King via that Ministry. As a result, the old SPDG, or presidential information service, set up by Admiral Carrero Blanco during General Franco's last years, was disbanded. Of course, many of the same officers serve in the new service as in the old. I drew their attention to these cryptic items in *La Corneta*, but they say they have drawn a blank so far.'

'What about the Information Brigade of my own Ministry, Interior? Have they been asked?'

'Yes, Comisario. The DGS, or DSE as it is now called, is investigating, but hasn't come up with anything.'

'In that case, I fail to see how I can help, Mr Secretary. I have only a small team, experienced, it's true, in criminal investigation, but we don't have the facilities or contacts to take on a political plot, as this shows signs of being.'

'Ah, but that's the point, Superintendent. Naturally we expect the security services to keep us informed about plots to take over the State, but here we are concerned about the references in these cryptic messages to some of the royal palaces.'

Bernal showed surprise at this. 'But it isn't clear that the palaces are meant. At least it isn't obvious to me. San Ildefonso is the name of a church in Madrid and presumably in other places, as well as being the official name of La Granja up in the sierra. And El Pardo, as well as accommodating the Franco Museum, is also the garrison of the top armoured division. In the case of a city like Segovia, it could be the barracks are meant, and not the royal castle. It isn't as if any of those palaces are lived in by the royal family.'

'No, that's perfectly true, but you must admit that it's a coincidence.'

'Have the army cipher experts worked on these mysterious messages?' asked Bernal.

'Yes, they have, and they've tried putting them through the deciphering machines, but they can't make head or tail of them. They take the view that they aren't in cipher, but rather in a code, the meaning of which depends on a predetermined equivalence known only to the senders and the recipients.'

'But what about MAGOS?' queried Bernal. 'That has the everyday meaning of the Magi, the Three Kings of Orient.'

'The experts consider that to be the call-sign to the recipients.' The Secretary turned to his desk and took a wad of papers from a dossier. 'The three colours mentioned they take to refer to different sub-groups of a secret organization, or to different phases of a proposed plan, and *A.1* could be the code-symbol of the sender.'

'And the three place-names which may refer to the royal palaces?'

'They simply don't know, Bernal. That's why we need your help.'

'Perhaps you'd explain more precisely what you have in mind, Mr Secretary.'

'It's a question of the security of the palaces, especially, of course, those used by the royal family. At this time of year, this one, the Zarzuela, is the main residence, but both Don Juan Carlos and Doña Sofía visit the main Palace of Oriente for official functions, such as receiving foreign ambassadors, civic and military representatives and so on. You wouldn't be responsible for the King and Queen's personal safety, because we have no reason to think the usual system of bodyguards is inadequate. Nevertheless, any incident of an unusual nature at the two Madrid palaces I've mentioned, or at any of the others, will fall within your power of investigation, but your role is to inform, not to act; the King will do nothing that is unconstitutional.'

'And have there been any incidents?' asked Bernal, suspecting that there was more to come.

'Only a very minor thing, so far. Late yesterday afternoon the main electric power failed here at the Zarzuela. After half an hour we got the emergency generators going, and we are still running on them until the generating company restores our mains supply.'

'Haven't you asked them what occurred?'

'Yes, of course. They attribute the failure to a snowstorm in the sierra yesterday, which caused a break somewhere below Segovia and above the village of El Pardo, which is also affected.'

'Is there any reason to suspect sabotage?'

'Not according to the electricity company. They say it's not unusual in the high sierra, but it's the first time anyone here remembers such a blackout. What has made us suspicious are the coded messages I've shown you. The effect of the power cut was to deprive us of outside communication except by one ordinary telephone line from the *centralita* or small exchange we have here. You can imagine what the importance of that would be in a national crisis.'

'As a first step, Mr Secretary, I suggest that you ask the electricity company to rig up an alternative cable from a different section of the grid, even when they've repaired the normal line. In the meantime, I shall make some inquiries myself into the causes of the power failure.'

'That's an excellent suggestion, Bernal. I'll act on it at once.'

'I shall also need a list of the King's engagements for the next month, and, if possible, the planned whereabouts of the royal family.'

'I have all that ready for you in a file, Superintendent. There is also the question of how you should report. I can arrange for a scrambler system of the latest type to be installed at the telephone in your office. Here is a list of the various cipher settings for it for each day, starting, I suggest, on Tuesday 1 December. Only the King or I will answer the scrambler telephone corresponding to this secret number.'

'Let's hope they don't cut the line!' joked Bernal, as he left.

Sitting back in the taxi that had been ordered to pick him up at the Somontes gate, Bernal wondered what he was letting himself in for in the royal service. The six years of the restored Bourbon monarchy had brought many rapid changes in the forms of government, civil service and institutions, but hardly any in personnel. He reflected, with some surprise, that the transitional period they were living through had already lasted longer than the Second Republic from its declaration on 14 April 1931 to Franco's rebellion against it on 18 July 1936, and then quite immense reforms had been attempted—far too immense, he thought—which had finally crumbled into the débris of the Civil War. Most of the recent changes in

Spanish society had taken place in the latter years of the Franco dictatorship, but had little directly to do with it: the so-called 'boom' from the mid-'fifties to the late 'sixties, when rapid industrialization and secularization had occurred. Would the *poderes fácticos*—the 'factive powers' as the press termed them: the Army, the Church, the bankers and industrialists—allow the reforms inherent in the new Constitution of 6 December 1978 to proceed? Not if any of their essential interests were affected. The present uneasy truce he attributed to a conflict of interest among the 'factive powers', whose combined resources could easily rout the political parties, Bernal thought, because they'd become no more than castrated paper tigers since the attempted coup d'état of 23 February, or '23-F' as the press had dubbed it.

FEAST OF ST ANDREW THE APOSTLE
(30 November)

On the Monday morning, Superintendent Bernal had his usual workday second breakfast in Félix Pérez's bar, having merely nibbled at the stale bread fried in home-pressed olive oil provided by his wife, and having imbibed little of the ersatz coffee she ground from toasted ilex-acorns. He was ever more appalled to see the interior of his favourite bar being tarted up by the new owners, and he observed that it was now invaded by two gleaming electronic machines labelled 'Crash Road' and 'Hell Drivers' respectively; he mourned the recent removal of the Real Madrid Football Club mementoes from the far wall and the disappearance of the red-and-white bunting that had surmounted them. Were all the old places going to be refaced in stainless steel and plastic, so that his grandson would never know the Madrid that had preserved, in the days of want, so much of its unimportant, but still appreciated, past? He decided not to linger over the Monday newspaper, the *Hoja del Lunes*, in view of the urgency of outlining the King's commission to the members of his group.

At 8.20 a.m. Bernal reached his old and rather battered office in the Gobernación building just off the Puerta del Sol, knowing that in a few months they would be leaving it for good, to be re-installed in gleaming but impersonal aluminium and smoked glass in the new building in the Chamberí quarter. The old Dirección General de Seguridad, restructured in the early part of Franco's dictatorship, had been retitled the Dirección de la Seguridad del Estado and its constituent parts reorganized. As usual when civil service reform took place, many of the existing staff were promoted, extra staff were engaged, and new buildings were to be provided. The grey-uniformed Policía Armada or armed police had been renamed the Policía Nacional and had been issued with smart brown and beige uniforms with brown berets. Bernal remembered the old tradition of the *madrileños* in giving colour nicknames to the police: the *guindillas* or 'Guinea peppers' with their red trousers when he was a small child, the *grises* or 'greys' in Franco's time, and now the *marrones*—'candied chestnuts' or 'browns'—though in a working-class bar in his native quarter of Lavapiés he had first heard them punningly, if rather lengthily, described as *cafés con porras* or 'coffees with fritters, or truncheons'.

Bernal found his senior inspector, Francisco Navarro, already at work in the outer office, as he had always found him during the previous twenty-five years.

'*Buenos días, jefe.* I'm just completing our report on that domestic homicide in Vallecas. It will be ready for you to check by mid-morning.'

'It's good of you to come in so early, Paco. We must try to clear the decks for an important case that has cropped up. But first come into the inner office and close the door.'

Bernal was fairly sure that Navarro wouldn't raise any difficulties over the royal commission. He was stolid and quietly spoken, essentially a desk man, who hardly ever strayed from the office, where he was brilliant at keeping all parts of an enquiry together on card-file and in folders of field reports. Now in his early fifties, he had served Bernal like a faithful spaniel, while bringing up a family of ten children who were firmly under the control of his vivacious wife Remedios.

'We've got a very unusual task, Paco, but it's entirely a matter of volunteering. I should emphasize that none of the group is obliged to take part.'

Navarro looked mildly surprised, but betrayed no other emotion as Bernal went on to outline the request made by the King's secretary. Bernal had not wondered much about his group's political affiliations and had certainly never inquired into them, but he was reasonably certain of Navarro's loyalty to his chief.

'I suppose we must take it on, *jefe*. It's really a great honour to be asked.'

'I'm relieved to hear you say so, Paco. It has caused me a great deal of heart-searching, I don't mind telling you. The biggest responsibility I feel is for the future careers of you all, though not for my own, at my age. After all, if the investigation should go wrong—'

'When have they ever gone wrong?' joked Navarro. 'We shall have to tread softly, that's all. In any case, we shan't be expected to act on anything we dig out, shall we? We're only being asked to provide an alternative information service.'

'I hope that's so,' said Bernal. 'How do you think the others will react? Are any of them extremists either to the right or to the left?'

'I'm sure not, *jefe*.' Navarro hesitated a little. 'There's

Elena Fernández's father, of course. He's pretty right-wing. But she's a sensible girl, intent on her professional career.'

Bernal had had Inspectora Fernández on the edge of his mind even when he was at the Zarzuela Palace the previous day, but after reflection he had also tended to take Paco's view of her.

Through the glass partition dividing them from the larger office, Bernal could see that two more of his team had reported for duty: the tall, peasant-faced Inspector Juan Lista and the ordinary-looking Inspector Carlos Miranda. 'Send Lista in next, Paco. I'd better explain it to them one by one. In the meantime, here's the royal warrant card already made out for you, and I'd like you to be looking at this file passed to me by the King's secretary.'

Juan Lista immediately expressed his willingness, even eagerness, to participate in the enquiry. His nimble mind at once pounced on the possible political ramifications. 'I hope it won't turn out to be another madcap *coup de main*, like the three or four rumoured to be brewing in the spring, *jefe*.'

'Were there as many as that, as well as the *tejerazo*?' Bernal used the popular term for the temporary take-over of the Cortes building on 23 February by Lieutenant-Colonel Antonio Tejero.

'So they say. It was just that they were planned for different dates, and none had any kind of unanimity of support.'

'Rivalry among the various saviours of the nation, do you think, Lista?'

'Possibly, *jefe*, or too much staying on the sidelines waiting to see if the bandwagon would roll.'

'You realize I shall want to keep this inquiry strictly along criminal lines? Of course politics will be involved, but we shall concern ourselves only with the legality of people's actions and report accordingly. We don't have to take sides.'

'I suppose not, *jefe*, but in this country just by doing nothing one is in a sense taking sides.'

Bernal handed Lista the appropriate royal warrant, and told him to send Miranda in.

'I'll put you in the picture first, Carlos, and then you'll have to make up your mind about your own involvement in this investigation,' said Bernal, who recalled that Miranda had been transferred to his group in 1970 and had shown that his true vocation lay in working in the field, especially in shadowing suspects. His self-effacing manner was certainly the key to his success in that, his chief thought. 'You realize that I have no wish to compel you, should you think the inquiry would jeopardise your career in any way,' Bernal added, after explaining the salient points.

'I'll go along with the others, *jefe*,' Miranda replied quietly. 'We've always sunk or swum together until now.'

'In that case, here's your special warrant, signed by the King. Paco will show you the very small amount of documentation we have on the matter. I can see Elena has arrived, but not Ángel yet.'

'It's still too early for our *señorito*, chief,' joked Miranda. 'He'll be still ungumming his eyelids from some late-night debauchery.'

As Inspectora Elena Fernández entered Bernal's office, dressed in a fetching beige suit trimmed with sable, and discreetly exuding a Parisian scent, Bernal nerved himself to face a refusal, though he already had an idea of how usefully Elena could be deployed.

'Please sit down, Elena. A difficult matter has arisen, and after hearing in outline what is proposed, you may wish to decline to take part in it. If that becomes your decision, I don't want you to feel that your career would be at all affected. Almost certainly I could get you temporarily transferred to another group, or even seconded to the local office of Interpol, for you to gain experience there.'

Elena Fernández looked grave, yet pent up, as she heard him out before she said anything. Bernal finished his account, then openly referred to the possibility of divided loyalties.

'I know that your duty to your father and his political views must be given full consideration, and I shall entirely understand if you choose to stand down.'

Elena thought about it for a short while, while Bernal somewhat nervously lit a Kaiser. Then she began to talk very rapidly. 'I was the first woman to be honoured by being appointed to the rank of Inspector in the Criminal Brigade and I want to be treated like my male colleagues in every respect, *jefe*. My ambition is to show our superiors that a woman can be just as good an investigator as a man, perhaps a better one, given certain natural advantages.' Bernal could certainly appreciate some of those, which presented themselves appealingly before him, and, as on previous occasions, he suddenly felt a strong fatherly wish to protect her vulnerability, as though she filled the place of the daughter he had never engendered.

'As for my father,' she went on firmly, 'I love him and respect his views, but he belongs to the old, hidebound, pre-Civil War Spain—' So do I, thought Bernal, but remained silent. 'And I get impatient with the older generation—of both political extremes—who refuse to see the realities of modern industrialized society. For them, as for most tourists, my place ought still to be at home seated behind a *reja* embroidering cloths, with the occasional outing to the bullfight, dressed in mantilla and high comb, to throw carnations to the matador, or an evening at the *tablao flamenco* to dance with castanets and cast fiery glances at the guitarists. I refuse to be typecast like that, and it's time they all grew up!' she ended explosively.

'I'm a member of their generation too, Elena, but I hope you don't think—'

'No, of course not, *jefe*, not for a moment. You have a special way of looking at the world, with a sort of quiet scepticism, as though you've seen it all before. And if the democratic monarchy offers the country its best chance of stability and of growing out of all those ridiculous feuds, then I'll be more monarchist than the King.'

The last member of the team arrived sheepishly late. Darkly handsome, lithe and witty, Ángel Gallardo had no doubt undertaken a tour of the nightclubs, taking mental notes for the Vice Group's files, as he always claimed; and Bernal was aware that he kept up an unrivalled knowledge of the *hampa* or demi-monde of the city. He agreed without demur to participate in the royally inspired investigation, and at once pocketed the special warrant card.

'We'd better have an immediate conference to decide how to proceed, Ángel,' said Bernal.

When he addressed his group, as informally and un-assumingly as ever, the Superintendent did not again refer to the unusual position in which they found themselves, but went straight into the case. 'We've little to go on, but two ways of proceeding suggest themselves. The electricity generating company must be approached and the power-cut that occurred yesterday at the Zarzuela Palace should be checked out. Perhaps, Lista, you would undertake that.' The tall inspector nodded his assent. 'Then we have these cryptic messages published in *La Corneta*. More of them may yet appear, and it would be useful to find out who is inserting them, and, of course, what they signify. It would hardly be sensible to make a direct approach to the editor, given his known political views. We'll have to use more undercover methods. Elena, with your background, you might see whether you could get some humble job in their offices, ideally as a filing clerk. You had some secretarial training, hadn't you, before you joined the service?'

'Yes, chief, I had, but I was no good at shorthand. How will I explain why I've left my post here in the DSE?'

'Should the question arise, as it almost certainly will, you might say you've resigned through disillusionment with all the changes that have occurred. I'll arrange for Personnel to confirm your story in case they check it back.'

He turned back to the whole group and looked graver for a moment. 'Never forget that these quite small groups of people who may want to overturn the State have immense *enchufe* or connections, often at very high levels. Don't proffer a cover-story that won't stand up to expert checking-out. If you're successful, Elena,' he went on, 'you'll have to report to Paco or to me at specified times in places we shall arrange, because it would be far too dangerous for you to come in and out of this office. I want you, Ángel, to back Elena up in any way that may occur to you both.'

'What about technical services, *jefe*?' asked Navarro.

'I've got authority to use Varga's department, and the forensic institute if need be. I'll be relying on you to co-ordinate the investigation here, as usual. Lastly, can I say that whatever is involved here is likely to happen soon, during the next month or so. I can't believe that they have chosen the call-sign MAGOS by chance, and it must refer to Epiphany, 6 January. So we haven't got much time to crack it open.'

Shortly after this conference, a telecommunications engineer arrived to install a new red telephone and scrambler equipment, and he finished by explaining its workings to Bernal and Navarro.

At 11.15 a.m. Lista phoned in from the offices of the

electricity company. 'They've located the break in the line, *jefe*, in the hills above La Granja Palace at San Ildefonso, and the repair's just been carried out. The serious bit is this, *jefe*: the linesmen have reported by radio that they discovered a charred corpse near the scene.'

'Have they called the Civil Guard in, do you know, Lista?' asked Bernal.

'I don't think so yet. I'm still here in the manager's office and I could ask him.'

'Put him on the line, Lista, if you can. It would be better if we handled this without interference from the outset.'

After some discussion with the electricity company's chief, Bernal assured him that he would take full responsibility, and asked him to contact his linesmen by radio and tell them to wait for him at San Ildefonso.

'Things are moving faster than I thought possible, Paco,' Bernal commented. 'You'd better ask Varga to come with me with his scene-of-crime team.'

'What about Dr Peláez, *jefe*? He'd surely be more useful to you than any local doctor.'

'You're quite right, Paco. You might rustle up the whole outfit: pathologist, photographer, the lot. Oh, and I expect there'll be snow up there. They say the scene is high above La Granja Palace, near that reservoir the locals call "El Mar". You could request special clothing for us and chains for the vehicles.'

Just after noon the small convoy of an imposing black Seat 134 bearing Bernal, Dr Peláez and Miranda, and the latest type of Range Rover driven by Varga and his technical team, left the city on the A.6 motorway. In under half an hour they were passing the brand-new Casino de Madrid, which had opened in October with great publicity. Bernal never ceased to be amazed at his compatriots' itch to gamble, which thirty-six years of Francoism had tried to curb. He knew that there were now more than three hundred bingo halls in Madrid alone, and he had read in *El País* that in the last financial year Hacienda—the State Treasury—had received for the first time in Spanish history more revenue from its 20 per cent tax on bingo cards than from the State Lottery.

'We're getting like Las Vegas,' he remarked to Miranda gloomily, shaking his head at the gleaming, windowless building.

'Oh, not quite, chief,' laughed his colleague. 'My wife made me take her there on her birthday, just to see what it was like, she said. I gave her five thousand pesetas to play with, and she came back after an hour on American Roulette with over a hundred thousand, while I was steadily losing on Blackjack. She wants me to change the car for a larger one with the winnings.'

As the cars swept up into the sierra, the sky became blotted out by falling snow, and they crawled the last ten km. to San Ildefonso, which had an Alpine appearance, reinforced by the large cedar of Lebanon—its branches beginning to strain under the thick white layer—which stood imposingly in front of the royal palace at the top of the one main street the village possessed.

They soon found the electricity board linesmen comfortably ensconced in the only restaurant open there in the winter months, setting to work on an enormous *fabada*—a rich stew of the large white beans for which La Granja was famous, cabbage, fat bacon and black sausage. Bernal urged his men to eat before they proceeded to make the difficult ascent to El Mar, though he begged them not to take too long over it because of the worsening weather and early dusk that would come upon them. Asking only for a *tortilla a la francesa* for himself considering that anything more than a plain omelette would do violence to his uncertain duodenum, he sniffed enviously at the bean stew being downed with gusto by the area manager and the foreman.

Sipping a Mahou beer, he asked them about the break in the power line. 'Do you think it was accidental or deliberate?'

'At first we thought it was caused by the blizzard, Superintendent, or by a strike of lightning, because such breaks are common under these conditions,' the manager replied.

'Was there any sign of lightning damage?' Bernal asked the foreman.

'Yes, sir, there was. The metal supports of the pylon bear signs of melting under great heat, and there are the typical droplets of metal, though I've seen that caused by a high voltage cable as it falls and then earths through the metal pylon. You'll realize that it's almost impossible to distinguish between the two kinds of scorch mark.'

'But did you notice anything that suggested that the break in the cable had been caused deliberately?' Bernal persisted. 'After all, the remains of a human being you found there suggest that he was up to no good. Why else would he be in such a spot in these conditions?'

'I didn't notice anything, but the arc-ing would have obliterated any signs, most likely.'

'Did you see any vehicle tracks in the snow?' Bernal went on. 'It's hardly conceivable he would have walked up there in a blizzard on his own. It's possible that an accomplice drove off after things went wrong.'

'None of us saw any tracks, Superintendent, but the snow was coming on thick when we got up there and would have covered them by then.'

'Are you sure that all your linesmen are accounted for?' Bernal asked the area manager. 'This charred corpse couldn't be that of any employee?'

'We've done a complete roll-call, Superintendent, and everyone is accounted for. The helicopter crew didn't spot the break until almost five o'clock yesterday afternoon, and this was the only team I sent in by surface.'

'We'll have to check out the villagers then,' said
Bernal, 'in case a palace gardener or a shepherd went up
there for any reason.'

By 2.0 p.m., Bernal, Dr Peláez and Miranda were
piling into the Range Rover with Varga's technical team,
while the linesmen's jeep led the way through the ghostly
landscape to the palace gates. They paused briefly for
Bernal to speak to the palace administrator, to whom he
showed the royal warrant. Then they drove slitheringly
across the grounds to the rear of the eighteenth-century
pile and took a side-track up the steep hillside. The snow
was stopping now and the pale rays of the winter sun lit
up a breathtaking view of the Versailles-like formal
gardens, dotted with classical statuary and many complex
fountains, their painted lead centrepieces whitened by the
blizzard. Bernal remembered reading of Philip V's wry
remark on returning to this, his favourite palace after a
long absence and being shown the marvels of the finest
fountains in Europe, installed by his second wife Isabella
Farnese to surprise him: 'They've cost me thirty millions
and amused me for three minutes.'

Beyond the brow of the first hill the chained vehicles
gradually reached the edge of the frozen reservoir and the
line of small pylons beyond, which were not visible from
the palace. The jeep came to a halt by some dark
markings in the snow below the spot where the cable had
been repaired, and they all zipped up their thermal clothing
before descending into the deep snow.

'Here's the place, Superintendent,' shouted the
youngest of the linesmen, Julio Prat. 'That's where I saw
the body.'

'You'd better go first, Varga, with Dr Peláez, before
we trample over everything,' said Bernal, 'though the
snow is going to make things difficult.'

'I've brought brooms and spades, *jefe*, to clear the
ground.'

'Watch out for tyre-tracks underneath, Varga. We might get impressions of them.'

Bernal asked the foreman to explain how they had effected the repair and to point out where they had positioned their vehicle. 'Would this be the obvious spot to arrange a break in the cable, if you wanted to do so deliberately?' he asked.

'It's certainly the nearest place to the track that is out of sight of the village and the palace, Superintendent.'

Julio Prat intervened. 'From the very top of the pylon I could just see the lights of the village when I climbed up early this morning, but it's very unlikely anyone would notice anything from so far away.'

'How would you arrange a deliberate break, assuming you wanted to sabotage the line?' Bernal asked the foreman.

'It would be very difficult to do without some expert knowledge, and a small amount of explosive; *goma-2* or plastic would be best.'

'And where would you position it on the pylon?'

'Assuming you didn't want to blow up the whole thing, you'd need an insulated ladder and clothing. Then you could place the charge just under the smaller insulator and run a fuse to ground level and from there to any point you wanted. A timing mechanism would be best, to allow you to get clear.'

Bernal pondered on this. 'And if you wished to be able to bring about the break in supply at a particular moment later on?'

'I see what you mean. Yes, the wire wouldn't be noticeable and you could hide the triggering device in the rocks over there. We'll have a look if you like.'

'That would be most helpful.' Bernal shouted to Varga, who was advancing cautiously with the pathologist to the darker mark of the transverse cross on the slope below the pylon: 'Watch out for a fuse wire, Varga. They may have used it to cause the explosion.'

The younger linesmen were searching the area of the rocks, while the foreman asked Bernal, 'It's not really my business, Superintendent, but why would anyone want to interrupt the supply? Could they have been Basque terrorists?'

'That's what we are here to find out. I take it you know the places this cable supplies?'

'It's a minor branch of the Segovia grid, and runs down to El Pardo and a few villages to the north-west of the capital.'

'Now you can see why I'm here,' replied Bernal enigmatically.

By this time Varga had uncovered the charred remains and the police photographer moved in to take the official photographs. Dr Peláez began to turn the cadaver over, but almost at once allowed it to settle in its former, strangely pugilistic position, with forearms stuck out and one knee raised.

'It's too risky to examine here, Bernal,' he shouted. 'It's very badly carbonized. We'll have to slide it into the fibreglass tube and take it to the lab.'

When Varga and his assistant had succeeded in doing this, the chief technician carefully examined the ground on which the cadaver had lain.

'There's a kind of wooden frame here, *jefe*, but it's almost burnt away. Can't think exactly what it was.'

Bernal descended the slope with difficulty to take a closer look.

'There are two long cross-pieces, chief,' said Varga, his heavy breath congealing whitely in the freezing air, 'and each arm is more than four metres long. It looks as though they were nailed together.' The technician gently poked one of the wooden arms with a probe. 'I can see the remains of wooden pegs at half-metre intervals.'

'Could it have been used as a primitive kind of ladder?'

asked Bernal. 'A wooden frame would have been safer than a modern metal ladder if they used it to climb the pylon.' He looked back at the relative positions of the frame and the cable-post. 'It could have been thrown here by the explosion.'

'You're almost certainly right, *jefe*. There are a few droplets of molten metal on this piece.'

'How will you get all this back to the lab? We should have brought the van, but I wanted to keep as low a profile as possible.'

'We'll wrap it in polythene sheeting and tie it to the roof-rack. There'll be room in the electricity company's van for the cadaver.'

'Search for vehicle tracks and footprints and get what impressions you can, Varga. There must have been more than one man involved.'

Bernal returned to confer with the pathologist. 'Do you think we'll be able to do an ID, Peláez?'

'There was a tremendous explosion, Bernal, quite close to the victim's head, and most of the upper part of the skull has disintegrated. It seems to have been accompanied by a powerful electrical charge, which has carbonized the whole body. Many thousands of volts it must have taken. Even the plastic dentures have melted.'

'No natural teeth, then?'

' 'Fraid not, and the hands are completely charred. I hardly think it'll be possible to take even dermal prints, but I'll have a shot at it in the lab. The clothing has all been burnt, except for the rubber soles of the boots, which show signs of melting. If this chappie was clinging to the wooden frame balanced against the pylon when the charge passed through him, his whole body must have conducted the current to the main metal structure of the pylon.'

'And the pugilistic attitude of the body?' asked Bernal.

'It's quite commonly found in corpses charred in house

fires. The posture always amazes those who haven't seen it before, and makes them think that some criminal assault was taking place at the time of the conflagration, but over the years I've seen a number of such cases. It's really caused by muscle reflex in the limbs.'

Varga now shouted up to Bernal. 'We're in luck, chief. There are some tracks underneath this layer of snow, and last night's frost has hardened them for us. The vehicle used seems to be some kind of jeep or Land-Rover, to judge by the tyre-marks, with chains on the rear wheels. I'll try to get a plaster cast of the front-wheel tracks.'

'Any sign of a fuse wire?'

'No, chief, but perhaps they didn't have a chance to fix it.'

Bernal looked anxiously at his watch and at the failing light. 'We'll have to leave soon, Varga, before it gets completely dark.'

At 5.30 p.m., while his team warmed themselves over coffee laced with brandy, Bernal thanked the electricity company's employees for their co-operation, and asked them to preserve complete silence over the affair.

After finding out from the jovial bar-proprietor that the village mayor lived a few doors away, but at that hour would probably be at Mass, celebrated in the evening at the Colegiata, Bernal led Miranda once more into the icy evening. 'It would be best if Peláez and Varga and his men returned directly to Madrid, Miranda. We'll keep the car if they can manage with the jeep.'

Dr Peláez indeed refused to be parted from his latest gruesome acquisition, and the living and the dead were crammed into the small vehicle.

When Bernal and his inspector entered the chilly church, they were immediately astonished by the baroque elegance of its Italianate frescoes and sculptures. Beyond the chancel they could glimpse the red vestments of the priest celebrating Mass at the high altar, but at first could

see no worshippers in the imposing pews, until the celebrant reached the Pax, when three people got up from
their kneeling position and stood as the priest began to
read the Communion proper for the day: '*Venite post me:
faciam vos fieri piscatores hominum* . . .' (Still unreformed by
Vatican II, Bernal noticed; his wife Eugenia would feel at
home here)—'Come ye after me; I will make you to be
fishers of men . . .' That's what he had been for nearly
forty years, thought Bernal, a fisher of men, casting his
net and examining dispassionately what it brought up,
trying not to be sick—he had never had a stomach strong
enough for the task.

As the parishioners emerged, Bernal and Miranda
waylaid the village mayor. A *serrano* of the old school, he
insisted on inviting them to his house for refreshment.
Without revealing to him their grisly find on the hillside,
Bernal explained that they were checking on security at
the royal palaces.

'Have you noticed any strangers in the village, Don
Venancio?'

'No, not really. We get hardly any visitors in the
winter.'

'Your house is a stone's throw from the palace entrance;
have you noticed any strange vehicles go in or out, such as
a Land-Rover or jeep?'

'This morning the electricity company van went in.
The palace superintendent told me they had been repairing a
cable on the upper slope. A great fight we had ten years
ago to get them to place the pylons out of sight of the
village. They would have been an eyesore.'

The three of them sat awkwardly on straight-backed
Castilian chairs with uncomfortable slung leather seats,
sipping the *vinillo* he had courteously offered them from a
small cask, and warming their chilled limbs in front of a
log fire.

'Do any shepherds or goatherds go up into the sierra

above the palace?' asked Bernal.

'Not any more. Years ago we had a flock of sheep up there in summer, but the farming has declined in recent times. The climate's against it, and the younger men have left for the city.'

'Tell me, if you would, about the palace gates. Are they normally shut at dusk?'

'Yes, that's so. The superintendent of the palace will confirm it. It's opened again at nine a.m.'

'But is there any other way an entry could be made into the grounds?'

'Only by the servants' gate, at the back of the church. The lane comes out behind my house. That is not usually locked until eleven p.m. Come to think of it, yesterday morning I thought I heard a car with chains coming down the lane as I was getting up. Soon after first light it was, but I didn't chance to look out.'

'We'll take it up with the palace servants,' said Bernal smoothly. 'Do you remember anything else?'

'Yesterday I was awakened by some noise, something like a deep vibration through the house. I thought it was thunder, and there was a storm later on when the snow started. I mentioned it to my wife, but she couldn't have heard it. She's been very deaf of late.'

As they made their way back to the inn, treading gingerly on the crisp snow, Bernal mentioned a possible timing to Miranda. 'It looks as though a vehicle with chains on the wheels went up to El Mar before dawn yesterday to install the explosive device. Soon afterwards, things went wrong, and one man was killed, fulminated by the electrical charge. His accomplice or accomplices then made their getaway before the village was up.'

'Perhaps the vehicle would have been a familiar sight at that hour?'

'That's possible. I'd like you to stay here overnight, Miranda. I'm sure they'll have a room for you at the *fonda.* Mix with the locals in the bar and find out what you can. Try and get the feel of the place, their political views, any local resentments, that sort of thing. You'd better say you're an inspector of buildings, come to see what work is required at the palace.'

'OK, chief. Do you think the mayor or the palace super-intendent will talk about our visit?'

'I don't think so; they seem discreet enough. Report in tomorrow before lunch. Our driver will take me back to town now to see what Varga has come up with.'

FEAST OF ST BIBIANA (2 December)

Quite out of breath, Bernal was shaking the water off his commando-style raincoat in the sacristy of his parish church, after his wife had once more impressed him into porterage of a hamper of religious vestments.

'We simply had to bring the white ones, Luis. Father Anselmo will need them for Thursday, for St Francis Xavier. What a good job the portress helped me to get them cleaned yesterday afternoon, before this rain came. Not that we don't need the blessed rain: I don't have to tell you how half the livestock in the country is dying for lack of it. And we've made so many special prayers of inter-cession all this autumn. See how they're being answered!'

A little too enthusiastically, perhaps, thought Luis, who was busy planning a hasty withdrawal. As soon as Mass was under way and the priest reached the gradual: '*Fluminis impetus lætificat civitatem Dei*—The stream of the river makes the city of God joyful,' Bernal crept out into the street where conditions were distinctly joyless. He dived into Félix Pérez's bar where he ordered a large break-fast coffee and a croissant, and, huddled with other shel-terers from the storm in that special, dank smell of dampened dust and dripping raincoats, he watched the rainwater stream across the Calle de Alcalá.

He glanced down surreptitiously at his half-sodden copy of *La Corneta*. The *quiosquero* had been giving him strange looks for the past few days when he had started asking for an extreme right-wing newspaper instead of the liberal—or almost libertarian—*El País*, which even uniformed policemen read in public nowadays. How ironical it was, thought Bernal, that only four years earlier, at the time of the first democratic elections, you could get beaten up just for carrying a copy of *El País* or *Diario 16* in this mainly right-wing district, and now they looked at you askance for doing the opposite.

He checked the personal column, but found no further cryptic messages. He noted, however, the bitter editorial about the continuing arrest of the officers allegedly implicated in the failed coup d'état, and the lightly veiled antimonarchist sentiments in the suggestion that a third Spanish Republic need not be a Marxist one. The King had stuck his neck out in defending the new democratic constitution, and it was clear that the Old Guard weren't going to forgive him in a hurry.

When Bernal got to the office, Paco Navarro presented him with Dr Peláez's detailed forensic report on the charred remains found at La Granja. The cause of death was given as electrocution, which had been at once succeeded by an explosion that had badly damaged the cranium. The cadaver was that of a white male Caucasian, aged 35 to 40, 1.68-70 m. tall and 63-65 kilos in weight. No distinguishing marks could be ascertained owing to the severe post-mortem charring. Identification would be virtually impossible: the limbs were so badly damaged that not even dermal fingerprints could be obtained. There was no sign of any earlier surgical intervention, or, indeed, of bodily illness. The hair had probably been dark brown or black, the eyes brown.

'It's a poor do, Paco,' sighed Bernal. 'We'll not get an ID from this.'

'It seems not, *jefe*, though Dr Peláez told me on the phone that he's going to try, as a long shot, comparative tomography of the facial sinuses.'

'Comparative tomography? That's a new one on me. Did he say what it consists of?'

'It's some way of X-raying the planes of the maxillary sinus cavities.'

'No doubt he'll let us into the secret in due course. Has Varga reported?'

'Yes, chief, and it's just as bad. The tracks of the jeep-tyre will only be of use if we find the vehicle to match them up with. The tyres are Michelin X, and you can guess how many million are in use throughout the country.'

'And the explosion?' queried Bernal. 'Was it the result of a lightning-strike, or was it induced?'

'Definitely induced, *jefe*. He's found traces of *goma-2* plastic explosive, of a type commonly used in terrorist attacks. The trouble is, it's quite often stolen from quarries and mines, so the chances of tracking it to source are minimal.'

'Was there any trace of a cable or fuse, do you know?'

'Varga found none. He suggests that they probably hadn't got around to fixing it when the explosion occurred prematurely.'

'Well, at least I can report to the King's secretary that the electricity supply was being deliberately interfered with, although we can't tell when they intended to interrupt it.'

'Before you ring him, *jefe*, you might like to look at this map of the grid which Lista brought in yesterday from the generating company. It shows each place supplied by the power line, including El Pardo and the Zarzuela Palace.'

'I wonder if they've fixed up an alternative supply from

a different part of the grid yet. There may be further attempts.'

Bernal used the red scrambler telephone for the first time and his call was at once answered by the royal secretary, to whom he began to impart the latest news.

'I'm glad to be able to tell you, Bernal, that the Company has begun to fix up an alternative cable to which we can switch in an emergency. I've also had our own generator overhauled.'

'What about the telephone lines?' asked Bernal. 'Wouldn't it be wise to ask the Telefónica to do the same?'

'That's an excellent suggestion, Superintendent, especially in view of what occurred at the Palacio de Oriente this morning.'

A warning note sounded in Bernal's brain. 'What has happened at the main palace?'

'The telephone went out of action at about eight-thirty a.m., owing to flooding in the underground cable. I'm sure it was just because of the very heavy rain.'

'I'd better get down there at once,' said Bernal. 'Just to be on the safe side.'

'That's most kind of you, but I think it was probably a coincidence.'

'I don't believe in coincidences in cases like this,' replied Bernal.

After putting down the red telephone, Bernal turned to Navarro. 'Is Lista available?'

'Yes, chief, he's with Varga in the lab.'

'Tell him to order a car. We're going to the Oriente Palace.'

The rain still lashed the Puerta del Sol as they set out, and the few pedestrians in the Calle del Arenal scurried into the shop doorways to avoid being splashed by the passing vehicles.

'Take us to the Prince's Gate, in the Calle de Bailén,'

c.]

Bernal instructed the driver. The smartly uniformed members of the King's Guard saluted from their sentry-box as the Seat 134 passed over the cobbled forecourt and under the arch to the right of the sumptuous façade of Sepúlveda granite, recently cleaned for the restored monarchy. Bernal noticed that it took on a pinkish tinge where it was wetted by the rain, which contrasted more strongly with the facings of white Colmenar stone. The palace doorkeeper examined Bernal's royal warrant, saluted politely, and explained the whereabouts of the *centralita* or internal telephone exchange. The black limousine swept across the elegantly proportioned inner palace yard and deposited Bernal and Lista under the colonnade. They were fortunate in finding the two engineers from the Compañía Telefónica still there, talking to the female operator.

'We're from Security,' Bernal explained, showing them his DSE badge. 'Could you explain to us how the break in the telephone line occurred?'

'There was a very heavy shower at eight a.m.,' said the older of the repair men, 'and it put a number of lines out of action where the drains couldn't cope. The water was pouring out of the Plaze de Oriente across Bailén when we got here, and we found that it was flooding the junction-box.'

'Does the cable come along the Calle de Bailén on the palace side of the street?' asked Bernal.

'No, sir, it runs from the Calle de San Quintín on the north side of the square, under Bailén, and then to the box which is accessible from the ramp that leads down to the Sabatini Gardens, below the north side of the palace.'

'Will you show us the place?' asked Bernal.

Lista and Bernal examined the junction-box with care. 'The security is poor, isn't it?' Bernal remarked to the two engineers. 'This lock is old-fashioned and anyone could force open the metal door and cut the line.'

'Ah, but they'd have to know it was there, wouldn't they? And in any case the guards would see them coming down the ramp.'

'Was there any sign of tampering?' asked Bernal.

'No, none at all. Though it's true that this particular box has never flooded like this before, as far as our foreman can remember. But it was a cloudburst more than a shower.'

Bernal was not satisfied. 'We'd better talk to the palace clerk of works, Lista. We'll ask him to explain the layout of the cables.'

This official proved most accommodating, and was actually able to produce copies of the original architectural plans drawn up by Filippo Juvara in 1735 with the changes made by Saccheti the builder, together with the plans of the nineteenth-century alterations and additions. 'Here you can see the arrangement of the telephone cable and the electricity supply line installed last century, Superintendent. Of course the equipment was renewed in the nineteen-thirties, and again more recently.'

'Have you a plan of the drainage system of the Plaza de Oriente and the Calle de Bailén?' asked Bernal.

'Ah, that's a little more difficult, because it comes under the ægis of the Ayuntamiento, but we may have a copy of the city council's map of the sewers in the archive. I'll just send my assistant to search.'

When the clerk returned, Bernal asked him whether the only telecommunication between the palace and the outside world was the telephone cable.

'As far as the civil household is concerned, there is only that arrangement, but we have six lines.'

'Unfortunately they all run through the same cable,' Bernal commented.

'The military household has radio communication as well, with the aerial mounted on the roof, so we were not altogether cut off,' smiled the clerk.

'Nevertheless the security of the cable is not good,' Bernal pointed out.

The young assistant now returned with a carton tube, from which the clerk drew out a rather yellowed plan. 'This should give us the information. Yes, here you can see the surface drains in the square outside. Of course the gardens should absorb a good deal, but it hasn't rained for so long until today that the earth must have been hardened and impermeable. You can see that the surface drains descend to a main storm drain under the middle of Bailén, which has its outfall below the ramp leading to where the royal mews once stood, and thence under the Campo del Moro gardens to a pipe leading down to the River Manzanares. We've never had problems before this.'

'Then why should there have been flooding today?' queried Bernal.

'It's possible that the surface drains were obstructed by fallen leaves or dirt,' said the clerk tentatively.

'Let's go and check on your theory,' said Bernal. 'We can ask the royal guards if they observed anything at the time of the heavy shower.'

The sergeant-at-arms recalled the two guards who had been on early morning duty from the guard-room for Bernal to question them. They both remembered seeing a wide stream of flood-water crossing the street from the square, and noticed how the wheels of the passing vehicles caused waves to advance towards the palace forecourt, whence the water was diverted down the ramp leading to the gardens before it could reach the sentry-box where they stood.

'Let's go across and examine the surface drains,' Bernal said to the clerk of works. 'The rain has eased off now.'

The finely trimmed trees in the square appeared to be recovering from their regular annual battering on 20

November, when thousands of Francoists foregathered to wave national flags and listen to speeches from their leaders. Among the forty-four statues of former Spanish monarchs, there stood out most impressively Pietro Tacca's equestrian bronze of Philip IV, based on a drawing by Velázquez; the equilibrium of its 18,000 lbs of bronze had been worked out by Galileo, and the steed with such an august pedigree astonished the visitor by standing on one rear hoof. In all but two of the thirty-six surface drains positioned under the pavement edges, Bernal and the clerk of works discovered that old bricks had been packed in to block the outflow of rainwater.

'You see, my suspicions were correct,' Bernal expostulated. 'These bricks can't have floated into the drains. It's been done deliberately.'

'But how could the perpetators know what the effect of the flooding would be?' objected the clerk. 'Even I couldn't know for sure.'

'Doesn't the electric cable run in near that same point?'

'Yes, but it wasn't affected, as it happened.'

'I agree the drains were blocked deliberately, *jefe*,' Lista chipped in, 'but how would they know when it was going to rain? With the drought we've been having, they could hardly expect it.'

'But you're both missing the point,' exclaimed Bernal. 'Imagine you wish to cut the telephone and electric cables leading to the palace, but you have no access to the plans and no way of knowing where the underground lines enter from the street. You provoke a flood to see if they are affected. The winter rains are over a month late, so you have to be patient. The daily watering of the streets by the *regadores* is quite insufficient to bring about what you want. You watch the weather forecasts each night, and when a rain-bearing depression is approaching, you put your plan into effect.' Bernal glanced nonchalantly around at the rooftops of the houses facing the square.

'They've surely seen the telephone engineers arrive and go down to the junction-box in the ramp, and they're probably observing us at this very moment.'

The clerk looked about him uneasily. 'I'd better get back and telephone the Ayuntamiento to send their men to clear out these drains, Superintendent.'

'A good idea. We'll all go back. Then we'll leave in the car, Lista, and I'll drop you out of sight of the palace and this square, near the Opera House will do; then you can return on foot and question all the *conserjes* in the houses that provide vantage-points, and find out if they have noticed anything unusual: any new tenants, or workmen going up to the roof.'

Just after midday, Bernal used the red telephone for a second time to report to the King's secretary and to urge him to improve the telecommunications at the Oriente Palace, preferably by having a second cable connected from the Paseo de la Virgen del Puerto below the palace gardens.

He then asked Navarro about Inspectora Fernández's assignment.

'Elena's managed to report via Ángel, chief. He says she lied unashamedly to her father and tried the cover-story out on him. He swallowed it hook, line and sinker, and even rang the proprietor of *La Corneta*, who's a buddy of his, and got her a job in the filing room. She started there this morning. She points out that she's only in the archive section, which gravely limits her access to the most important areas.'

'At least she's in,' said Bernal. 'That's an excellent start. She's got terrific initiative, hasn't she?'

'And she's cool, *jefe*, ice-cool when the chips are down.'

'What about Ángel, what's he up to?'

'He's making pals with some of the military in the bars near the main barracks, and says he's keeping his ear to the ground. He's also acting as our line of communication with Elena.'

'Let's hope that it's only his ear that gets to the ground, and that he doesn't go two hundred per cent over the limit on his expense sheet as he did last month.'

'He said it went on his informers, who are getting greedier in view of the fourteen per cent inflation rate.'

'Thank goodness the royal household's paying for this investigation,' said Bernal. 'They'll have no idea how cheap we are, compared with the security services.'

After a light lunch with Navarro in Los Motivos restaurant in the Calle de Echegaray, Bernal took a taxi to the Justicia quarter, where he had a second apartment which he had kept secret from his family and friends. He was surprised not to find his mistress Consuelo already there, since she worked in a bank nearby and would normally have finished for the day by 3.0 p.m. He switched on the Hitachi music centre and inserted his latest acquisition—a cassette of Giordano's *Andrea Chénier* sung by Plácido Domingo. When he went into the kitchen to make some coffee he discovered a note written in thick green ink in Consuelo's hand: *'Luchi, have gone to doctor's. Don't be alarmed. It's nothing serious. Conchi.'*

'Luchi.' Only she called him that; it sounded virile and exciting, she said. His wife tended to call him Luisito when in good humour, just as his mother had done, or plain Luis when in ill. His younger son Diego, the wilder one, at present on a field course in the Guadalquivir estuary, tended not to call him anything, while his married elder son, Santiago, his mother's pet, always so formal and well-behaved, never called him other than Papá. Behind his back, Bernal knew, his men referred to him as 'El Caudillo—the Little Chief', because of his faint resemblance to the late Generalísimo, but they never dared more than *jefe* to his face. Seven forms of address, and only one could touch his heart.

He lay, sipping his coffee, on the luxurious silk-covered divan (if only Eugenia had Consuelo's knack as a decorator!), and let his mind drift on the soaring notes of the famous Spanish tenor, who, of all modern singers Bernal had heard, was closest in warmth and richness of texture to Caruso, with the possible exception of Bruno Prevedi. As he drifted into his siesta sleep, he wondered vaguely why Consuelo hadn't just gone to a chemist's if it was a touch of 'flu; they dispensed antibiotics as merrily as if they were selling sweets.

Before returning to the office that afternoon, Bernal rang his childhood friend Inspector Ibáñez of Central Records, and invited him to take *merienda* with him at 5.30 in the Cervecería Alemana in the Plaza de Santa Ana.

'It must be a political case, Luis, or you wouldn't have invited me here.'

'At least we won't be overheard, Esteban. I want to pick your brains, as usual.'

'I've always said to myself, "That's how Luisito has got on; that's why he's a *superpolicía*; always picking other people's brains!" Your mother, may she rest in peace, always said you'd go to the top. Do you remember how she used to drive the prostitutes out of that bar she bought with the indemnity money after your father was killed in the 1936 riots? "*¡Fuera de aquí, pelanduscas!*" she used to shout at them, "*¡Cacatúas p'al gato!*" She had a terrific line in insults.'

'She learned it all there. The bar hardened her.'

Bernal took out a copy of the cryptic messages from the personal column of *La Corneta* and handed it across the marble-topped table to Ibáñez, as they sipped draught beer from the large white jars. The Inspector's eyes lit up and they devoured the small print with relish.

'MAGOS—h'm, looks like an acronym, don't you think? Don't remember seeing it in the files. It probably stands for *Movimiento* something or other. *Autonomista*, perhaps? *Autoritario*? It'll be along those lines. There've been so many, Luis, you'd hardly credit it.'

'That's an interesting notion, Esteban. The army code-experts thought it was the call-sign. I thought it might point to the date of some proposed action: 6 January, Day of the Magi.'

'It could be that too, Luis, but that would imply the organization existed just for that one action. The fact it's printed in upper-case letters suggests an acronym. Can't guess at the − GOS − depends on the context. Which newspaper are these from?'

'*La Corneta.*'

'Ah, the old soldiers! Plenty of clandestine movements there. We've got a special section in Records on all that, run by the counter-espionage chaps. I'll see what my computer terminal will come up with. You know we're all computerized now? It's amazing what I can call up on my little screen when no one's about.'

'What do you make of the places mentioned, Esteban?'

'*San Ildefonso, El Pardo, Segovia*: all royal residences, weren't they? But none of them are used these days.' Ibáñez pondered over the names. 'El Pardo is the headquarters of the crack armoured division, of course, but Segovia only has a regular garrison, and there's nothing much at La Granja that I know of. I'll think about it some more.'

'And the colours mentioned after "*A.1*" in each message: Purple, Blue and Pink?'

'They could refer to groups of these chappies who are plotting something. I suppose there's no doubt it's another conspiracy? Haven't the CESID or the secret police come up with anything?'

'Nothing at all, Esteban. That's the disturbing thing.'

'Nearly everybody's up to something, as usual, mark my words, Luis. If I come across any clue in the central files, I'll give you a ring.'

'But arrange to meet me over a drink like this, casually, will you?'

'I get it—all very hush-hush. Have another *jarra* for old time's sake, Luis?'

'No, thanks. I'd better keep a clear head.'

Back in the office, Bernal found an excited Dr Peláez awaiting him.

'I've got a reconstruction for you, Bernal. It's only a guess at what that charred fellow looked like in life, but I followed the method pioneered by Glaister and Brash of building up on the basis of the X-ray photograph of the skull. Now if you could bring me actual photographs of the man you suspect of having ended up as this corpse, I could try with the photographer to fit one over the other. In the meantime, this reconstruction may be of some help.'

Bernal examined the drawing with a critical eye. 'It's not bad—as good as the old Identikit pictures.'

'More than that: I tried tomography and got a positive result.'

'You'd better explain it to me.'

'It's simple, really. I took X-ray photographs of the facial sinuses from various angles to see if there was any abnormality. It became clear that the deceased had at some time received treatment for severe sinusitis, or possibly for the removal of a benign sinus tumour.' He pinned some X-ray plates to the glass partition in Bernal's office and turned the head of a desk-lamp to shine from behind them in the outer office. 'There you are: see the distorted shape of the left maxillary sinus cavity? It's almost square, instead of being a narrow curve.'

'But how do we use this information?' asked Bernal.

'You can go to the oto-rhino-laryngologists, of course,— the ear, nose and throat specialists—and see if they can match these plates with any of their patients, especially those they've treated during the last couple of years.'

Bernal's interest grew. 'You mean they might recognize the dead man just from an X-ray?'

'Of course! Just like dentists can recognize their patients from a photograph of the dentition. If the *otorrino* is worth his salt, he'll spot him all right!'

Soon after Dr Peláez breezed out, Miranda arrived from La Granja with his report.

'The villagers are predominantly old, now, *jefe*, and many of their children have come to the city to work or study. The remaining agriculture seems to leave them reasonably well off, but that's partly because of tourism in the summer months. I didn't notice any extreme political views, but they were hardly likely to reveal their opinions to a stranger whom they thought was an official of the Patrimonio Nacional. I spent a lot of the time playing cards in the bar; there's no beating them at *mus*, I can tell you. I lost a packet.'

'It will hardly qualify as expenses, Miranda,' said Bernal. 'Had they noticed any strangers in the vicinity?'

'Some chaps in a military jeep, they said, early on Sunday morning. A farmer who had done the milking noticed it going up the hill towards the palace. He didn't manage to see the regimental badge on the vehicle's wings; it was still dark at the time. So I went up to the palace and questioned the servants. One of them thought he heard a car enter by the side gate before dawn, but none of them heard or saw it leave.'

'What about the side gate? Isn't it locked at night?'

'Yes, but it's opened in time for prime in the Colegiata at seven a.m., almost an hour before dawn. Most of them went to that office, so the jeep probably slipped out while they were at their devotions.'

'Do they remember seeing army vehicles in the area before now?' asked Bernal.

'I questioned them about that, but they say they only

see the Guardia Civil on most days, and they know the sergeant and corporal on that patrol.'

'Perhaps we should conclude that this was an isolated incident up there, but I'm still concerned about the security of that cable. The people responsible may well attempt a break somewhere else along its length. By tomorrow the Zarzuela Palace should have the added protection of the alternative supply, but it would be worth keeping a watch on that branch of the Segovia grid if only we had the manpower,' sighed Bernal. 'Although then we should draw too much attention to the operation.'

Navarro intervened. 'Might it not be best to follow up Dr Peláez's X-rays, *jefe*? I've been looking in the telephone directory, and there aren't very many oto-rhino-laryngologists.'

'You're right, Paco. That's the most promising line. It could lead us straight to them. When Lista comes in, we can split up the list into sections and we'll share out the work. How many copies of the X-ray photos did Peláez leave?'

'Three of the reconstruction, chief, and five X-rays, though they're not all taken from the same angle.'

'Never mind. If the shape of the deformed sinus is as individual as he claims, any one of them should do. Has Ángel rung in this evening? He could do some of the leg-work.'

'Yes, chief, and he says he's hoping to be taken on as a van-driver at *La Corneta*. It's the best he's been able to do there, but it might have advantages for us in allowing him to pass messages more easily between Elena and the office.'

'You're right. He'd better go ahead and take the job. Ask him to try and get a copy of the delivery list. The really useful thing would be to get hold of the list of sub-scribers—those who get it sent to them by post each day. Elena might manage that.'

At 7.0 p.m. Lista reported back. 'I've questioned all the *conserjes* in all the houses in the Calles de San Quintíin and Pavía which face the Oriente Palace. Some of them have automatic porters now, more's the pity, so I had to chat up some of the housewives; I concentrated on the ones who live on the attic floors.'

'Did any strangers go up on to the roof or to a balcony overlooking the square in the course of the morning?' asked Bernal.

'None of them could recall it, but I suspected one of the portresses of lying about it, so I went up to the tenant of the top floor front in that house, and she told me that she glimpsed two men in blue overalls on the flat roof opposite her kitchen window. She assumed they were from the television rental firm seeing to the aerials, but later she thought it odd one of them was looking across the square with binoculars.'

'What time was that?' asked Bernal.

'She first saw them a little after eight-thirty, when they were sheltering under the eaves from the downpour. They were still there at nine-thirty when she went out to get the bread.'

'That's when you and I were with the clerk of works,' exclaimed Bernal. 'So my initial theory must have been correct: they were observing the effects of blocking the storm drains and they must have seen the telephone van arrive, as well as our later inspection of the square. They probably slipped away after that, before you got to that house.'

'I went back to the portress and cross-questioned her. She absolutely denies having seen them, claiming she went to the market around that time, despite the very heavy rain. I'm sure she was handsomely paid to hold her tongue.'

'We could bring her in and loosen it for her,' said Navarro.

'But if she's determined to be uncooperative, or is even sympathetic to whatever cause those men in overalls represent,' said Bernal, 'she'll never agree to try and identify them.'

Later that night, as he turned up his collar at the corner of the Puerta del Sol and made his way along the Carrera de San Jerónimo, Bernal realized how little he had progressed. Before leaving the office, he had discussed the incident of the mysterious rooftop observers in the Plaza de Oriente with the royal secretary on the scrambler phone, and had persuaded the latter to agree to order an extra telephone cable to the main palace by a different route. The secretary also promised to send over the latest CESID reports on state security.

After stopping to buy two packets of Kaiser cigarettes, Bernal's eyes were caught by the large antique lanterns outside Lhardy, the famous old pâtisserie and restaurant, and turned into the welcoming warmth for a quiet restorative. He poured himself a glass of white port from the silver container and chose a shrimp vol-au-vent from the imposing German-silver and crystal stand, which had little doors that lifted to supply hot *pinchos* and *tapas* of various kinds. What a civilized sense of 'self-service' Monsieur Lhardy had possessed, mused Bernal, and how he would have hated the modern equivalent: the automated and plasticized cafeterias that now dominated modern Madrid. As he settled with the *dependiente* at the door, he thought it must be the last place in the world where they took your word for what you had consumed.

When he got home, he found the flat in darkness, apart from a glow of warm light coming from a cupboard in the dining-room, which his wife had converted into an oratory dedicated to Our Lady of the Sorrows. Without disturbing her, he turned on the television set in time to catch the *Telediario*, which was mainly devoted to the events in Poland. Soon Eugenia emerged, and said brusquely: 'I'll just warm up some carrot stew for you. Do you want some of the whiting left over from lunch?'

'No, just a little of the stew,' he assured her.

'Well, get the wine out of the cupboard and help yourself, but mind you set out the cutlery.'

When she returned with the lukewarm stew and embarked on a protracted grace, he half-heartedly muttered the responses while keeping half an eye on the television news bulletin. He was suddenly riveted by a report on a lieutenant-general who was shown descending the steps of an army helicopter to inspect a line of troops: '*The new chief of the Central Artillery Division, Lieutenant-General Emilio Baltasar, took over his command today. In a speech to his men, he emphasized those duties of obedience and loyalty essential in every soldier, and praised the Division's unfailing devotion to the late Generalísimo during forty glorious years—*'

Baltasar! The surname resounded in Bernal's head. Why hadn't he thought of it before? The third of the Magi, the black king of Orient, who brought myrrh to the Infant Christ for his burial. Tomorrow he would have him investigated, discreetly of course.

COMMEMORATION OF ST BARBARA
(4 December)

Footsore from his morning's perambulations, Bernal emerged from the Concepción Clinic, and realized he had come to the end of his section of the list of ear, nose and throat consultants. From a call-box in the Plaza de Cristo Rey he phoned in to Navarro to see if any other member of his team had obtained more success in identifying the charred body found at La Granja.

'There's been no luck so far, *jefe*,' Navarro told him, 'but Elena's sent us a report; Ángel has just rung me. She managed first thing this morning to get a look at the personal column files, having made friends with the girl who takes the adverts in at the desk. She found nothing filed under MAGOS, but she didn't get to see the invoice book. She says that when she has a chance, she'll look up the entries dated a few days prior to the publication of each cryptic message and see who was charged for the insertion.'

'Good, let's hope she comes up with something soon. By the way, why didn't you put the Clínica Angloamericana on my list? It's just round the corner from where I am.'

'There was no ENT consultant listed there, *jefe*. I thought they probably called in specialists as required.'

'I might as well check while I'm up here in Vallehermoso, Paco. I'll see you in an hour.'

In the low red-brick building tucked discreetly in a wooden hollow, Bernal asked the white-uniformed receptionist whether the clinic administrator was available, and handed her his official visiting card.

'I'll just see if he's free, Comisario,' she answered, with a trace of an American or English accent, he wasn't sure which. She soon returned and ushered him into a pleasant office.

'It's most good of you to see me without an appointment, Doctor—uh—'

'Dr Gregory. I'm the hospital administrator, Comisario,' replied the tall blond man, with a foreign accent that was certainly English, thought Bernal, to judge by the aspiration of plosives and the diphthongized o's in his otherwise fluent Castilian.

'It's simply to find out if you have an oto-rhino-laryngologist on the staff. We're concerned to identify the victim of an accident.'

'Yes, we do, but he is also a dermatologist. A very clever chap who's a fellow-countryman of yours, Dr Galiano.'

'Does he have his office here?'

'Oh yes, he is here most days. Actually he's seeing one of our patients at this moment. I'll send for him.'

'Please allow him to finish his rounds. I don't want to interrupt your routine.'

'Not at all. I'm sure he'll be glad to help.'

Dr Galiano shook hands with Bernal, who came at once to the matter in hand, and produced the sinus X-ray taken by the police pathologist.

'Does this bring to mind any patient of yours, Doctor? Perhaps one whom you've treated during the past year or two?'

'It looks familiar, certainly. Do you mind if I look in my files?'

After a few moments Dr Galiano returned with a very large brown envelope, from which he extracted some X-ray plates. After pinning them up on an illuminated panel, he placed the plate taken by Peláez alongside them.

'You see? I thought it looked familiar. Here's one taken before I operated on the left maxillary sinus. You can see the dark area of the tumour clearly, and here's one taken subsequently.'

Bernal could see that the later X-ray certainly corresponded closely to Peláez's, and the outline of the skull seemed very similar, but he wasn't sure how much they normally differed.

'You are quite sure, Doctor?'

'Quite sure. I'd always recognize my own handiwork.'

'Who was the patient you treated?'

'A nice young fellow, of good family, you know; his father's very well off and a member of the nobility. They certainly paid on the nail, which isn't always one's experience, eh? Here's his file-card: José Antonio Lebrija Russell de Villafranca, aged 33 when I did the operation. He'd had upper respiratory problems for some time, and the pain grew intense with the formation of the tumour, naturally. But he had no trouble afterwards. One of my few successes.' He laughed. 'But what's happened to him? How have the police come by this X-ray?'

'It's a question of identification of a victim of an accident, who was severely burned, I'm afraid. Here's the pathologist's reconstruction of the face.'

'My God, killed in a car crash, I suppose. This drawing's pretty good, you know. Dr Peláez's work, presumably.' Bernal nodded. 'You know Lebrija's father is one of the grandees of Spain? The Marqués de la Estrella. It's an Anglo-Spanish family. José Antonio was the youngest son, I believe.'

'Do you know what he did for a living?' asked Bernal.

'He was an artillery instructor, and spent much of his time in the open air. That aggravated his sinus problems, especially in the winter months. What a shock it will be for the family.'

'I'd be grateful if you'd not mention this matter to anyone for the moment,' said Bernal. 'Naturally our pathologist will want to check these X-ray plates if you'd be so good as to lend them to me.'

'Of course you can take them. Please give Peláez my best regards; we were fellow students, you know. And you can rely on my absolute discretion in the matter, Superintendent.'

Bernal took a taxi back to the Gobernación building in the Puerta del Sol, and told Navarro to get Peláez on the phone. 'Call Lista and Miranda in; I think we've got an ID. Find out what you can about the Marqués de la Estrella and his family after that, Paco, but be discreet about it.'

On hearing of the likely identification, Dr Peláez opted to come up to the main police photographic laboratory. 'Their equipment is better than mine, Bernal, and we'll probably need to use the special enlargers. You must try to get hold of a good full-face photograph of the chap you think it is.'

Before Peláez arrived, Navarro had contacted Lista and sent him to the Documento Nacional de Identidad for the official *carnet* photograph of José Antonio Lebrija Russell. Bernal decided to watch Peláez and the chief photographer at work.

'This official photo of the supposed deceased isn't quite good enough for the superimposition method, Bernal,' said Peláez. 'You'll have to get us better ones, a portrait if possible, or failing that a selection of snapshots for us to choose from.'

Nevertheless they succeeded in superimposing the post-mortem X-ray of the head over the second of Dr Galiano's X-rays taken in life and got a perfect match. 'Galiano's right,' called Peláez. 'There can be no doubt it's the same skull.'

By noon Bernal and Miranda had set out in the official limousine for the elegant Chamberí quarter, where the Marquis's town house was situated in the Calle de Zurbano. The façade looked undistinguished, with all the shutters closed, but as he rang the bell under the outer arch of the porte-cochère, Bernal noticed a small television camera trained on them from above. Through the intercom a male voice asked them their business.

'I am Comisario Bernal of the DSE. I wish to see the housekeeper.'

'Please show your badge to the camera above your head, Comisario,' said the disembodied voice. Bernal complied.

After a pause, a small door inset in the large double-doored gate was opened and an old retainer wearing a green apron invited them in. A cobbled drive open to the sky led from the main gate between large buildings, for the most part in the elegant Isabelline style, and they were surprised to see large trees in the garden in the far distance, since the outside of the dwelling gave no clue to its size and complexity.

The porter brought them to a glass double door to the left of the drive.

'Please wait in the library, señores. The majordomo will attend you shortly.'

Miranda whistled softly when they were left alone. 'It's immense, chief. Just look at those marble pillars!'

The library was high and very long, in classical French style, with a gilt staircase leading to an upper gallery. Near the door gleamed a fine collection of rich bindings, and between the long rows of morocco-bound books there reposed at random intervals precious objets d'art in the baroque style: nacre shells mounted in gold, urns of coloured marble, elaborate lamps of La Granja crystal. Arranged at intervals along each side of the room were groups of comfortable armchairs and work-desks with Louis XVI chairs, and all of it was suffused by green light emanating from the garden at the furthest extreme.

The majordomo soon appeared and invited them to be seated.

'We are here on a delicate mission,' Bernal explained, 'and we should like to know if the Marquis is in Madrid.'

'I'm afraid not, Comisario. His lordship is on a shooting expedition at his country estate near Jerez. Her ladyship is here, but is at her devotions in the chapel at present. It is a special day for the household, since St Barbara is our patron. We have a special Mass.'

'Could you perhaps tell us where the Marquis's children are?' asked Bernal.

'Only the two daughters are in residence at the moment. The eldest son, Don Miguel, is with his father in the south, and the second and third sons have their own establishments abroad.'

'And the youngest son?' queried Bernal. 'That would be José Antonio?'

'That is correct. He's at the cadet school of his father's regiment.' The majordomo looked temporarily pained.

'Or we think he is there. We were surprised not to see him here this morning, Superintendent, for the celebrations. He's never missed them in previous years. It's quite an elaborate affair, with a special luncheon for the guests afterwards.' He became suddenly anxious. 'Nothing has happened to him, has it?'

'I can't say for sure,' replied Bernal cautiously. 'But it would help if you could let us have some recent photographs of him.'

'You mean you have someone in custody who might be him?' asked the majordomo incredulously.

'Rather worse than that, I'm afraid. An unidentified accident victim, who was very badly burned.'

The servant's face became suddenly stricken. 'I'll get the photograph album for you.'

As they waited, Bernal and Miranda were astonished to see a small but richly robed procession coming along the interior alley of the house. At the rear was a bishop in a red chasuble with gold orphreys over dalmatica and tunicle of the same hue, who wore a white mitre and carried his tall crozier in the shape of a crook, and who was preceded by a chaplain and a deacon also vested in red.

Seeing the holy water they carried for the Asperges and a silver censer emitting incense, Miranda commented: 'They're making for the private chapel over there, *jefe*. It must be a solemn Mass they're going to celebrate.'

When the majordomo returned with the photograph, Bernal said, 'I see the bishop has come to say Mass.'

'Ah yes, he's an old friend of the Marquis, and comes up every year especially for this commemoration, to please the *marquesa* really.'

After they had chosen photographs of Capt. Lebrija that Bernal considered suitable for Dr Peláez's purposes, they took their leave of the servant under the portico. From the open door of the chapel they could hear the opening words of the introit: '*Loquebar de testimoniis tuis in conspectu regum, et non confundebar*—I spoke of Thy testimonies before kings, and I was not ashamed.'

When they got back into the official car, Miranda said, 'Did you spot the five cars parked in the inner courtyard back there, chief? Three of them had SP public service plates and *matrículas* belonging to the army.'

'I expect some of the *marquesa*'s guests are from the artillery. I know you've got a photographic memory, Miranda, but you'd do well to write down those registration numbers you've memorized straightaway. When we get back you can check them out to see who was brought here in those official vehicles.'

'Why the artillery, chief? The numbers don't reveal the regiment or division, do they?'

'I thought you'd been brought up as a good Catholic, Miranda,' said Bernal, as his inspector looked even more puzzled. 'St Barbara, of course. The special Mass is for her. She's the patron saint of artillerymen.' Bernal had in fact cheated a little, since he had found out from Navarro before leaving the office that the Marqués de la Estrella was honorary colonel of an artillery regiment and that his lordship's two main passions were firing cannon and shooting wildlife on his southern estate.

Back at the Gobernación building, Bernal rang Inspector Ibáñez of Central Records to invite him to lunch at Lhardy at 2.0 p.m. As soon as he replaced the receiver, Ángel Gallardo arrived, dressed in blue overalls and a workman's cap.

'I was making a delivery of the last edition of the newspaper to the kiosks here in Sol, *jefe*, and thought I'd bring you this from Elena.' He produced a thick buff envelope.

'You watch your cover won't get blown, Ángel,' admonished Bernal.

'They know I used to work here, and sometimes call in

to the cafeteria to see my old buddies, chief. I wouldn't be surprised if they were beginning to see me as a way of getting info out of the DSE should they need it.'

'Be careful, just the same. What's Elena sent?'

'She managed to get a Xerox copy of the subscriber list. She's really *enchufada* in that place. The editor will be inviting her to sit on his knee next.'

'She should take care not to get rumbled,' said Bernal. 'We're dealing with ruthless people.'

'She's doing fine. Don't worry about it. Is there anything special you want me to take back to her?'

'Ask her to find out anything she can about the Marqués de la Estrella and his family, and to see if they're connected in any way with *La Corneta*. Especially if the youngest son has any involvement with the newspaper. His name is, or was, Captain José Antonio Lebrija Russell de Villafranca—to give you the shortened version of his noble surname. It's well nigh certain his was the charred corpse we found up at La Granja, but we're keeping it strictly under wraps for the time being.'

'OK, chief, will do. Anything else?'

'Find out what you both can about the central artillery division. It may be that a handful of officers are up to something. And don't come in here again. Stick to the agreed procedure, understood?'

When Ángel made a jaunty exit, Navarro handed Bernal a long blue envelope sealed with pink wax which bore the impression of the royal seal.

'The King's secretary sent that over by special messenger, chief.'

Bernal slit open the envelope and perused the contents with interest:

MILITARY INTELLIGENCE DIVISION: COUNTER-INFORMATION SECTION

First Military Region: General Staff
Information collection date: 19 November to 2 December
Date of report: 4 December
Declassification: Group 2
No. 53. Evaluation: A-1.

1. *Current views and attitudes of the officers and men*
1.1 *Commissioned Officers*

There is currently absolute discipline and obedience to the commands of the General Staff. There is continuing concern, however, about the civil government's apparent inability to take stronger measures or adopt tougher policies in the following matters:

> The process of devolution in the provinces and separatist attitudes
>
> Insults to the national flag
>
> Terrorism and apologists of it
>
> Attacks on the armed forces or its members in the mass media
>
> The high crime rate and the worsening of social mores
>
> The deepening economic crisis, aggravated by strikes
>
> Attacks on the sanctity of family life
>
> Loss of national prestige abroad.

It is recognized that some of these evils are international phenomena at the present time, but the officers and high command are disturbed by the lack of effective response to them by the civil arm. Nevertheless it is not the Army's wish to undertake any kind of action that falls outside the strictly military sphere, nor is it its wish to submit the civil authorities to any kind of pressure; rather it has observed and will continue to observe complete obedience and respect.

1.2 *Non-commissioned Officers*
Their views are identical to the Officers'.

1.3 *The Troops*
The rank and file have kept complete discipline and obedience to orders. Those who are permitted to spend the night out of barracks at their home addresses in a few cases show signs of being influenced towards left-wing standpoints by their families or by the perverse influence of the mass media, but the officers and NCO's do their utmost to combat these tendencies.

Bernal could see that there was a great deal more in the same vein, but the general message was that everything, in the central region at any rate, was calm on the military front, and that there was no indication of any plot against the Government or the Constitution.

He passed the report over to Navarro. 'Have a look at this, Paco, and see how peaceful everything is.'

Dr Peláez now entered, beaming with triumph. 'With those photos you got for me I've tried out the method of superimposing the blown-up picture of the suspected victim over the X-rays of the skull and they match in every detail, Bernal.'

'Will such an identification stand up in court, Peláez?'

'It might do. I could produce accounts of similar cases in other countries where such evidence has been admitted, if the judge were to ask for them.'

'It may not come to that. I'll have to take advice from the highest authority.'

'I understand. But you'll want an official forensic report in the usual way?'

'Yes, please, but I don't think it will go to the judge of instruction. Or not yet, anyway.'

After Peláez had left, Bernal asked Navarro to call in

Miranda and Lista for them to review the position together.

'We need to investigate the last known whereabouts of Captain Lebrija,' he told them, 'but we don't want to put the MAGOS conspirators on their guard. They must know about his death at La Granja on Sunday and the circumstances of it from the accomplice who got away after the explosion, yet there is no sign so far that they have informed his family or the college where he was an instructor. We ought to avoid barging in uninvited.'

'But they must expect a search for him sooner or later, *jefe*,' objected Lista. 'The family will report him missing.'

'I'm not sure it's that sort of family,' replied Bernal. 'Its members are scattered at three residences in Spain alone, as well as at a villa in Paris and an apartment in New York. It would take some time for the loss of the unmarried son to be noticed.'

'Now we've paid a visit on them,' said Miranda, 'and asked the majordomo about his whereabouts and told him of the accident victim, they will surely make enquiries themselves today.'

'Exactly,' said Bernal. 'Let them make the first moves. I've given the majordomo our number. Once he's talked to the Marchioness and they've inquired at the college, they'll come back to us, I'm sure. Then we can go in and investigate at the family's request, which is a much less suspect way of proceeding.'

'What if they ask whether we've managed to identify the burnt cadaver by forensic means?'

'Then we'll deny it for the moment,' said Bernal. 'If necessary they can inspect the remains, and we'll watch their reactions, knowing, of course, that a normal identification is impossible.'

'Wouldn't that be a bit heartless, *jefe*?' suggested Navarro.

'Heartless it might be, but it's so important to observe

the way they would react. In the event—unlikely, I realize—
of their claiming to recognize the charred corpse, we
would know they were involved in the affair. If they
don't, then there's no real harm done. Let's give them
until six p.m. before we start enquiring at the college.'

At lunch with Inspector Ibáñez, Bernal asked him what
he'd managed to find in the official records about the
MAGOS messages.

'A blank, Luis, or rather, not quite a blank. An almost
blank screen, yes, but a code number appears on my
terminal which signifies "*No information available: Reserved
to higher authority*." That usually means that there is
something on file, but it can only be retrieved by the top
echelons.'

'That's very interesting,' said Bernal. 'The top
echelons I've been in touch with claim there's no
information at all.'

'If you can get the right computer key, the information
will be yours,' said Ibáñez. 'I also tried the three palace
names, but got nothing of any possible interest to you.
The colours drew a complete blank.'

'Will you try an important family for me, Esteban?
One of the grandees?'

Ibáñez sat up. 'With pleasure. Which one? You know
the late Caudillo kept full files on them all, as well as on
the lesser nobility. I think he was worried they'd try to
bring the old King back, or put one of the Carlist claimants
on the throne.'

'It's the Marqués de la Estrella, the Lebrija Russell
family.'

'They're rich and very powerful, Luis. Be careful.
They're out of your league if it's a crime you're
investigating.'

'But it's not a crime, in the ordinary sense, Esteban, or
won't be, if it prospers.'

Affairs of state, they'll be the death of you, Luis. Why

don't you take the nice pension and go and live in
Estoril?'

'Not yet, Esteban, not yet. I'm too hooked on them. Anyway, I'd be bored playing roulette in Portuguese each
night, though Eugenia would probably be pleased to go
off and pray at Fátima every whipstitch.'

'How is she, Luis? It's been a long time since I saw
her.'

'Just the same. You wouldn't notice any change except
for one or two more grey hairs.'

They chatted on about old times under the large Chinese
lantern in the upper dining-room at Lhardy, which was
officially regarded ever since it was fitted out in the 1850s
as The Japanese Room, and in the end had their usual
tussle about whose turn it was to pay the bill, both claiming
that honour.

After he took his leave of Ibáñez, Bernal made for his
clandestine apartment in the Calle de Barceló. Consuelo
was mysteriously missing, as she had tended to be in
recent days, but just as he was becoming concerned for
her, she arrived loaded with parcels.

'I've just been doing some preliminary Christmas
shopping, Luchi. It's better than getting caught up in the
rush nearer *Reyes*, and I've got a large and scattered
family to find suitable presents for.'

As he kissed her, he noticed how blooming with happi-
ness she seemed, as though she were younger than her
thirty-three years. After they had taken coffee and retired
to the luxurious divan, he told her something of the case
on which he was working, since he had frequently found
that she helped to crystallize his thoughts and sometimes
contributed to a solution by bringing her own viewpoint
to bear.

'All this is in the utmost secrecy, you realize, Conchi.
It's a very delicate affair.'

'Of course. Isn't it exciting! And the grandee, Estrella,

you say? I think he's connected with the Banco de Castilla where I work. He may be one of the directors. I'll check tomorrow. Those old *latifundista* families were founded by a pack of brigands, really. They made fortunes for centuries as absentee landlords in the centre and south of the country, allowing the landless peasants to starve while they lived it up at the Court, not to mention Biarritz, Monte Carlo and Paris! Now their descendants are doing jolly well out of the new industrialization, and many of them have got fantastic banking and commercial interests.'

'Please try and curb your revolutionary fervour for a day or two, and find out what you can about the Lebrija family's affairs, will you, Consuelo?'

'With pleasure. As the manager's personal assistant I've got access to all the files. Anyway, he's been charming to me today and most accommodating about a special request I've made.'

'And what was that about?'

'I'll tell you when it's all confirmed. Not before, OK? It will be a big Christmas surprise for you.'

When he returned to the office rather later than he had intended, Bernal discovered that the Marquesa de la Estrella had already telephoned, and had left a message: Would Comisario Bernal do her the honour of calling again for her to receive him?

'I told her ladyship you would be over as soon as you could, *jefe*,' said Navarro.

'Ask Miranda to order the official car, would you? We've let them sweat enough, I think.'

Twenty minutes later the Marchioness received Bernal and Miranda in her private sitting-room, the décor and furnishings of which were all of gold and palest yellow, in the Second Empire style, perhaps original, Bernal judged, as he perched unhappily with Miranda on an exquisite chaise-longue.

'I so much regret I was unable to receive you this morning, Comisario. It was a very special day for our family.'

'It's good of you to receive us now, señora marquesa,' said Bernal in his politest voice. 'I understand how very concerned you must be for your son.'

The *marquesa* pulled her black Manila shawl more tightly round her shoulders with a slightly trembling hand encrusted with antique rings, though her back was ramrod straight. 'Yes, we are, of course. We have checked with the military college at Ocaña and José Antonio has not been seen there since Saturday evening, Comisario; nor have we seen him here. But I understand you think he may have been involved in some accident—' she paused uncertainly.

'We simply can't be sure, señora, but we have an unidentified victim of an accident which occurred at San Ildefonso, and it's possible a military vehicle was involved—'

'Should I accompany you to try to make an identification?' She hesitated once more, only just controlling her strong emotion.

'No, señora, I don't think that would be advisable. Would his lordship or one of your other sons be available, perhaps?'

'My eldest son will be taking the late Aviaco flight back from Jerez tonight, Comisario.'

'Well then, no doubt he will come with us tomorrow. I very much hope we are mistaken, but one must be prepared for the worst.'

'I shall pray, Comisario. We are all in God's hands.'

When they emerged into the Calle de Zurbano, Bernal suggested to Miranda that they check out the military college that evening, and told the driver to take them to Ocaña.

They beat the rush-hour traffic, leaving the city by the

south exit with a quarter of an hour to spare, and the experienced chauffeur pushed the Seat 134 to a steady 120 k.p.h. on the A.4 motorway, with the result that they crossed the River Jarama at Seseña in just over half an hour, and in less than ten minutes they reached the Tagus at Aranjuez, that green oasis in an arid landscape, just east of the confluence of the two rivers. Young people thought of the place nowadays, Bernal supposed, as a source of early strawberries and asparagus, but he could recall with clarity what a stricken sight it had presented in February 1937, when it was the Republican headquarters during the bitterly fought Jarama campaign, and a key-point in preventing the Nationalist forces from cutting Republican Madrid's only road to Valencia and the east coast.

They sped through the now dark and quiet streets and rejoined the road that led in a few kilometres to the small town of Ocaña, with its once notorious *Penal* or prison. They stopped in the town square for a coffee, and sought and were given directions to get to the military college. There Bernal showed his official DSE badge at the main gate, and they were presently received by the Director, who held the rank of colonel.

Bernal explained that they had been requested by the Marquesa de la Estrella to inquire into her son's where-abouts.

'We were expecting him back on Monday, Super-intendent, to begin artillery practice with the cadets admitted this term, but one of the lieutenants had to take the class. He told me on Saturday evening when he left that he was going up to the sierra on a hunting trip with some friends.'

'Were the friends brother officers, and are any of them missing too?' asked Bernal.

'No one else has failed to report, Superintendent, and quite honestly I didn't ask who was accompanying him.'

'May we see Captain Lebrija's room?' asked Bernal. 'Perhaps his servant will recall what clothes he was wearing.'

'Of course. I pray that nothing has happened to the captain. He's one of our most valued instructors.'

As they passed the officers' mess, Bernal noticed that the table was laid with silver and as yet unlit candelabra as for a banquet. The colonel observed the direction of Bernal's gaze and hastened to explain: 'It's our patron's day, Superintendent, the feast of St Barbara. We shall be sorry if Captain Lebrija misses it this year.'

Bernal and Miranda went through the motions of examining Lebrija's room, and questioned his batman about the clothes he had been wearing.

'He went in his informal hunting clothes, sir, and took his sporting gun. All the captain's uniforms are still here, and he keeps the rest of his civilian clothes at his private residence in Madrid.'

Bernal looked idly at the bookcase and quickly noted the contents: works on military tactics and gunnery practice, the biography of José Antonio Primo de Rivera, founder of the Falange Party, a number of recent works on General Franco and his family, a number of right-wing bestselling novelettes, back numbers of *El Toque*, and a pile of old copies of *La Corneta*. There could be no doubt about the late captain's ideological bent.

'Did Captain Lebrija keep private correspondence here?' he asked the servant.

'Only the occasional letter addressed to him at the College. He had a small pigskin case of writing materials.'

'Is it here now?'

'I don't see it, sir. I'll just look in his bedroom.'

Bernal realized it would be impossible to do a thorough search without giving cause for suspicion, so he acted on sudden impulse and picked out the copy of *La Corneta* dated 14 November, quickly folded it in four, and stuffed it into his overcoat pocket, just as the servant returned.

'No, it's not there, sir. I've looked everywhere.'

'It doesn't matter. Thank you very much. We shan't trouble you further.'

At the bottom of the main staircase, near an impressively filled row of locked rifle-racks, the college director was hovering anxiously.

'Do you think any of Captain Lebrija's friends or colleagues might be able to tell us anything, Colonel?' asked Bernal.

'I hardly think so, Superintendent. I questioned them after the Marquesa telephoned and they know nothing.'

'Are any of them close friends of his?'

'No, not really. Lebrija was rather distant and correct in manner, you know.' Bernal noticed with interest that the colonel used the past tense about the missing captain. He clearly knew much more than he was admitting.

The colonel hesitated, then gave the impression that propriety demanded he offer something more concrete. 'He only seemed close to his spiritual adviser.'

Again the past tense, Bernal noticed. 'Would that be the military chaplain?'

'No, his adviser was Father Gaspar, of the Apostolic House at Aranjuez. He comes here regularly to teach the cadets on the spiritual side of army life.'

Bernal decided it was unwise and probably useless to press him further, and they took their leave.

Outside in the forecourt, Miranda looked longingly at a row of military jeeps parked opposite the entrance. 'Couldn't we take impressions of the front tyres of those, chief, and find out if one of them was used up at La Granja?'

'It's tempting, Miranda, but much too dangerous. And I don't see any way of getting tyre-casts without the college authorities knowing.'

'I could slip back later tonight, *jefe*, while they're at the regimental dinner.'

'But these guards won't go away, Miranda. I'd bet they have these kids marching up and down on guard duty all night, as part of the training. The game's not worth the candle.'

As they were driven back northward to Madrid, Bernal switched on the rear reading-light and extracted the copy of *La Corneta* from his pocket. 'See what I filched, Miranda. Let's have a look at the personal ads.' They both saw at once that the first MAGOS message: '*Purple A.1. San Ildefonso*', was ringed in red ink. 'So it's pretty clear now. Captain Lebrija was definitely involved in the MAGOS ring. I'm so relieved we've got some kind of confirmation for the King's secretary, even if we don't know yet what it all portends.'

When the official car left Bernal at the corner of his street, he decided to have a Larios *gin tonic* in Félix Pérez's before facing one of Eugenia's scratch suppers. He also took and ate two fish canapés from the plate on the bar, just in case the later offering should prove inedible.

As he opened the door of the apartment, he could hear Eugenia on the telephone in the chilly tiled corridor. 'Well, you just make sure you go to Mass tomorrow morning, Diego, without fail, while you've got the chance. Here's your father, who's just come in.'

Bernal took the receiver and greeted his son. 'Where are you?'

'They've brought us into Seville for the night. The sudden rain swamped our tents, I'm glad to say, and we'll have to dry everything out tomorrow or when it stops.'

'You're very fortunate to have rain down there. It must be the first for two years. How is the course going?'

'It's quite interesting. We've been helping the geologists sink borings to see how much natural gas there is in the Marismas. It's hellishly boggy down there, and full of snakes and scorpions. A good job you lent me those strong boots.'

'Have you got enough money?' asked Bernal, being almost certain that Diego would have spent the 20,000 pesetas he'd given him as pocket money, even though he'd only been gone a week.

'Yes I have, actually. There's been no chance of spending it until tonight.'

'In that case don't let it burn a hole in your pocket, and don't go mad in the Triana quarter with your wild friends.'

'Where's that?' queried Diego, feigning a tone of complete innocence. 'By the way, Papi,' (Bernal was surprised to be so addressed; the matter must be serious, he thought), 'we've seen a lot of military manœuvres going on in the marshes by the River Guadalquivir.'

'Military manœuvres?' queried Bernal, with quickened interest.

'Yes, and I didn't recognize the uniforms. Blue, with a red flash on the shoulder and beret. Perhaps they're a sort of GEO or special commando.'

'I'll enquire about it, but don't stick your nose into anything military, now. Where and when did you see them?'

'For the past three days, just west of Trebujena, about half a kilometre from the river, in the salt-pans. It's completely uninhabited round there.'

'All right. Mind what I said.'

Later that night, as he slowly chewed the tough, cold omelette of leftovers, which was burnt on the underside, Bernal pondered on what his son had observed. He went to get an Almax folding road map from a drawer, and turned to the bottom centre fold of the area bordering Seville, and Cadiz provinces, which he studied with close interest.

ADVENT: SECOND SUNDAY (FEAST OF ST NICHOLAS, 6 December)

The shrill bell of the telephone awoke Bernal just after 7.0 a.m. and he felt around sleepily for his slippers on the cold tiles of the bedroom floor. Eugenia had already risen from the large brass matrimonial bedstead and was nowhere to be heard. He lifted the receiver from the old-fashioned wall-rest and murmured, '*Dígame.*'

'*Jefe*? It's Elena. I'm sorry to ring you so very early, but I didn't have the opportunity to get in touch with you last night. There's another MAGOS message come in for insertion in the personal column on Tuesday, 8 December. It arrived too late for the Sunday edition today, and tomorrow being Monday *La Corneta* won't be published.'

'You did right to telephone me, Elena. Did you jot the message down?'

'Yes, chief. Have you got a pencil?'

'Hold on a moment.' Bernal found himself in the usual predicament in that house of having nowhere other than the umbrella-stand on which to balance his notepad, while trying to prop the receiver under his chin as he wrote. 'Go ahead.'

'It reads: MAGOS (in capitals), *Purple. A.3. Aranjuez.*'

'*A.3*—are you sure? The first three messages all ended with *A.1.*'

'Quite certain, *jefe*. I saw the copy on the advertising girl's desk, marked ''*For insertion in the next issue*'', and she had added ''*8 December*''.'

'Did you see who had paid for the insertion, Elena?'

'That's the best bit of luck, chief. It said: ''*Charge to Editor's personal account*''.'

'That's very interesting indeed. Are you working to-morrow?'

'Yes, chief, but I'm feeling quite frustrated just cutting up the various editions and marking the bits for the biogs. of the people mentioned in the various reports.'

'Have you got free access to the files?'

'To the archives, yes, but not to the current files up-stairs in the Editor's office.'

'Would you look up something in the old files you can get at? It's the Marqués de la Estrella and his family, and their social activities and business interests. The family name is Lebrija Russell. There are, or were, four sons, and two daughters.'

'OK, *jefe*, I'll see what there is and send a Xerox copy over with Ángel.'

Making his way back to the bedroom, Bernal realized that his wife must have gone to early Mass and would come back later with the bread. Although it was Sunday, he now felt too alert to go back to bed, and decided to have his usual altercation with the ancient gas geyser in the kitchen, in the hope that more than a trickle of warm water would penetrate the clogged pipes and reach the shower in the broken-down bathroom. Would he never persuade Eugenia to move to a modern apartment, or even to bring this one up to standard, as most of their better-off neighbours had done?

By the time he was finishing dressing, the phone rang again.

'This is Navarro, *jefe*. I came into the office to get up to date with the filing of the various reports we got yesterday. The King's secretary has just rung to say that the Delegate of the Patrimonio Nacional has reported the discovery of a corpse in the grounds of the palace at Aranjuez early this morning.'

'Aranjuez? We must get down there as soon as possible. Will you get in touch with the palace administrator down there and tell him we'll be taking over the investigation? Has he called in the Guardia Civil, do you know?'

'Not yet. The royal secretary told him to do nothing until he heard from us.'

'That's good. Warn Peláez and Varga, will you? And get Miranda and Lista in. I'll see you in the office in ten minutes.'

As the taxi took him around the triumphal arch built by Sabatini for Charles III, which still bore the marks of French cannon-balls from 1808, Bernal was surprised to see so many people up and about on this cold but bright Sunday morning, and he commented on the fact to the taximan.

'It's the Day of the Constitution, yet another national holiday!'

Then he remembered that the Government of Calvo Sotelo had asked all the municipal councils to arrange celebrations and cultural activities to commemorate the 1978 Constitution which had been proclaimed on this day. The radio and television news bulletins the night before had re-broadcast part of the King's speech of accession made on 22 November 1975, and Bernal had interpreted all of it as an attempt to eradicate the propaganda effect of the large fascist parade that had been held in the Plaza de Oriente on 20 November, the anniversary of Franco's death.

While the taxi bowled along the Calle de Alcalá, Bernal thought hard about the cryptic messages and their sequence. The first message, published on 14 November, had mentioned San Ildefonso, and Capt. Lebrija's charred body turned up there in the grounds of the royal palace on 30 November; why the delay of fifteen days? The second and third MAGOS messages, published on 20 and 27 November, had mentioned El Pardo and Segovia respectively, but absolutely nothing had happened at either place as far as they knew. Now Elena had discovered the contents of the fourth cryptic message two days before its publication was due, and it referred to Aranjuez; by a remarkable coincidence a corpse turns up there in the grounds of the royal palace, without any of the possible recipients of the fourth message knowing of its contents. There was simply no logical pattern that he could discern. Perhaps the change from *A.1.* mentioned in the first three messages to *A.3.* in the shortly to be released fourth was significant? If so, he had no idea what it might imply. At all events, the palace at Aranjuez was of no possible strategic importance. It hadn't been lived in by anyone apart from the servants since Alfonso XIII's time. The same could be said of La Granja, apart from Franco's garden parties held there every year on 18 July, but the connection there was surely not the palace itself but the relatively easy access to the power cable, which supplied the new King's permanent residence of La Zarzuela nearer the capital.

It was true that Aranjuez was near Ocaña and the military college where Capt. Lebrija had worked as an instructor, and that his spiritual adviser happened to be from a religious house situated in the royal town. What was his name? Ah, Father Gaspar, he remembered. Bernal suddenly sat up and shook himself slightly. Gaspar, the name of the second of the Three Kings of Orient: really, it fitted too absurdly. The code-word MAGOS referring to the three kings, then Lt-Gen. Baltasar taking over command of the central division, now Father Gaspar. When, he wondered, would Melchior turn up?

In the office, Navarro asked him whether he had breakfasted.

'No, I haven't. Perhaps you'd ask the desk-sergeant to send us up some coffee and croissants, Paco.'

'I've contacted Dr Peláez, and he wants us to collect him at his chalet in the country at Perales. It won't be far out of our way. His assistant will come on direct to Aranjuez with the mortuary van. Should we inform the local examining magistrate there?'

'Not if we can avoid it. We could use the royal warrant to override the normal procedure. After all, the body has been found on land belonging to the Patrimonio Nacional, and it's quite likely that the King has a prerogative over the local jurisdiction.'

'Varga is preparing his scene-of-crime team and equipment. He'll bring the technical van. Who will you take with you? Both Miranda and Lista would be best.'

After the breakfast had been brought up, Navarro asked Bernal about the previous day's visit to the Instituto Anatómico Forense.

'Of course, you don't know about that. I watched Captain Lebrija's eldest brother closely when he viewed the charred remains. He was very cool, but behaved strangely, I thought. It would have been clear to anyone that an identification was out of the question, yet he claimed, almost at once, that the body could well be his brother's. Only afterwards did he think to ask Peláez how we had come to suspect that the corpse might be José Antonio Lebrija's, so we explained about the technique of comparative tomography. I certainly gained the impression that the heir to the Estrella Marquisate had been informed about his youngest brother's death beforehand. He showed no sign of grief, though.'

'That's the aristocratic training coming out, perhaps. I suppose that Captain Lebrija's accomplice at La Granja had already let the family, or some of its members, know last Sunday, after making his escape from the scene?'

'I'm sure that's what happened. Perhaps the *marquesa* didn't know at first; her shock seemed to be genuine. But the accomplice probably contacted the *marqués* and the heir down at the family seat.'

'That could imply that they are involved in the MAGOS

affair, chief.'

'It could well. But are they only on the fringe of it because of Captain Lebrija's involvement? That's what we must find out. Did you get any more on the Marquis's interests?'

'A little. For a start, the whole family are staunch supporters of the conservation of the Latin Mass.'

'Ah, that accounts for what Miranda and I witnessed on Friday and the presence of that reactionary bishop at their house.'

'The Marquis's late father was a well-known monarchist and member of Alfonso XIII's court, a supporter of the dictatorship of Primo de Rivera in that reign. The old marquis fled to Paris when the Second Republic was proclaimed in 1931 and died abroad. The present marquis returned to join the insurgents as soon as Franco raised his standard in North Africa. Estrella rose to the rank of artillery colonel by 1939, then took over the management of the extensive Andalusian estates.'

'And his business interests have diversified since?'

'Very much so, especially from the 'sixties on, with the new industries. He's a director of three banks, a shareholder in a number of Spanish utility and armaments companies and in various multinationals. He and his sons are also members of a Catholic apostolic organization, which hasn't obtained papal recognition so far.'

'Find out all you can about that religious organization, Paco.'

'OK, *jefe*. By the way, Inspector Ibáñez of central records rang to invite you to lunch if you were in today. It's his turn to pay, he says.'

'Thank you, Paco. I must let him know we've got too much on so far as today's concerned.'

After they had driven out of the city through the poor south-eastern suburbs and joined the A.3 motorway that soon petered out and reverted to being the old N III

Valencia highway, Bernal once more found the bare and dreary landscape reminding him of the Civil War. The road hardly seemed to have changed in forty-five years. It was along this bitter road of flight and later exile that in November 1936 the only working-class prime minister ever to rule in Spain, the 'incorruptible' Francisco Largo Caballero, had departed with his Socialist Cabinet for Valencia, whence he had governed Republican Spain until his colleagues enforced his resignation in May 1937. Some of those same colleagues had spitefully denied him even the luxury of a car in 1939, and at the age of 68 he had found himself obliged to walk to France, only to be handed over afterwards to the Nazis and transported to the Oranienburg concentration camp. Not only did he survive that experience, but 'The Spanish Lenin', as Moscow had earlier dubbed him, returned to Paris and wrote his memoirs just before his death in 1946. When Bernal had been persuaded by Consuelo Lozano to witness the final translation of Largo's remains from the Père Lachaise to the civil Cementerio del Este in Madrid on 14 April 1978, he had been impressed, not so much by the million people lining the streets in respectful silence, with only the occasional muted shout of ¡Viva la República! which was quickly suppressed, nor by the seemingly endless procession of purple and red flags, but by the quite unexpected reappearance of the steely features of Largo, embalmed in his glass-topped coffin. No one would have been really surprised if he had lifted the lid and given one valedictory clenched-fist salute before reaching his final resting-place, for in life he had talked almost incessantly of 'the will of steel' required to achieve the Revolution, and he had demonstrated that will unsurpassedly in his old age.

The day brightened as they reached Perales on the north bank of the River Tajuña, and Bernal spotted Dr Peláez at the door of his chalet, gazing myopically up the road through his thick pebble lenses. As the car drew to a halt, he gave a late wave of recognition and dived to the verandah to pick up his black bag.

'So you've got another one for me, eh, Bernal?'

'It's a drowning, apparently, in the grounds of the palace at Aranjuez.'

'When was it discovered?'

'Early this morning.'

'I suppose they've fished the cadaver out of the water?'

'Yes, but with considerable difficulty,' said Bernal. 'The palace administrator said the current in the Tagus is powerful along that stretch, especially after the recent rains.'

'Who made the discovery?'

'One of the palace staff.'

'And is the deceased male or female?'

'Male, middle-aged, balding. No ID yet.'

After they had crossed the bridge that led into Aranjuez and reached the main avenue called the Calle de la Reina, the car and the technician's van turned right to pass alongside the Parterre Gardens, where they found awaiting them the mortuary van, which had been driven directly from Madrid by Peláez's assistant. Bernal's car led the way up to the elegant eastern façade of the palace. Here they found the administrator standing under the imposing portico, flanked by two lackeys dressed in the royal livery of dark blue and gold.

Despite the sun's attempts to filter some warmth through the tall elms and plane trees, now almost totally bereft of their autumn leaves, the air felt sharply clean and nipped one's face. The overnight frost had not yet melted on the lawns where the sunlight had not reached.

Bernal greeted the administrator and shook hands.

'We're glad you have been able to come so quickly, Comisario. We were told not to take any further action until you arrived.'

'The body has been moved, I take it?' said Bernal.

'I thought it right to have the gardeners recover it from the water, in case it was carried off by the current. They placed a tarpaulin over it on the river bank.'

'Where exactly was it found?'

'In the Jardín de la Isleta, to the north-west of the palace.'

'And who discovered it?'

'One of the under-gardeners, just after first light, at seven-forty.'

'I shall need to interview him first of all, so that he can show me the precise position of the body when he caught sight of it. What was he doing out in the grounds at that hour on a cold morning?' Bernal inquired.

'He's an addict of *el footing*, this new fad that has come to us from the Anglo-Saxons,' said the administrator rather apologetically. 'I find the idea of it quite peculiar, Comisario, but he gets up every day at that hour and runs round the whole of the Island Garden wearing a *chandal*—I think he calls it—a kind of woollen suit.'

'A track-suit,' said Bernal. 'No doubt the sport is very invigorating, if you have the right physique.' He smiled, though the only kind of physical exercise he himself indulged in was practised in his clandestine apartment. 'Perhaps you'd lead us to the spot,' he suggested to the administrator. 'Can we take the vehicles?'

'Yes, the paths are negotiable with care.'

'Would you be so good as to ride with Dr Peláez and me and show us the way?'

The three vehicles entered the narrow wrought-iron gates leading to the Jardín de la Isla, turned left past the Fountain of Hercules and took the first long path that stretched north-westward to the Garden of the Little Island. Bernal was amazed to see the large rose-beds still showing late red blooms, rimed with a frost that had not been so severe as to wither the petals, but merely to coat them with a white sparkle in the filtered rays of the sun.

'I've brought a plan of the entire gardens for you, Comisario,' said the administrator, 'so that you can see the layout.'

'That's most thoughtful. Perhaps you'll mark on it when we stop the exact place where the body was found.'

The car pulled up at a point where they could see three gardeners standing guard near the tip of the Little Island, the western extreme of the gardens overlooking the Tagus and the green-painted road-rail bridge.

'We'll let the pathologist and the technician do the initial examination,' Bernal commented to the administrator. 'Did you look at the body yourself?'

'Yes, to see if I could recognize him. Naturally I was anxious about the safety of our employees. But he is quite unknown to me and to my staff. He's only dressed in his underclothes, Comisario, which seems very peculiar. It looks like a suicide, since no one is likely to go for a swim early on a winter's morning.'

'Have there been suicides by drowning here in the past?' asked Bernal.

'Not to my knowledge, Comisario. Certainly not in the grounds of the royal palace.'

'Could a stranger have got into the grounds during the night?'

'I've considered that possibility. It would be very diffi-cult. All the gates were locked—I've checked that point with the gardeners. The ha-ha or flooded ditch which cuts off the garden on one side is five metres deep, with iron railings on each side, and on the northern boundary the Tagus is very wide and deep. I wonder if he could have fallen out of a boat.'

'I see from the plan that the river describes two large bends, something like an old-fashioned handwritten V, with the town bridge at its base. Now this water that flows through the Ría de los Molinos which has waterfalls marked on it where it passes close to the palace, is it taken from the river?'

'Yes, that's it, Superintendent. The water is extracted from the Tagus by a sluice-gate near the boating bridge where the jetty is, and passes over a wide, shallow cascade known as Castañuelas—the Castanets—because of its shape and the noise it makes. That water from the Ría rejoins the main stream over there—' he pointed at a spot beyond the tip of the small island—'just below the place where the body was first seen.'

'The current in the main river certainly looks strong at this point,' commented Bernal.

'It is powerful, but varies according to the way the river curves. There are quiet eddies where angling is possible.'

'The most likely thing is that the body entered the river here, or upstream of here,' said Bernal. 'Do you think there's much chance of it having come along the Ría from the palace and then having been swept back a little, in the eddy caused by the confluence?'

'I don't think so, Comisario. Apart from the presence of the shallow waterfall, the artificial channel is much slower running than the main river stream, because the sluice-gates control the rate of flow.'

'Well, that's most helpful. We needn't detain you here any further, but before you go, perhaps you'd introduce me to the under-gardener who discovered the body. My driver will take you back to the palace.'

'That's most kind,' said the administrator, who, unlike the youngest member of his staff, was no devotee of *el footing*.

The young man, still dressed in his blue track-suit, was a short, cheerful lad, whose natural exuberance was only slightly subdued by the circumstances. Perhaps he was intent on enjoying the attention he was about to receive, Bernal considered. He always took a special interest in the discoverer of a corpse, first because he or she was usually the only person to have observed the scene of the crime precisely as the perpetrator had left it, and secondly because of the real possibility that the person who reported a crime was the author of it. But perhaps this case was no more than a run-of-the-mill suicide.

'What is your full name?' Bernal began, as Miranda took shorthand notes.

'Hernán Álvarez Oliveras.'

'How long have you worked here at the palace?'

'Two years, sir, since I left school.'

'Were you born in Aranjuez?'

'Yes, sir, and I've lived here all my life. My father also works for the Patrimonio Nacional.'

'So you know the gardens well?'

'As well as I know anything,' said the young man confidently.

'Do you take the same route every day when you go running?'

'Yes, sir, on most days. It's jogging really, to keep myself in good shape, especially in the winter months.'

'Show me on this plan the way you normally go.'

'We live in the staff quarters there, sir, behind the Queen's mews. I pass the rear or west façade of the palace, across the bridge there and into the Jardín de la Isla; then I run along the path by the Ría and turn at this point—just where we are standing—and take the river towpath north-eastwards, following its curve round to the south. That brings me back to the bridge by the palace. I usually go before breakfast, at first light; sometimes a little earlier, in the false dawn. It was quite frosty this morning, but I soon warm up,' he said, smiling, and Bernal suddenly envied the brimming physical energy of youth, which he had come to feel he himself had never really possessed.

'And when you got to this point you noticed the body?'

'Yes, sir. The sun had just risen, and as I turned the

corner at the point of the Little Island, just over there, the rays picked out something white in the river, nearer to this bank than the other, and it seemed to be caught on that tree-branch that touches the surface of the water.'

'So you went to the edge of the bank to get a better look?' Bernal had studied the footprints on the grass and had noticed the spiked marks left by the running-shoes.

'Yes, and I could see it was a corpse, floating upside down, dressed in white vest and long drawers. I realized I couldn't hope to reach it without a rake or a long hook, and in any case, if I dislodged it with a broken branch, I thought the current might sweep it further downstream.'

'That was most wise,' said Bernal in a congratulatory tone, which caused his interlocutor to blush with pleasure. 'So you decided to go for help.'

'Yes, sir, I ran back to the head gardener's house, and found him having breakfast. He came with my father, and we brought a long hook and a grappling iron. They decided to recover the body from the water in case it broke loose from the overhanging bough. We covered it with a tarpaulin while the head gardener went to inform the administrator.'

'And did you recognize the deceased?'

'No, sir, I'd never seen him before, nor had the rest of those who've taken a look at him.' He suddenly shivered. 'I've never seen a drowned person before.'

'Don't let it prey on your mind. Some of us have to see them every day. Thank you for telling me everything so clearly. Inspector Miranda here will make up a deposition for you to sign.'

Dr Peláez was still labouring over the cadaver with his thermometers and other instruments, while Varga and his assistant were making a minute search of the river bank, so Bernal lit another Kaiser and decided to question the head gardener and the under-gardener's father who had brought the corpse ashore, but they had nothing material to add to Hernán Álvarez's statement.

In the meantime, Lista had, with Bernal's approval, set off along the river towpath north-eastwards towards the town, searching the undergrowth carefully as he went.

After the last of the official photographs had been taken, Peláez closed his bag and came over to where Bernal was waiting.

'Let's talk in the car, Bernal, it's damp and chilly out here. The water temperature is only just above zero, and the air temperature is plus two.'

'And the cadaver?' asked Bernal.

'Still some warmth in the organs. Almost six degrees.'

'So how long is it since he died?'

'That rather depends on whether he's been in the water from the moment he died. He has gooseflesh all over, of course, but the "washerwoman's skin" or sodden wrinkling is only very noticeable in the fingers, and it hasn't extended to the whole hand. I'd say about ten to twelve hours, as a rough guide. Between eleven p.m. last night and one a.m. this morning. I'll check the stomach contents later, and see how recently he'd had his evening meal.'

'But why are you doubtful about whether he died in the water or not, Peláez?'

'I thought at first it was a straightforward case of drowning, but there are some severe lacerations and a large cut at the back of the scalp which show signs of hæmatoma. Now it's quite common for victims of drowning to show injury: the corpse may hit against rocks or submerged branches or other objects, or come into contact with boats and their propellers, but in such cases there should be no external or internal bleeding, since the wounds are occasioned after death.'

'Could this person have fallen or jumped in by the town jetty and been carried over the sluice gate perhaps?' asked Bernal. 'It's just feasible he would then have been drawn over the waterfall and expelled from the Ría into the main river just below here, and the back-eddy could have pushed him upstream as far as that overhanging branch. We could try a reconstruction using a weighted dummy of similar size.'

'Try it out by all means, but I'm still concerned by these wounds, Bernal. You'll have to wait until I can dissect them in the lab to see if they were sustained while he was still alive, which I suspect. Unless he was drugged or very drunk, it's not likely he was bumped along as you suggest, however suicidal he was feeling, because the natural instinct to save himself would have taken over on such a long and uncomfortable watery ride.'

'But he did die by drowning, Peláez?'

'I'm not sure. You'll have to wait until I do the autopsy and see whether there are signs of asphyxia: there should be tell-tale red pin-points in the lungs. I'll also do the old Gettler test of the sodium chloride content of the left and right ventricles of the heart. That is usually accepted by the courts as conclusive proof of drowning. I'll get the Institute of Toxicology to test the organs for drugs, but don't expect a final report from them until the day after tomorrow. I'll phone some preliminary comments through to you tomorrow.'

'Thank you, Peláez. Doesn't it strike you as odd that he took off his outer clothing before jumping in?'

'Pretty odd, but not unknown in suicides by drowning. Obviously no one in his right mind would go for a swim in a river in December, let alone between ten p.m. and midnight, but it's curious the way the unbalanced mind retains an association of ideas. Your chappie dives in intending to kill himself, but partly undresses to give himself buoyancy, as though he's going for a swim. It may occur like that, especially when the attempt at felo-de-se is not genuine, when it's really a cry for help. And I'd expect that to occur in a fairly public spot, where the feigned suicide bid is likely to be thwarted by an able-bodied onlooker. Of course it can quite easily go wrong. That's why we sometimes find partly dressed corpses in self-induced drownings. But all this is idle speculation until I can get the cadaver back to the institute and cut it up to have a look-see. Shall we have to wait for the examining magistrate?'

'No, I've got full authority. You'll let me have your report tomorrow?'

'I'll try. Any way you'll have it first thing on Tuesday. The analyses may take longer. It depends on how busy they are at the Institute of Toxicology.'

After Dr Peláez had superintended the lifting of the body into the mortuary van and he and his assistant had left for Madrid, Bernal conferred with Varga the technician.

'There's very little for you, *jefe*. I'm pretty sure the deceased didn't enter the river from this section of the bank. The footprint evidence entirely confirms the young man's story, and those of the two gardeners. All I've got for you is this scrap of paper the dead man was clutching in his right hand.'

'Oh, Peláez didn't tell me about that. Is there any writing on it?' asked Bernal eagerly.

'It's just a soggy scrap or corner of a larger sheet which was written in fountain-pen ink, which the water has obliterated. I'll get it under the ultra-violet light and try infra-red photography.'

'And there's nothing else at all?'

'No, nothing. I've taken samples of the river water and of the soil and vegetation in case we need them for comparison later.'

'In that case we'd better go and see how Lista's getting on in his search of the tow-path. Where's Miranda?'

'He crossed the bridge to have a look at the path on the north side.'

'It's a pity we haven't brought a full team,' sighed Bernal, 'but the main thing is to conduct this investigation discreetly, without raising a hue and cry in the neighbourhood. We certainly don't want the press to come in on the act.'

'I'll go and join Lista, *jefe*, if you like, and send my assistant over to Miranda.'

'No. Lista's got the longest stretch of river bank. You take your assistant and go to help him, and I'll assist Miranda. Let's agree to meet back here at the car at eleven a.m. I'll send one of the gardeners to fetch us coffee for that time.'

As the sun rose higher in the clear azure sky, the day became quite pleasant, though there was still a damp nip in the air near the river. Just before 11.0, after a fruitless search of the north bank, Bernal and Miranda heard themselves being hailed by Lista from the Jardín de la Isla.

'I've got something, *jefe*,' he shouted in some triumph, holding up a black garment. Bernal and Miranda hurried to join him. 'I found it in a thicket near the town bridge, just below the point where the sluice draws water from the main river into the Ría that passes the royal palace. There are a few tears and snags in the wool as you can see.'

'Good Lord, it's a cassock!' exclaimed Bernal. 'A very rare find. Is it big enough to have fitted the deceased?'

'I think so, *jefe*,' said Lista, stretching out the garment at the waist. 'It's damp from the frost, but it's not sodden, so it hasn't been in the water, nor has it lain long in the woods, certainly not in the rains of last week.'

'Anything in the pockets?' asked Bernal.

'Only twelve pesetas, a rosary, and six lumps of white sugar, wrapped in papers marked *Envase especial para esta casa*.'

'Although the wrappings claim the sugar is wrapped especially for this establishment, I suppose the name of the café isn't given, as usual?'

'That's right, *jefe*. You could probably find them in hundreds of thousands of cheap bars or cafés.'

'But there won't be many bars in Aranjuez. It's worth a try later, if you have time.'

'I've handled the objects as little as possible, with tweezers, in case Varga can get fingerprints from them. He's having a go now in his van, but the surface areas are very small.'

'I expect he'll try the cassock itself back in the lab, Lista, with his new electron autography method, so handle it as little as possible. But that looks to be a very rough weave, so he may get nothing. Ah, I see the coffee's coming. Take the cassock to Varga, Lista, and don't mention our find to the gardeners.'

The latter had now appeared, bearing two trays with vacuum jugs and pottery mugs, and a plateful of croissants, the sight of which gave Bernal a sudden appetite, which he had not felt for many months. It must be the country air, he thought.

As he sipped the coffee, he chatted in apparently idle fashion with the father and son about Aranjuez and its population and industries, and then asked them about the religious houses. 'Now the Franciscan Sisters, are they still at the Convento de San Pascual?'

'Oh yes, Comisario,' said the older man.

'And at the church of San Antonio, are there still daily masses?'

'Indeed there are. I go myself.'

'There aren't any other convents, are there?'

'There is a new house, Comisario, just across the river from the jetty. The brothers have converted an old mansion.'

'Would they be the Cistercians, now?' asked Bernal.

'No, sir, they belong to a new order. They call it the Casa Apostólica.'

'Are there many brothers?'

'About thirty, we think, but most of them remain enclosed and don't come out into the town. We see only
Father Gaspar, the Prior, coming and going on matters of
business, and Father Dámaso, who attends to the domestic ordering in the shops.'

'How interesting,' said Bernal, without actually
showing himself to be too interested. 'I've never heard of
that order. What colour habits do they wear?'

'Just a black soutane, Superintendent, with a red braid
girdle and a wooden cross hanging from it.'

'It's not an ordinary cross, though,' chipped in the gardener's son, 'I've seen Father Dámaso's cross close to.
It's shaped like a German Cross—like the Iron Cross—at
the top and ends in a dagger-point at the lower end. It's
almost like a paper-knife.'

After they had finished their coffee, Bernal sent Varga
back with Lista to photograph and search the river bank
near the spot where the religious habit had been found,
while he decided to go with Miranda to pay a call on
Father Gaspar.

As they strolled along the avenue that had inspired the
blind composer Joaquín Rodrigo to compose his *Concierto de
Aranjuez* when spending his honeymoon in the delightful
town, before it was temporarily ravaged by the war,
Bernal pointed out to Miranda some grooves in the paving
near the palace wall.

'Can you guess what used to be there, Miranda?'

'There were quite large grooves made in the paving,
and then filled in. They're exactly parallel and about one
and a half metres wide, and run up to the main portico of
the palace.'

'And you can't guess what they were for?'

'No, I can't, unless there was a kind of tramway used
in the construction or rebuilding of the palace.'

'You're on the right track,' joked Bernal. 'When the
second railway to be built in Spain was finished in 1851—

it ran from Atocha to Aranjuez and people called it "*el fresa*" or "the strawberry line"—they ran a single-track extension right up to the palace here, and even into the main entrance hall, where they laid silver-plated rails. Isabella II inaugurated it, and the banker Don José de Salamanca paid for it.'

'Good Lord, it must have got quite smoky in the palace from the engine fumes.'

'I don't think so. They used to back the royal coach up the line from the station. It was a regular manœuvre.'

'Couldn't she have used a horse-drawn coach from the station?'

'No doubt she used to, but she must have hated travelling on the rough roads, because of her chronic cystitis, caused—the gossips said—by her frequent love-affairs with the royal guards, who infected her. Most of the royal coaches, and the thrones, of her reign had built-in commodes.'

'And with the crinolines she wore I suppose nobody would notice when she relieved herself.'

'Autocratic as she was, the people adored her for possessing all the old Spanish vices.'

Although it was less than half a kilometre to the Casa Apostólica, Bernal decided that they should go in the official car, in order not to reveal that they had been investigating anything close at hand.

The new religious order must enjoy considerable financial backing, thought Bernal, when they pulled up at the high wrought-iron gate of a well-restored eighteenth-century mansion set in large grounds. It was some time before the bell was answered by an aged black-garbed monk or friar, they weren't certain which, who asked the police driver their business.

'Mass has just begun,' he explained rather crossly, 'but you may enter and wait.'

Bernal indicated that they would, and the main gate

was opened for them to drive into the forecourt.

'You may await Father Gaspar in the parlour if you wish, Superintendent,' said the monk.

'Can we come to the church, or is it not permitted for lay people to enter?'

'Men may enter, but not women. If that is your wish, please follow me,' he replied, apparently somewhat mollified by their wish to attend the office, and then led them to the newly built church, to the right of the original house.

As he and Miranda entered, indicating to the monk that they would be happy to remain in the back row of pews, Bernal caught some of the words of the introit, which were said in Latin here too, he noticed: '*ecce Dominus veniet ad salvandas gentes*—behold the Lord shall come to save the nations . . .' intoned the white-vested celebrant, flanked by a deacon and sub-deacon likewise attired in the white proper for the day.

When Bernal was busy counting the number of monks seated in the chancel, Miranda nudged him and pointed out a small group of uniformed worshippers sitting in the right transept. As they knelt to pray, Bernal whispered, 'Slip out, Miranda, and see if you can spot the vehicles they came in. Ask our driver to chat with theirs and find out who those military chaps are.'

After the post-communion, but before the last gospel was read, Miranda returned and slid into the pew at Bernal's side.

'They've got a large Seat and a jeep parked round the back, *jefe*,' he whispered. 'Our driver has gone to have a smoke with theirs.'

'Good. I hope he asks about their strange uniform.'

When the last prayers had been said, they were once more approached by the aged monk who invited them to follow him to the parlour.

'Father Gaspar won't be long, Comisario. He has to

remove his celebrant's vestments before he can come to you.'

While they waited, Bernal gazed at the dismal nine-teenth-century coloured prints of scenes from the life of Christ, and wondered if he dared light a cigarette.

'There's an ashtray, chief,' said Miranda, noticing his superior officer's nervous fingering of a packet of Kaiser.

'Perhaps we'd better wait until the Prior gets here.'

When at last Father Gaspar appeared, Bernal rose to shake hands, closely observing as he did so the prominent red braid girdle he wore, from which hung a gold crucifix of curious dagger-like shape, with three squared-off cross-ends at the upper extreme.

'Do sit down, Comisario,' said the tall cleric politely. 'This is Inspector—?'

'Miranda, my assistant.'

'Will you take some refreshment?' He produced a de-canter and three glasses from a cupboard and poured them some wine. 'It's only a humble Moriles, I'm afraid.'

'That will be most welcome, Father.'

'Please smoke if you wish.'

The Prior was of large stature, white-haired and thin-faced, with a pointed nose, and he exuded a sense of power and burning fanaticism.

'How can I be of service to the Criminal Brigade of the Judicial Police?'

'We need to ask you a few questions concerning Captain Lebrija Russell's tragic death. What state of mind was he in when you last spoke with him? I under-stand you were his spiritual adviser.' Bernal obtained the impression that the Prior was relieved by the question, almost as though he had feared a worse one.

'It was indeed a very tragic occurrence.' Bernal noted that neither this nor any of the other witnesses connected with Lebrija showed any curiosity about the details of the supposed accident. 'Surely, Comisario, there's no question that his death was other than accidental? It would be unthinkable. He was entirely assured and self-possessed; never worried or depressed. Furthermore he was in a state of grace,' he said with a tone of finality.

'Ah, you saw him just before his departure from the college at Ocaña, then?'

'Not quite. He called here on his way to Madrid, made confession to me, and joined us at vespers. He said he would try to attend Mass at San Ildefonso the next day, which was the first Sunday in Advent.'

'I don't think he lived long enough to do that,' said Bernal. 'It seems that he died early on the Sunday morning.'

The Prior crossed himself. 'May his soul rest in peace, and may God preserve us all from a violent end.'

'Did Captain Lebrija often come here?' Bernal went on.

'Very frequently. He sometimes came for a week to undertake spiritual exercises. He was well liked by all the brothers.'

'How many are there in this house?' asked Bernal. 'I'm afraid I'm not familiar with your Order.'

'I'd better explain. Our Order was founded only in 1932 at Cologne, and we do not yet enjoy papal recognition. In Spain we have only two houses, with thirty-two brothers at this house including myself, and a smaller number at a second house in Seville.'

'Are all your brothers here today?' asked Bernal, noticing a look of anxiety pass across the Prior's face.

'I certainly believe so, Comisario, but they may not all have been at Mass. Some have to hew the wood and draw the water, you know,' he ended with a laugh that had a nervous, false ring to it.

'I'm sorry to be so curious, but what is the role of the Apostolic House?' Bernal asked.

'The original Apostolic Fathers were, of course, the

Christian writers of the first century, who had been in contact with the apostles of Our Lord himself. Emulating them, we see our mission as a rearming of society to counteract the laxity and wickedness now so prevalent in every sphere of life. We seek influential lay contacts— converts if you like—who can sow the seed of moral reform everywhere: in commerce, industry, the armed forces, broadcasting, journalism and so on. These lay members have very close ties with us.'

'I see. That is how you came to be the spiritual adviser to Captain Lebrija at the artillery college?'

'Yes, and to a number of other officers there. You will have seen some of them at Mass this morning. We have to rebuild our leaders' faith and give them a firm moral basis for their actions in the face of the rapid secularization of our social structures.' The Prior's eyes burned like those of a saint in an El Greco painting.

'Thank you, Father, for the explanation. I'm glad to hear that you are certain Captain Lebrija was not in any way depressed. His death is still something of a mystery, and the Marchioness his mother is most anxious for us to clear it up.'

'Whatever occurred, Comisario, I'm sure he did not commit felo-de-se. For us his death is a great tragedy; he played such an important part in our plans for stiffening the resolve of our army leaders. We shall be saying a Requiem Mass for him the day after tomorrow.'

When they got into the car to return to Madrid, Miranda asked their driver what he had managed to get out of the drivers of the military vehicles parked at the rear of the priory.

'They say they know very little, Inspector. When I asked them about the special blue uniforms with the red flashes on the epaulettes, they said that they sometimes changed the usual artillery uniform for certain occasions, and it belonged to a hush-hush branch like the GEOs or special operations group.'

'But it's quite different from the GEOs' uniform, isn't it?' Bernal commented.

'Yes, sir, you're quite right. I've never seen anything in the armed forces or police like it. That red flash is very distinctive.'

'What exactly is it like? Did you get a close look?'

'Yes, sir. It's pointed like a dagger at the outer edge, and has a triple head like a thick-armed cross.'

'Like a German Iron Cross?'

'That's it, sir. Like the medal some of those generals who served in Franco's Blue Division wear on official occasions.'

As they approached the southern outskirts of Madrid, Miranda asked Bernal what else he would like him to do.

'Nothing more for today, except to hand in your reports and depositions to Paco Navarro for his files. I expect Lista and Varga won't finish down there until sunset. We'll go over what we've got on both cases tomorrow.'

As the car nosed its way up the Calle Mayor through the Sunday evening strollers taking the usual *paseo*, they saw that a tall Norwegian spruce had been erected by the Ayuntamiento in front of their Ministry in the Puerta del Sol.

'It'll soon be Christmas, Miranda. We haven't got much time to get to the bottom of this murky business.'

FEAST OF THE IMMACULATE CONCEPTION OF THE B.V.M.
(8 December)

While breakfasting unhappily on the meagre offering of fried bread and ersatz coffee Eugenia had brought, Bernal shivered in the cold living-room of their apartment and cursed the *calefactor*, whose job it was to stoke the ancient boiler in the patio on the ground floor. The noise of his shovelling normally awoke them of a winter's morning, and even so the pipes and radiators in their eighth-floor flat wouldn't usually receive any hot water until a couple of hours later; today when it had turned much colder he hadn't appeared at all.

Through the *reja* of the small window that gave on to the terrace, where some brave but battered geranium flowers shivered in the keen wind, Bernal could see Eugenia bent over the *brasero* or brass brazier, blowing on the small pieces of matchwood she had crossed together in order to ignite the lumps of charcoal. As soon as it was well alight and had stopped smoking, she would bring it into the room and place it on the wooden frame under the circular table. Ours must be the last household in Madrid to use the non-electric *mesa camilla*, he thought, watching her efforts with the usual mixture of guilt and irritation. Everyone else used modern heaters of some kind, but she refused to contemplate using such wasteful new-fangled devices, and he had all but given up arguing with her.

'There you are, Luisito, get your legs under the table-cloth and you'll soon warm up!'

He raised the heavy red rep cloth for her to position the brazier correctly, and then gingerly balanced his feet on the rungs underneath, hoping the fumes wouldn't rise up and asphyxiate him.

'I'll have to be going shortly, Geñita.'

'You must help me fold some vestments first. It's the feast of Our Lady today, and Father Anselmo especially wants the blue chasuble.'

After disappearing into the oratory cupboard, she emerged staggering under the weight of exquisitely embroidered cerulean-blue ecclesiastical robes.

'Those are really superb,' exclaimed Bernal. 'They

can't be used very often.'

'No, Luis, they aren't. And according to that Second Vatican Council they need not be used at all any more. Those cardinals confirmed the reduction of the liturgical colours to five. But Father Anselmo is very traditional,' she said with obvious approval. ''If it has been done for a thousand years, why change it now?'' he asks. So for the Feast of the Immaculate Conception today he will use blue vestments instead of white. It will be a change from the Advent purple, at any rate.'

Connections began to form themselves in Bernal's mind. 'What are the five usual colours, Geñita? And when are they used?'

'But Luis, you must have noticed the different colours for the various days, even with your Godless upbringing!' She decided to humour him for once, since she judged the instruction she was giving to be very worthwhile. Perhaps there was hope for him yet. 'Let's start at the beginning of the Church year: in Advent, from the Sunday nearest to St Andrew's Day on 30 November, to Christmas Eve, the vestments and the altar cloths are normally purple or violet as a sign of penance. They change to white on Christmas Day as a symbol of joy in the coming of Our Lord and that colour continues up to the infra-octave of Epiphany on 14 January. From the second Sunday after Epiphany the colour is green, symbolizing hope, until the sixth Sunday or Septuagesima, when it becomes purple again for the Lenten fast. It stays purple until Maundy Thursday. The white of celebration is again used from Easter Day until Whit Sunday, when red, signifying the fire of the love for God, is used until Trinity Sunday, which is white. Then green is used right through until Advent comes round again. There, I hope you've learned something useful!'

Bernal was left reeling a little from the explanation, but asked 'When you were cleaning the vestments I didn't see any green ones. Why was that?'

'White can always replace green, or indeed any of the others in case of need. Some churches are too poor to have vestments in all the colours.'

'You said there are five liturgical colours normally used, but you've only mentioned four: purple, white, green and red.'

'The other one is black, but that's only worn on Good Friday, and on the Commemoration of all the Faithful Departed on 2 November, and of course, for Requiem Masses and funerals. You mustn't forget that the colour for the season of the year is often overridden by the colour proper for the day. If it's the feast of any martyr, for example, the vestments will be red, and if it's the feast of a virgin who isn't also a martyr they'll be white, and so on.'

'But why are these robes blue, then? You haven't ex-plained that.'

'It's an old tradition for feasts of Our Lady that are of the degree of double of the first class, such as today.'

'And pink? Can the vestments ever be pink?'

'Yes, Luis,' said Eugenia in a long-suffering tone. 'On the third Sunday in Advent.'

'Which is when?'

'Next Sunday, of course. Now will you let me get the breakfast things washed up, so that we can carry all these vestments to church in time for Mass?'

'Yes, yes, all right. But where will I find a list of the colours for each day?'

'In the Roman Missal, of course, at the beginning, where it gives the Liturgical Calendar. Look, I'll find you an old one that belonged to my mother.' She went to a cupboard in the rather battered sideboard. 'Here you are. It's pre-Conciliar, in Latin and Spanish, published by Acción Católica in nineteen-forty-five. The new one is much simplified and is only in the vernacular. Father

Anselmo doesn't use it much.'

'No, I don't expect he would,' muttered Luis, poring over the tables at the front of the missal.

'Can I go to the kitchen now?' she asked in considerable puzzlement, gazing at him with her head cocked on one side and her arms akimbo, but he had already sunk into a brown study.

After a while he went in search of his copy of the MAGOS messages, and began comparing them with the liturgical calendar printed in the missal.

The first message contained the words *Purple A.1*, and the fourth message, which *La Corneta* would be publishing that very day had *Purple A.3*; he remembered querying the *A.3* with Elena Fernández when she had read it out to him over the phone. Omitting the days marked *Feria*, which had no colour given against them in the table, he checked the number of days in Advent where purple vestments were indicated. The first was the first Sunday in Advent, which this year had fallen on 29 November. Could that be *Purple A.1* mentioned in the first MAGOS message, published on 14 November? If so, then the fourth message's *Purple A.3* might be the third day in Advent marked for purple vestments.

He counted down the calendar page: there were many red and white days for various saints, then he came to 20 December, which was the second 'purple' day. There was no other until 24 December, which was the last day of Advent, so that could well be *Purple A.3* in today's message.

Bernal now tried to work out the other messages. The second, published on 20 November, read *Blue A.1*. None of the days were indicated for blue vestments, but Eugenia was certain that today, the Feast of the Immaculate Conception of the Blessed Virgin Mary, was traditionally 'blue'. He checked the latter part of the missal under the Masses proper of saints, and there it was: *8 December:*

White or Blue. Certainly it was the first 'blue' day in Advent and apparently the only one at that season.

Now he tried the third message published on 27 November: *Pink A.1*. The table of the liturgical calendar did not mention pink at all. What had Eugenia said? It could be used on the third Sunday in Advent—next Sunday in fact. He checked in the first section of daily Masses proper of the season: *Advent, Third Sunday: Purple or Pink*. He flicked through the remainder of the fine bible-paper pages looking at the rest of Advent: pink was only mentioned for that Sunday. So the third message could signify the first (and only) 'pink' day in that season.

Now he drew up a schema on a blank sheet of paper:

Message Published	Text	Date Meant?
14 November	MAGOS Purple A.1 San Ildefonso	29 November
20 November	MAGOS Blue A.1 El Pardo	8 December (today)
27 November	MAGOS Pink A.1 Segovia	13 December
8 December	MAGOS Purple A.3 Aranjuez	24 December

He looked at his handiwork critically: there was always a gap of between sixteen and eighteen days between the publication of the message and the date apparently proposed for some action unknown to him. He wondered why: to give the recipients of the messages time to prepare? Perhaps.

In the case of the first message, something had indeed happened at San Ildefonso early in the morning of 30 November, which was close enough, and at all events Capt. Lebrija and his accomplice must have set out from Ocaña, stopping off at the priory in Aranjuez, on the evening of 29 November. So that tied up. Furthermore, that first message printed in the personal column of *La Corneta* on 14 November was ringed in red ink in Lebrija's copy of the newspaper. That was the only piece of concrete evidence that connected the MAGOS with San Ildefonso and with Capt. Lebrija, but it was conclusive, outside any coincidence.

What puzzled Bernal beyond measure was the body found drowned at Aranjuez on 6 December. According to his partial decodification of the messages, nothing should occur at Aranjuez until Christmas Eve, but the corpse had turned up two days ago, well before its time, when no action was apparently being proposed by the liturgically encoded dates—or else he had made a mistake. However, there was now a chance to check his theory. Something might happen at El Pardo today, he realized. Should he warn the King's secretary and have him put out an alert? Bernal thought he would then look foolish if nothing occurred after all. None the less he would contact the Zarzuela to see if any warnings had been received from the CESID or any of the other security branches; they had far more resources at their disposal than he had.

Eugenia sharply interrupted his calculations. 'We'd better be off with these vestments, Luis. You can help me carry the hamper.'

He submitted with better grace than usual, intending to check the liturgical calendar printed in his late mother-in-law's missal with Father Anselmo's more expert and practical knowledge of the topic.

In the lower hallway they dragged the heavy wickerwork basket out of the ancient hydraulic lift, having themselves descended by the eight flights of stairs in order not to over-strain the elevator's mechanical resources. The portress emerged from her doorway—resplendently arrayed in shiny black bombazine and wearing a large gold medallion of Murillo's bust of Our Lady of the Sorrows.

'*Buenos días, don Luis.* It's a sunny day for the fiesta, Doña Eugenia, thank the Lord. Are those the blue vestments? They'll look so wonderful now we've cleaned them. I've already been round to the church to put the white lilies before the altar.'

By the time the three of them reached the sacristy, they were out of breath. There Bernal managed to consult Father Anselmo about the colours for the various days, while the two *beatas* fussed with chasuble, maniple, stole and girdle. After getting a somewhat long-winded and ultra-pious confirmation of what he had already gleaned from Eugenia and from the daily missal, Bernal felt obliged to stay at least for the opening of the solemn Mass that was to be sung in Latin. Once more he remarked the chance appropriateness of the introit proper for the day: '. . . *quia induit me vestimentis salutis: et indumento justitiæ circumdedit me*—for He hath clothed me with the garments of salvation, and with the robe of justice He hath covered me . . .'

Quite soon Bernal slipped out by the baize-lined side door and into the Calle de Alcalá, where he stopped to buy a copy of *La Corneta*, getting the strange look from the *quiosquero* to which he was becoming accustomed. At the bar counter in Félix Pérez's where he ordered a large *café de desayuno* and a croissant, he scanned the personal column and found the fourth MAGOS message in a prominent position: 'MAGOS *Purple A.3. Aranjuez*', printed exactly as Elena Fernández had seen it ready for the copy room two days earlier. No doubt the King's secretary would see it too; should he be informed of Bernal's explanation of it at this stage? The thought that the calculations he had made might be erroneous still dogged him, but if they were right this fourth message called for some unspecified action on 24 December, and if they were wrong, then it was still anybody's guess. It would be safer to wait and see what the day would bring, since his decoding suggested that the second message called for some action on 8 December, that very day.

In his office at the Gobernación, he found Lista and Miranda assisting Navarro with a mound of reports and filing cards.

'We're keeping the two homicide enquiries entirely separate, chief,' said Navarro. 'I've put everything relating to Captain Lebrija on that side of the room, and I've cleared Elena's and Ángel's desks for the reports relating to the unknown cadaver found at Aranjuez.'

'That's fine, Paco. What are you doing about the reports on *La Corneta* and the MAGOS messages?'

'I've left them on the spare table in your office for the moment, since we've got so little on them.'

'I think I've got something to add,' said Bernal, 'but it's very tentative at present. Have we received the full report from the Instituto Anatómico on the Aranjuez corpse?'

'It came this morning and it's on your desk. The analyses still haven't arrived from the Institute of Toxicology, but they should be here soon.'

Bernal set to work on Peláez's long report, which was in his usual telegrammatic style:

Deceased: recovered from R. Tagus at Aranjuez. White male Caucasian, height 1.77 m., weight 82 kg., approximate age 45-50, stout build, rounded broad shoulders, dark hair greying at temples, dark brown eyes; discernible physical disease suggests chronic mild alcoholism: maxillary purpura, duodenal ulceration, incipient hepatic cirrhosis. Profession difficult to determine: no callouses on hands or feet, no deformation of legs, slight stoop suggests scholarly occupation, bald patch on crown of head not due to alopecia but shaved some 15 days prior to death (for religious reasons? has appearance of tonsure).

Bernal thought that Peláez was pretty smart to have spotted that, since he had left the scene before Lista's discovery of the abandoned cassock and had not since been informed of the find.

Good natural teeth, two premolars and one canine with gold fillings, complete set apart from extraction of all four third molars or wisdom teeth (photograph of dentition enclosed for checking with dentists' records). Broad, plain gold band on annular finger of right hand (manufactured in Seville according to jeweller's mark); gold neck-chain with plain gold cross pendant around neck (these objects sent to technical laboratory). Stomach contents show that a meal consisting of Spanish omelette, steak, fried potatoes and salad, accompanied by more than a litre of red wine, had been consumed within one hour and one and a half hours of the time of death. These contents, together with all other organs, and blood samples, sent to the Institute of Toxicology, and further blood samples sent to official hæmatologist for routine checks.

Cause of death: No asphyxial hæmorrhages on face, neck or scalp, and no water in bronchial passages or lungs nor 'pinpoint' marks on pulmonary surfaces; the victim did not die by drowning. Many of the abrasions on exposed parts occurred after death, probably by contact with natural objects in the river, a few had bled and had thus been occasioned before death. Seven heavy blows had been delivered on the back and top of the cranium. The first three blows had been dealt by a right-handed person standing behind and to the left of the victim, the instrument being fairly broad, smooth and blunt. These initial blows had produced extensive cerebral bruising, certainly sufficient to stun the victim temporarily, though possibly insufficient to cause complete loss of consciousness. Four further very heavy blows were delivered from above, while victim was either in a sitting or semi-prostrate position, the instrument being blunt but narrower than the first instrument. The second of these final blows was the cause of death, by fracturing the skull, fragments of which had entered the brain, producing massive hæmorrhage. The two last blows had been delivered after death.

Bernal whistled softly; not a drowning then, but a murder by bludgeoning, the corpse having been stripped of its outer clothing and thrown into the river. Peláez had added a handwritten note appended to the official typewritten report:

'Suggest you search for a bloodstained rifle. The first blows were possibly struck with the flat side of the butt, and the final homicidal blows with the narrow edge of the same weapon.'

Bernal noted that there was no mention of abrasions or lacerations on the forearms or palms of the hands which were usual if there had been an attempt at self-defence. This omission suggested that the killer had lain in wait for the victim in the dark, probably between 10.30 p.m. and midnight to judge by the evidence about the time of the victim's evening meal, and then had jumped out and attacked from behind, first knocking the victim to the ground in a dazed condition, and then finishing him off when he was semi-prostrate. Bernal noticed that no shoes had been found. It would be necessary to drag the river to look for them, and for the weapon, though if Peláez was right about the latter having been a rifle, was it likely that the perpetrator would have disposed of an object of such value in that way? Surely he would wipe it clean, in which case it would probably still bear minute traces of the victim's blood and perhaps some hairs from his head, which the murderer would have overlooked. In his mind's eye, Bernal saw again the row of locked rifle-racks at the artillery college at Ocaña, and wondered if he would ever be in a position to get hold of those weapons for Varga to examine. He decided to call his inspectors together for a conference on the pathologist's report.

When they were gathering in the outer office, Varga came in.

'I've got the technical report for you, *jefe*. I was able to get some good shots of the scrap of paper the Aranjuez victim was clutching in his right hand. The black light didn't help much, but the infra-red photographs are very clear. It's the upper left-hand corner of a handwritten sheet of very ordinary notepaper.'

Bernal examined the enlargement, which read:

Sr Direc . . .
Ministe . . .
Pue . . .
Ma . . .

and which clearly referred to the addressee. The jagged piece of paper also had part of the text:

Exce . . .
Le comu . . .
urgen . . .
la Op . . .

Bernal handed it over to Navarro, commenting, 'It seems to be part of a letter addressed to the director or permanent secretary of one of the Government ministries. Probably ours, don't you think?'

'I don't see how you can tell, *jefe*,' said Navarro.

'Well, the second line of the address refers to *Ministerio*, I agree you can't tell which, but the third line must be the street and the fourth must be *Madrid*. Now I can't think of many street-names starting with *Pue* unless the word is *Puente*, *Puerta* or *Puerto*—"bridge", "gate", or "port" or "mountain pass"—of which there are a number in each case, but the only Ministry situated in such a street that I can think of, without checking the street-index, is the

Puerta del Sol where we are.'

'Here's the *Callejero*, chief, let's check, but I'm sure you're right.' Navarro did some hasty counting. 'There are twenty-six starting with *Puente* and there's no Ministry in any of them as far as I know.' He went on down the list. 'There are forty-one beginning with *Puerta*, and—' he did a longer count—'and seventy-one with *Puerto*. The only other possibilities are two beginning in *Puebla*, one in *Pueblo* and one in *Pueblos*.'

'Ah, I forgot about those,' said Bernal. 'Now check the list of Ministries.'

'You're quite right, *jefe*, ours is the only one with an address starting with *Pue*.'

'It's a pity we haven't got more of the text of the letter,' sighed Bernal. 'Obviously it began "*Excelentísimo Señor*— Most Excellent Sir", then started to impart some piece of urgent information: "*Le comunico a S.E.* . . . *con urgencia*—I communicate to your Excellency with urgency", don't you think? But what about the rest? "*La Op*" could be completed in a number of ways, but notice the capital *O*. It's not likely to be *la Ópera*, since it's hardly credible anyone would write to the Interior Ministry about the Opera House or Opera Square with *urgency*. It could be the Opposition, but it's hard to see what could be urgent about the left-wing political parties. It's much more likely to have been *La Operación*—some plan or operation.' He turned to Varga and asked, 'Was there anything on the back?'

'Very little, chief, only a few letters. Here's the other infra-red photo.'

Bernal examined the enlarged photograph carefully:

. . . ención.
. . . nción.
. . . isos.
. . . ta.

. . . ón.

. . . ción.

. . . n.

'I can't make much of it. It's clearly a list of some kind, with each entry taking up most of a line and ending in a full point, but the word endings are so common, there's no way of guessing what words were there. What did you make of the hand, Varga? It's copperplate, isn't it?'

'Not quite, *jefe*. It's a florid italic script you don't see very often these days, and it's written with a fountain pen in blue-black permanent ink.'

'That's surprising, isn't it, when most people use ball-point pens for convenience these days, with disastrous results for legibility, as we all know.'

'The handwriting expert says the writer must have been in his fifties or more, and wrote shakily and with very uneven pressure, suggesting he was under some emotional strain and even, perhaps, suffered from some disease of the nervous system.'

'What an imagination those experts have!' exclaimed Bernal. 'The judges always take their evidence with a large pinch of salt.'

'The hand looks clerical to me, *jefe*,' commented Miranda, as the photographs were passed round. 'The priest who taught me in school used to write on the blackboard in a similar hand, with lots of serifs and curlicues.'

'That's what it reminded me of too, Carlos,' Bernal agreed. 'It's an old Church hand.'

'What should we do next, chief?' asked Lista.

'I suggest two courses of action,' replied Bernal. 'First, the Tagus must be dragged from the town jetty to the point where the body was found or even further downstream if possible. The main task will be to search for the murder weapon, possibly a rifle, and the dead man's shoes and any other pieces of clothing, a belt for example.

Second, we have to try and get an ID. The religious houses and churches at Aranjuez should be checked out for missing clerics, the local dentists should be shown the photograph of the deceased's dentition, and the men's outfitters and suppliers of religious garments asked about the old-fashioned underclothes and the cassock.'

'I'll organize the dragging operation, *jefe*,' said Varga.

'And Juan and I could do the other inquiries,' added Miranda.

'I'll come with you,' said Bernal, 'but you'd better stay here, Paco, to coordinate things. I'm concerned about the motive for this killing. It can't have been robbery, since the gold ring and the gold pendant and chain were left on the corpse before it was tipped into the river. It's unlikely, in any case, that a priest would carry large sums of money, especially not at that time of night. I think the local bars should also be asked whether they sell postage stamps; some of them do that in country places to help out customers when the post office is closed.'

'What makes you think the deceased was going to buy a postage stamp, chief?' asked Navarro.

'Oh, you may not have read Varga's report about the pocket contents, Paco. The victim had some wrapped sugar lumps, a rosary, and twelve pesetas—just the price of a stamp for an internal letter, probably the one that was snatched from his hand before he was disposed of. Perhaps he was going to get an envelope as well, since the sheet appears to have been loose in his hand.'

'You three had better set off for Aranjuez straightaway,' said Navarro to Miranda, Lista and Varga. 'The chief has got another job to do first.'

When they had left, Bernal asked Navarro what job he had referred to.

'The King's secretary wants to see you urgently, chief. He phoned just before Varga came. I told him you'd be there in half an hour. He says there's a bit of a flap on.'

'I'll go up there by taxi, Paco, but have the official car ready in an hour or so to take me to Aranjuez.'

Taking not the first nor the second, but the third taxi he found cruising along the front of the Gobernación building, Bernal jumped in and his heart sank at seeing the ever more common notice in the ashtray: '*En beneficio de todos, se ruega no fumar*'; he put the packet of Kaiser back into his pocket with ill grace. Why was it one always wanted to smoke more desperately when it was not allowed?

As the driver made an illegal turn to get round the Puerta del Sol towards the Calle del Arenal, Luis noted that workmen had erected a tall ladder in the flower-beds around the fountain in the square to place strings of coloured lights and decorations on the Christmas tree. It was curious how this German and Scandinavian tradition had caught on in Spain and had been grafted on to the native Yuletide ornaments, not to mention the commercial introduction of *Papá Noel* into the main department stores, as a prelude to the much older Iberian tradition of the gift-bearing Magi who came on Twelfth Night, when the children put their shoes on the window-sills expecting Melchior, Gaspar and Balthazar to fill them with goodies, and then hardly slept a wink until they could see what *Los reyes* had brought.

Bernal had noticed that the taxi-driver had given him the usual inquisitive glance when he asked him to take him to the Zarzuela Palace, but he'd decided not to offer any explanation. After his official badge had been examined by the royal guards, who he saw had been reinforced by four brown-uniformed National Police carrying submachine-guns, the King's secretary came straight over and led him to the small white Fiat.

As he drove Bernal up the long paved driveway to the Palacio de la Zarzuela, the official rapidly explained what the flap was about.

'Since early this morning, Comisario, we've been getting reports that leave has been cancelled in a number of barracks in four of the nine mainland military regions, but the Chief of the General Staff has not issued any such order. The King has asked for an immediate inquiry.'

'Where did the first reports come from?' asked Bernal.

'From El Pardo, and then Segovia and Valladolid in the north. Later we got similar reports from Valencia and Seville.'

'El Pardo was the first, was it?' repeated Bernal, with some satisfaction; perhaps he would after all reveal to the royal secretary his provisional interpretation of the colour code in the MAGOS messages.

'Yes, it was. The Prime Minister has been in touch with His Majesty and has set up a new Cabinet committee to oversee all the security services. Its first task will be to find out who gave these orders, because there is no kind of emergency, either external or internal, that could possibly justify them.'

When they were seated in the secretary's office, with its extensive views of the Guadarrama peaks, now gleaming white in the strong sunshine, Bernal brought him up to date with his investigation into Capt. Lebrija's death and his connection with the Casa Apostólica at Aranjuez. He also gave him a brief account of the unknown corpse recovered from the Tagus and handed him a copy of the pathologist's report.

'Have you any clue as to the nature and strength of this MAGOS organization, Comisario?' asked the secretary.

'I'm beginning to get the measure of it. I believe Father Gaspar, perhaps unwittingly, gave me a subdued version of its aims, as you'll see from my report on that interview. I think its power and influence may be far-reaching, and extend into most of the echelons of power, but its numbers may be very small. What's not clear to me yet is whether MAGOS is an alliance between ultra-conservatives in the

Church with a few wild, though deeply sincere, elements in the armed forces, or whether it is more widespread. Nor can we be certain about the name of the organization: does it refer simply to some action proposed for 6 January, or has it a more permanent character?'

'We'd be very pleased if you'd keep at it, Superintendent. We must try to find out what they have in mind to do.'

Bernal then remembered what Inspector Ibáñez of central records had said about the reserved information on the computerized central criminal files, and he explained the problem to the official. 'Could you provide me with the top secret computer keys, or seek the information on my behalf?'

'It actually says "*Reserved to higher authority*" on the screen, does it? We have a terminal here and our attempts produced no information at all about MAGOS. I'll look into it, if you'll leave it with me.'

'Very well. In the meantime I think you should reinforce the royal family's bodyguard. What are their movements up to 6 January?'

'We've already had the palace security strengthened with trusted units of the Policía Nacional. After the King's annual message to his people on Christmas Eve, the whole of the royal family will go for a brief skiing holiday in the Pyrenees, at Baqueira-Beret. They will fly back to Madrid on the morning of 5 January, in time for the Pascua Militar, which will be held as usual in the Palacio de Oriente on the morning of the sixth. Queen Sofía will take the royal children to the Plaza Mayor on the evening of the fifth, at the Mayor's invitation, to see the procession of the *Reyes* and they will greet the Three Kings of Orient from the balcony of the Casa de la Panadería.'

'That's going to be a devil of a headache for the security chaps, isn't it?' asked Bernal, with concern. 'The Queen and the Infantes will be exposed to possible attack for up to an hour or more, perhaps, and the Square will be packed with sightseers.'

'But the balcony of the Panadería is pretty high, and the houses surrounding the square will be searched in the late afternoon. In a way, the dense crowd will act as extra security men and make it difficult for a marksman to attempt anything from the square, certainly not with anything as large as a rifle. The height of the balcony would make it unlikely that a bomb could be thrown or a revolver used, because the section immediately in front will be kept clear for the procession itself, with the usual floats and *cabezudos* or *papier-mâché* giants.'

'Let's hope you are right,' said Bernal. 'Could you also explain to me the normal system of national alert in case of external or internal threats to State security? How is it organized in each branch of the armed services?'

'The Navy and Air Force are the first lines of defence in case of a foreign threat, of course. As far as sedition or riot is concerned, your own Ministry has the planned countermeasures. The nine mainland Military Regions, together with the three for the Balearics, the Canaries and the North African enclaves respectively, have a regular emergency procedure to follow, in seven phases, once the JUJEM or Junta of the General Staff gives the first order. It's known as *Operación Mercurio*. I'll ask for a copy to be sent to you under royal seal, if you like.'

'That would be most helpful, Mr Secretary.'

When Bernal called back at the office, Navarro had an urgent message for him. 'Father Gaspar has telephoned. He says that one of his monks is missing, a Brother Nicolás, who went away on Saturday evening in order to spend Sunday with his sister in Toledo. He was expected back yesterday morning, but did not return, and by today the monks became concerned. Father Gaspar says he rang the sister's house and discovered that Brother Nicolás hadn't turned up at all. Since he's inclined to be absent-minded, she didn't give it any importance.'

'Give me one of the photos of the corpse that was fished out of the Tagus, Paco. I'll take it to show to Father Gaspar. I'll bet a month's pay he'll recognize it as of his missing monk. I got a strong feeling on Sunday that he was keeping something back, and even lied at one moment during the interview, when I saw his ears turn red.'

'The car's waiting outside the side door, *jefe*. I arranged for Miranda and Lista to meet you in the Hotel Pastor at Aranjuez between one-thirty and two p.m. Here are the papers and the photo you'll need. *Hasta luego*.'

When Bernal arrived at Aranjuez, he told the driver to stop first at the town jetty, where he spotted two boats working their way very slowly upstream towards the weir. On one of them he could see Varga standing in the bows directing the dragging operation. As he waited on the quay, Bernal lit a Kaiser and turned up the collar of his camel-hair coat against the keen breeze.

After the boats tied up, Varga climbed the steps and showed Bernal a curious pile of urban and rustic refuse, including a number of odd shoes.

'It's amazing how people manage to discard or lose one shoe out of a pair, isn't it, Varga?'

'I expect a very logically minded detective would conclude that there are a lot of one-legged cripples about,' joked Varga. 'There's only one matching pair, *jefe*,' he said, holding up two worn black shoes, 'and they haven't been in the water long.'

'They probably belonged to our man,' said Bernal. 'Take them back to Peláez, will you? He'll see if they will fit the deceased.'

'Before we finish here, chief, I thought you'd like to see an experiment. I've made a dummy of the approximate weight and volume of the corpse, and we can try throwing it over the sluice-gate and see how far it gets along the Ría past the palace.'

'Let's do that, Varga. I take it there was no trace of the murder weapon?'

'None at all, though we've dragged the main river thoroughly.'

Varga and his assistant went to their van to get the dummy, which was dressed in white underclothes and socks similar to those found on the cadaver. After launching it over the lock the three of them followed its progress, taking the footpath along the north bank of the stretch of artificial waterway that led to the Castañuelas waterfall. Quite soon they saw that it was too large to float over the first step of the cascade, so they fished it out.

'Won't the weight increase as it gets waterlogged, Varga?' asked Bernal.

'I've tried to allow for that, with lead weights.'

'Let's throw it from the town jetty,' said Bernal, 'and see how far the current will carry it down the main river.'

Again they followed the bobbing object, which was more than half-submerged, by taking the towpath on the south bank of the Tagus. They found they had to hurry when it got out into the stronger main current, and observed how it was carried towards the north bank at the first large curve, but was then caught once more by an undertow which carried it onwards down the long reach. At the second bend, the dummy came almost to a complete halt, and they thought it would beach on the southern bank, but it gathered speed again and sped along the final reach towards the green bridge. Bernal shouted to Varga that it would be swept past the point where the body had been discovered, and urged him to get his boat-hook at the ready.

'We could let it go a little further, chief; I can recover it from the bridge.'

Just when Bernal thought they would lose it for good,

the mannequin came to a stop at the confluence of the two streams, and after a while a back-eddy started to nudge it upstream once more, towards the overhanging branch, on which it finally got entangled.

'What a piece of luck!' exclaimed Bernal. 'Well done, Varga! Take some photographs, will you?'

After this had been done and the object recovered, Bernal told the technician that he was going to interview Father Gaspar and would expect him for lunch at the Hotel Pastor if he wanted to wait.

'I'd rather get back to the lab, *jefe*, once I've returned the boats to the palace boat-house.'

When the official car drew up at the gate of the Casa Apostólica, the same aged monk came to answer the bell.

'Father Gaspar is just beginning the Requiem Mass for Captain Lebrija, Comisario.'

'Ah, I'd forgotten it was today. I'd like to attend it if you don't mind. Perhaps the Prior would spare me a few moments afterwards.'

'I'm sure he will. We are all much concerned for Brother Nicolás's safety.'

'Did you see him leave on Saturday evening? I take it you are the gate-keeper.'

'That is one of my duties, Comisario. No, I didn't see him leave, which was strange because two of the brothers had been delegated to accompany him to the bus station. It was I who went with him on Saturday to buy the ticket.' The old monk was much more forthcoming than he had been on the earlier visit, Bernal noticed, and now offered an interesting confidence. 'Perhaps you should know, Comisario, that Brother Nicolás had been confined to his cell for ten days, by the Father Prior's command.' His voice lowered to a stage whisper. 'Because of his drinking, it was. Father Gaspar ordered us to search his cell daily to make sure he hadn't any alcohol hidden there, nor any money to buy some.'

'But he still took his meals with the rest of you in the refectory?'

'Oh yes, Father Prior allowed him to take wine with his meals, but no other strong liquor.'

'Was this a new state of affairs, Brother Nicolás being restrained in his cell?' asked Bernal.

'Not restrained, Comisario,' said the monk somewhat reproachfully, 'he was discreetly watched, that's all. Though after the quarrel he had with the Father Prior, we'd been ordered not to let him out of our sight. On Saturday evening he took advantage of our going to compline, Comisario. Such a thing to do, such a thing!' The old monk shook his head. 'But he was a most pious man, most pious. He even asked me to post a daily missal he was sending to his sister to aid her devotions, but I didn't tell Father Gaspar about it.'

Bernal remembered from previous cases what a hot-bed of tittle-tattle religious houses usually were, and encouraged the aged brother to tell him more. 'And what was the quarrel about, do you know?'

'Well, I'm not really sure, Comisario,' said the monk, looking about him to make sure there were no eaves-droppers. 'It was over some documents, I think, that temporarily disappeared from the Father Prior's room. A fortnight ago six artillery officers came from the college after the last office of the night—such an unusually late hour for a visit—and they were closeted with Father Gaspar for over two hours. I saw Brother Nicolás hovering in the cloister outside the Father Prior's door—he's an inquisitive man in the best possible way—but I'm not sure if he heard anything.' The old monk sniffed. 'At least he wouldn't tell me about it afterwards. But the next day after terce Father Gaspar called him in and they had an almighty row. I couldn't hear much of it, but the Father Prior was shouting about some missing papers, until Brother Nicolás seemed to placate him, saying they had been mislaid on the Father's desk.'

'And it was after that incident that Brother Nicolás was confined to his cell?'

'Yes, that's so, but it was for his own good, we all agreed about that. He had got into the habit of slipping down to the local bar after vespers, where he used to drink spirits and come back in a sorry state, but Father Gaspar found out and stopped him having any money. Then Brother Nicolás used to try and beg some from the rest of us. It was most pitiful to see him imprisoned in his vice.' He crossed himself, and indicated that they should now proceed to the church if they were not to miss the Requiem Mass.

Out of the monk's hearing, Bernal gave his driver instructions to park at the rear of the building if he could, and take note of the registration numbers of the vehicles parked there.

The priory church seemed fuller than on the previous occasion, and Bernal noted that the colonel who was director of the artillery college at Ocaña, together with a large contingent of officers and cadets, sat in the left transept, all of them dressed in proper regimental uniform, while on the right were the members of the Lebrija family, most of them attired in mourning black. The three veiled ladies he took to be the Marquesa de la Estrella and her two daughters, while the tall, rather stout figure alongside them was presumably the Marquis himself. The Order must think the Lebrijas very important to allow ladies in, he thought.

Bernal noticed that the altar was draped in black, and Father Gaspar and the deacon and sub-deacon also wore black vestments. No incense was burned at the introit and the acolytes bearing candles were omitted as is usual in the Mass for the Dead. The celebrant had by now reached the gradual: '*Requiem æternam dona ei,*' and Bernal listened with interest to the last words of it: '*In memoria æterna erit*

justus; ab auditione mala non timebit—the just shall be in
everlasting remembrance; he shall not fear the evil
hearing,' and recalled how puzzling he had found those
words, heard in the funeral Masses for his mother, and
for various relatives and departed colleagues. '*No temerá
oír malas nuevas,*' as the Spanish translation put it: 'He
shall not fear to hear bad news;' but what sort of news
good or bad was a dead person capable of hearing? It
seemed to Bernal to be exclusively a problem for the
living, until he had been moved to ask Father Anselmo,
his wife's confessor, who had explained that the words
came from Psalm 111, verse 7, and in their original context referred to the living man: 'Happy is the man who
fears the Lord . . . Bad news shall have no terrors for
him.'

After the responsory and the final prayer for when the
body is not present, Bernal found himself rather hastily
conducted to the same parlour as before. The old monk
appeared anxious to avoid his coinciding with the other
mourners now leaving the church.

Soon Father Gaspar appeared, and seemed more ready
to be helpful than on their first meeting.

'I'm so relieved you've come, Comisario. I called your
office to report that one of the brothers is missing. Nicolás
went away after supper on Saturday evening to catch the
last *coche de línea* to Toledo, and gave us to understand he
would return on Monday morning. By this morning I was
sufficiently alarmed to telephone his sister, who shocked
me by saying he had never reached her house. She
thought he'd decided not to go there after all.'

Bernal took out his file. 'Perhaps you would care to
look at this photograph, Father, and see if you can recognize the person.'

'Oh dear God, that's him,' said the Prior, crossing
himself. 'He looks . . . looks dead on this photograph.'

'I'm afraid he is. Perhaps you could arrange to come

and make a formal identification, or we could ask his sister—' Bernal hesitated.

'No, no. It's my duty to come. In any case I shall be travelling to Madrid with the Marquis and his family. How dreadful it all is! How did it happen?'

'He was found on Sunday morning in the river,' explained Bernal, as Father Gaspar crossed himself once more, 'but we couldn't then identify him. You will recall that you told me all your monks were accounted for.'

'But we had no idea then, none at all!' burst out the Prior, rather vehemently, Bernal thought. 'He was such a pious man, and of such a simple and innocent nature, almost childlike. He was greatly loved by all the brothers. He was a *sevillano*, you know. He took his vows at our Seville house.' He looked suddenly grave. 'Surely there's no suggestion that he committed—' the Prior almost whispered—'felo-de-se? He had a little weakness in that he was fond of his wine, but it was only a venial sin.'

'No, we don't think so.'

'Ah, an accident, then. At least we shall be able to bury him in sanctified ground.' The Prior lost his sudden air of relief. 'But he was unshriven, and died without the last sacrament. What a terrible thing!'

'Would it be possible for me to see his possessions?' asked Bernal.

'Possessions?' echoed the Prior wonderingly. 'You realize that once we have taken the vow of poverty, we have no worldly possessions. But you may inspect his cell if you wish, Comisario.'

Father Gaspar led him up the dormer staircase to the rows of bare, whitewashed cells. The late brother's contained a truckle bed, tidily made, with a large wooden crucifix affixed to the wall above it, a small bedside table with a worn, morocco-bound prayer-book, and a small wardrobe, which Bernal opened, observing that it contained two cassocks, a black cloak and hat, and two drawerfuls of white shirts and underclothes.

'Is it not odd that he went without his cloak and hat, Father?' Bernal commented.

'Somewhat odd, considering the cold evenings we've been having. But he was very absent-minded, and hardly noticed the weather. We didn't know that he had gone without them, because no one saw him leave.'

'Did he go much into the town?' asked Bernal.

'Hardly ever. Only when he went to catch the bus to go to Toledo, or to post a letter. On his two or three visits a year to his sister he would come to me for sufficient money for the journey.'

'And did he ask you for money on this occasion?'

'Oh yes, on Friday, when he went to buy the coach-ticket.'

'It's strange we didn't find that ticket on the body,' said Bernal. 'Did he take sugar in coffee, by the way?'

The Prior was clearly taken aback by the apparent inconsequentiality of the question. 'Now, come to think of it, he didn't. He used to collect the odd lumps that came his way and give them to poor people he met.'

'I see,' said Bernal. 'And can you tell me what was served here at supper on Saturday evening?'

'Steak, I think, but I'll see you have a copy of the refectory menu before you leave.' The Prior looked puzzled again at this question.

Bernal opened the drawer of the bedside table and took out the contents. A cheap notepad, an old-fashioned fountain-pen, a bottle of permanent blue-black Quink and a clean blotter. There were no envelopes.

'May I take these few possessions for examination?' Bernal asked the Prior. 'We shall return them later.'

'Take what you wish, Comisario.'

After Bernal took his leave of Father Gaspar, he returned to the car, where his driver handed him the list he had made of the *matrículas* of all the vehicles parked at the back of the priory. 'You'll see there were three limousines with Seville numbers, chief.'

'The family's vehicles, I expect,' said Bernal. 'After lunch, I want you to drive me to Toledo. I want to interview the dead man's sister.'

As Bernal sat in the comfortable lounge of the Pastor, sipping a Larios *gin tonic* and smoking a Kaiser, he wondered how long Miranda and Lista would be. He pondered on Father Gaspar's reactions during their interview. In contrast to their first meeting, he had seemed ostensibly concerned, but inwardly relaxed; he looked like a man who feared no danger to himself or to his organization. There had clearly been ample time to remove anything incriminating from the late Brother Nicolás's cell, though the notepad, fountain-pen and bottle of ink had been left as if they had been considered of no importance. Varga would, of course, check them with the scraps of paper found in the dead man's hand, and Bernal would ask the murdered monk's sister for a sample of his handwriting.

Bernal picked up the prayer-book, which was in fact a book of hours. He supposed that Father Gaspar would have examined it thoroughly before allowing him to find it there, if indeed it had really belonged to Brother Nicolás; there was no name inscribed inside the cover. Bernal flicked through the pages, but could see that none had been turned down, there were no markings of any kind, nor had any papers been left inside. He turned to the list of refectory meals for the previous week: the Saturday evening collation corresponded exactly to Peláez's note on the stomach contents of the deceased, though the neatly typed menu did not mention wine. Nevertheless Father Gaspar had admitted that Brother Nicolás liked his Valdepeñas; more than admitted, Bernal judged, positively offered the information about his alcoholism, probably in order to suggest the notion of a half-tipsy man accidentally stumbling into the river in the dark.

Inspectors Miranda and Lista now interrupted his musings.

'Nothing, *jefe*,' said Miranda, 'or virtually nothing, though the owner of a small bar did recognize the photograph as being of Brother Nicolás, one of the monks from the Casa Apostólica, who sometimes slipped out for a snifter after compline, but he hadn't seen him for some weeks. The bartender had noticed his habit of slipping sugar-lumps from the counter into the pocket of his cassock. We've not found any other bar where he was known.'

'Does that bar where he was recognized sell postage stamps?' asked Bernal.

'They keep a few to help their customers out, just as they sell lottery tickets and tobacco. It's only a small town, after all, and the *estanco* closes quite early.'

'None of the priests at the other convents and churches in the town knew him, chief,' said Lista. 'I've been to them all.'

'You'll be glad to know that Father Gaspar positively identified the photo,' said Bernal. 'Perhaps you'd come with me to Toledo after lunch, Carlos, for us to interview Brother Nicolás's sister. Juan can drive your car back to Madrid, and help Paco with the reports.'

After lunch Bernal and Miranda were driven in the smooth official Seat 134 out of Aranjuez by the N.400, which followed the south bank of the Tagus all the way to the old Visigothic capital of Spain. On the eastern heights of the city, as they passed the old Castle of San Servando, where El Cid had kept a vigil before meeting King Alfonso VI at an important assembly of the Court, Bernal tried to shake himself more awake from the near-slumber that had overcome him from the large Carlos III brandy he had taken and the lack of his usual siesta. They gazed at the famous view, immortalized by El Greco, and Bernal said,

'All we need now is the storm, Carlos.'

The driver parked the car with some difficulty in the Zocodover, the small, irregularly-shaped main square, which had once been the Moorish market-place, and which, Bernal remembered, had been renamed 'La Plaza de Carlos Marx' for a time during the Second Republic. As they emerged from the narrow alley that led to the upper square near the Cathedral, Bernal and Miranda stopped in surprise at the glowing window of an old-fashioned *confitería*, which was full of round boxes or drums of various sizes, opened to reveal Christmas eels—coils of burnt almond-paste, with eyes of glacé cherries or pieces of angelica, and delicious crystallized fruits filling the spaces between the writhing marzipan.

'You hardly ever see those on sale in Madrid, Carlos,' commented Bernal. 'I think I'll order a couple for the family, and the driver can put them in the boot. They're typical of Toledo.'

'I'll take one as well, *jefe*. I remember seeing them at Christmas in Corunna, too, when I was small.'

After paying for their order, they went on past the many tiny workshops where the artisans were hammering at damascened Toledo steel objects for the tourist market, and finally reached the cathedral. They had been surprised to learn that Brother Nicolás's sister lived inside the archi-episcopal precincts, on the first floor of the old cloister. They were greeted by the homely sight of washing hung out to dry in the upper cloister walk, where they discovered that Señorita Abad had a most roomy apartment. How happy his wife Eugenia would be to move to this, thought Bernal. There was no substitute for really living over the shop.

They were graciously received in old Castilian style and offered white wine for refreshment. Bernal now took his time over the difficult task of breaking the news of the death of the lady's brother.

'When was your brother last here, señora?'

'Over five weeks ago, on All Saints' Day, it was. He's very scatter-brained, you know, Comisario, but it's not like him to go off like this without saying a word to anyone.'

Bernal glanced at Miranda, who was taking notes of the interview. 'I'm afraid there is grave news, señora.' He handed her the photograph, which she perused.

'That's him, Comisario. But what's happened to him?' She put her hand to her mouth as she grew aware that she was looking at the photograph of a corpse.

'I'm extremely sorry to have to tell you that his body was recovered from the river quite near to the priory at Aranjuez.'

Señorita Abad crossed herself. 'Oh dear God! He must have had a drop too much and fallen in.' She took out a handkerchief and dabbed her eyes. 'How childlike he was. Always in the wars through his absent-mindedness. But when was he found?'

'On Sunday morning, señora, but only today have we been able to identify him.'

'That can't be, Comisario!' she exclaimed. 'He was due here on Saturday night, ready to spend his saint's day here with me on Sunday. He takes me every year to that nice restaurant on the corner of the Zocodover, you know. When he didn't turn up, I thought little of it, until Father Gaspar telephoned today to ask why he hadn't returned, when in fact he had never arrived. Yet he couldn't have died at the weekend,' she said. 'Look at this, Comisario. The postman delivered this an hour ago.'

She went to fetch a small parcel wrapped in brown paper, which Bernal examined with care.

'You see, Comisario? He must be alive!'

The parcel had clearly been opened and loosely re-wrapped. It was addressed to Señorita Abad at the Cathedral, and the postmark was badly blurred where the franking-stamp had touched the corner of the rough brown paper. Bernal took out a jeweller's glass and could see that the mark was somewhat clearer on the two glossy stamps bearing Juan Carlos I's head. He thought he could make out part of the word ARANJUEZ in a curve at the top, 11^{00} in the centre, and the lower part of the day and month, *06 Dic*, while the year was quite clear below.

'I'm afraid this was posted on Saturday morning, señora, well before he died. May I see what it contains?'

'Of course, Comisario. That's the oddest part, really. It's just his daily missal. There's no note or anything.'

'But it is his handwriting on the address?'

'Oh yes, I'm sure. I'll find you one of his letters for you to compare.' She rummaged in a drawer. 'Why would he put his missal in the post like that? Perhaps he really meant to send me something else? But he was intending to come here that very day!'

Miranda now examined the wrapping paper and compared it with Brother Nicolás's handwriting, while Bernal checked through the pages of the missal. He could see there were a number of markers of thin paper, each bearing different religious images and texts, like those often handed out at church doors after Mass, but he could spot no marks in pencil or ink.

'May we borrow the missal and the wrapping-paper, señora, as well as this letter from your brother?'

'Of course you can, Comisario.'

'Please don't build up any false hopes, señora. If you wish, we will take you to Madrid for you to make the formal identification, but Father Gaspar is also going, and if you prefer not to—'

'I have to come, Comisario, to satisfy myself that it is him. One must find strength for the trials God sends.'

FEAST OF ST EULALIA OF MÉRIDA
(10 December)

When Bernal reached the office that morning, Inspector Navarro handed him the toxicologist's report on Brother Nicolás.

'It arrived yesterday evening, after you had left, *jefe*, but I thought it could wait until today.'

'They certainly have taken their time over it. What are the main points?'

'No sign of drugs in the stomach contents, blood or organs, but there was quite a high level of alcohol, over 140 milligrams per cent. Since he was a regular drinker, it wouldn't have been enough to make him lose control of his movements, but it would have been plenty to make him very tipsy.'

'And therefore unwary, Paco. That's why he was not on his guard.'

'The most puzzling thing is this, chief. They found some river water in his stomach. They are sure because of the traces of silt and algæ in it, which match the sample Varga took from the river.'

'But that must mean he was still alive when he went into the water,' expostulated Bernal, 'and Peláez was sure that he had not drowned, but had been killed by one of the blows on the head. Was there any water in the lungs or bronchial passages?'

'No, Chief, only in the duodenum and stomach.'

'Peláez must have got it wrong, then, though it's not like him. The deceased must have gulped some water before death, and it's hardly credible that he would have climbed down from the path that passes the royal palace in order to drink some water from the river, which is very contaminated. You'd better ask Peláez to come up for a conference.'

After the call had been made, Bernal asked Navarro about Brother Nicolás's missal, which had been sent to the technical lab.

'Has Varga got anywhere with it?'

'Not very far. He says there appears to be nothing written in it. He's sent up a list of the pages where markers had been inserted in the section of Masses proper for the day.'

Bernal looked at the list with growing interest, and the series of dates Varga had typed out: 29 November, 8, 13 and 24 December, 1, 5 and 6 January. 'And is nothing written on the corresponding pages, or on the page-markers?'

'Not as far as he can make out, but he's trying further tests.'

'I think Brother Nicolás was trying to warn us about the MAGOS plot, Paco. Consider the first four dates: they correspond to my interpretation of the colour code in the MAGOS messages. Tell Varga to keep at it. The dead monk must have learned something in Father Gaspar's room that he was trying to pass on to the authorities by secret means.'

Before Dr Peláez arrived, Ángel Gallardo came breathlessly into the office.

'Didn't I warn you not to risk blowing your cover, Ángel?' said Bernal reproachfully. 'What are you doing here? Has Elena found out anything further?'

'I've only got a moment, chief. My mate's gone to phone his girl-friend and I took a chance to come up and tell you the news. There's something big brewing, not here but in Andalusia. We've been told to take a large van loaded with pamphlets specially printed on *La Corneta*'s presses down to Seville and deliver them to an address in the Calle de la Feria there.'

'Have you managed to see what the pamphlets say, Ángel?'

'Better than that, *jefe*, I've brought you one.' He produced a folded red and blue glossy sheet. 'I slit open one of the packages. There are also packs of large posters, but I couldn't get at those so easily.'

Bernal spread out the folded sheet and the three of them examined it. It was headed in large blue letters:

MAGOS. THE DAY OF NATIONAL SALVATION IS AT HAND!

All members are asked to make themselves ready for resolute action on 6 January. Final orders will be given at the regional meetings on Sunday 13 December.

Every day that passes sees our national life prostituted by the political parties that bring our country into disrepute at home and abroad, just as the late Generalísimo forewarned.

Every day sees our religion spat upon, and our priests and nuns ridiculed.

Every day sees our family life demeaned and the honest feelings of our mothers, wives, sisters and daughters degraded by overt pornography in the theatres, cinemas and newspaper kiosks.

Every day sees our people led into the wicked temptation of gambling on football pools, lotteries and bingo.

Every day sees our gallant soldiers and civil guards murdered by regionalist fanatics whose sole aim is to destroy the unity of the Fatherland.

Soon we shall put all this to rights. The old Spanish traditions will be restored. The moral reawakening of our country is at hand!

DO NOT FAIL MAGOS! IT IS THE LAST CHANCE TO SAVE THE NATION!

'It doesn't say where these regional meetings are to be

held,' commented Bernal. 'Are there more vans involved than yours, Ángel?'

'Yes, chief. Seven others have been loaded up, and I've talked to some of the drivers. One is going to Barcelona, another to Valencia, and a third to Valladolid. I didn't manage to find out about the others.'

'H'm,' muttered Bernal. 'It looks as if one vanload is being sent to each of the military regions. The central region can obviously be supplied nearer the time. Has Elena managed to find out where the meetings are to be held?'

'She says she's seen boxes of red and blue badges in the Editor's office, and there's clearly a lot of preparation going on. She's going to try and pump the Editor's personal secretary at lunch time.'

'When you get to Seville, Ángel, find out everything you can, especially the venue for the regional meeting next Sunday, and ring us back. You could stay there for the next four days. Couldn't you fake a breakdown with the van?'

'I'll cause one if necessary, *jefe*. I can always put sugar into the fuel tank. It would take a repair garage a couple of days to discover what was wrong.'

'In an emergency, contact the Seville police, but see what you can find out on your own first. Remember our role is essentially one of discreet observation. We haven't the authority to arrest anyone on mere suspicion.'

'OK, *jefe*, will do.'

Soon after he had departed, Dr Peláez arrived in somewhat aggressive mood. 'You've taken me from a most interesting autopsy, Bernal. What's the problem?'

'I'm sorry to drag you out, Peláez, but are you sure your findings about the cause of Brother Nicolás's death are correct? There's some conflict with the toxicologist's report.'

'You mean the Aranjuez corpse? Of course my findings

were correct. Aren't they always?'

'But look at this, Peláez. The Institute of Toxicology found river water in the monk's stomach and duodenum. Now you say he died from the blows to the head before being pushed into the river and that he didn't die by drowning. Can you explain how he managed to swallow water, if he was already dead?'

'H'm, I see. Yes, it is a poser. Let me read the report.'

Peláez held the typewritten text close to his thick pebble lenses to peruse it carefully. 'River silt and algæ, eh?' He pondered for a while. 'You realize there's no doubt whatsoever in the matter? Brother Nicolás did not drown. I found no asphyxial changes at all. I also ran the Gettler test, which, although it dates back to 1921, is still reliable and is always accepted by the courts.'

'Can you explain it briefly?' asked Navarro.

'You simply take blood samples from the left and right cardiac cavities of the suspected drowning, and compare the sodium chloride content. When a person drowns, the water tends to pass from the lungs into the blood stream. If he drowns in sea water, the salt level in the water will cause the sodium chloride level in the blood found in the left cavity of the heart to be notably higher than that in the right. If he drowns in fresh water—it doesn't matter if it's river or lake water or clean bath water—the reverse situation will be found. If the subject was already dead from other causes before being thrown into the water, then Smith and Glaister proved that water cannot enter into the left cavity of the heart, and the sodium chloride level will be the same in both cavities, just as I found in Brother Nicolás's case.'

'How then can we account for the river water in his digestive tract?' asked Bernal.

'We shall have to hypothesize. How about this as a suggestion? The monk comes out of the priory somewhat tipsy from the large quantity of red wine he has drunk at supper. He is on his way to buy an envelope and a stamp to send off a letter which he is carrying.'

'But why isn't he wearing his cloak and hat on this chilly evening?' objected Bernal. 'And where is the bus ticket he bought the day before for the trip to Toledo? The old janitor monk went with him to buy it.'

'Either he's in too much of a hurry to post this important letter, or his mild drunkenness prevents his feeling the cold. He's carrying the bus ticket in the pocket of his cassock. You didn't find it in the priory, did you? The murderer removed it from the body later.'

'Alternatively,' said Bernal, 'he had left the ticket in his cell and was going back for it, his cloak, hat and a small amount of luggage before the *coche de línea* left at ten-thirty p.m. Our problem is knowing exactly when he went to post the letter. Then Father Gaspar or someone else removed the ticket before we searched the cell.'

'Very well. I agree there are two possibilities on that point. At all events, he sets out from the priory along the path that leads to the town bridge and brings him near to the north-east corner of the royal palace. In an obscure spot he is suddenly attacked from behind and struck three times with something like the butt of a rifle. You haven't found the weapon, I take it?'

'No, we haven't. I can hardly call in all the weapons at the artillery college for you to test.'

'I do see the problem. Anyway, Brother Nicolás falls dazed by the blows, momentarily unconscious, perhaps. The attacker strips off his cassock, pulls off his shoes, and snatches the letter from his hand, inadvertently leaving a small scrap of it in the victim's tightly clutched right fist. I'm not sure why he strips off the outer clothing and the shoes, though.'

'Presumably to prevent an early identification. Even the black shoes might be recognized by someone close to him,' said Bernal.

'I don't understand why the murderer left the cassock neatly folded in the nearby wood, chief,' commented Navarro.

'Either he was disturbed, or he thought there'd be no systematic search if the local Guardia Civil treated it as a suicidal drowning,' suggested Bernal. 'He checks the pockets, though, and if the bus ticket was there, he removed it, leaving what he regarded as of no importance. In any case he hopes to delay identification.'

'Now let's look at the plan of the Aranjuez gardens,' said Peláez. All this happens on this stretch of the path where it runs alongside the Ría or artificial waterway. After being stripped of his religious habit, Brother Nicolás recovers consciousness and tries to break away from his assailant. During the struggle—'

'Lista found signs of a struggle on the bank,' interrupted Bernal.

'That's good. It helps my reconstruction,' said Peláez. 'He breaks away and falls into the shallow watercourse, gulping some of the water as he does so; remember it's the same water as in the main river. His attacker then renews the attack, delivering the fatal blow and three others from above. Certain now that his victim is dead or dying, he decides to carry him the few metres to the main river bridge, in order to throw him into the main current, which will carry him much further downstream, well away from the scene of the murder and, of course, from the priory. The overhanging branch was just bad luck; the corpse could have been carried many kilometres down the Tagus. How's that for an explanation!' said Peláez triumphantly.

'I think it's pretty good. Do you think there could have been more than one assailant? The footprints were so badly defined, and the surface of the path was so hard from the year-long drought—last week's rain hardly softened it at all—that Varga could get nothing positive.'

'There could have been two or more assailants, I suppose, but one strong and determined murderer could have carried out the whole thing.'

'I must say I get the impression of a hurried crime, not a premeditated one,' said Bernal, 'but we must recognize that hasty crimes are often the most successful, especially when there is no obvious connection between the killer and the victim, and no obvious motive. Perhaps Brother Nicolás was indiscreet at supper or just afterwards, and hinted that he was off to send some important information to the Ministry of the Interior. He was overheard, someone quickly followed him out or was warned by telephone to go and intercept him. I don't believe that Father Gaspar did it personally, but he may well have tipped off one of his military pupils, who decided to take immediate action. Probably the killing was more than Father Gaspar bargained for, which would account for why he looked so upset on Sunday.'

'Is there no chance of getting all the rifles in for inspection, chief? Some excuse could be invented.'

'If this were a normal case I should have proceeded in the normal manner, of course,' said Bernal, 'with a full scene-of-crime operation and massive search of the surrounding countryside. All weapons in use in the area could have been taken for examination, not to mention tyre-moulds from all the vehicles at Ocaña, which would have led us to Captain Lebrija's accomplice at La Granja, when they went to place the explosive on the power-line. But our orders are so restrictive: discreet inquiry and no more. All I can do is to give a full report to higher authority and wait to see what they order me to do.'

After Dr Peláez had left, Navarro was called down by the desk-sergeant to sign for a special delivery. He returned bearing a large blue envelope, which had the royal arms on the back and four large wax seals on the flaps.

Bernal opened it and found the details of Operation

Mercury, which the King's secretary had promised to send him. It was headed SECRET, and began:

MINISTERIO DE DEFENSA

COMMITTEE OF THE CHIEFS OF THE GENERAL STAFF

Date of issue: 1 December 1980
Declassification: Group 4
Number: 131.X.2Q

OPERATION MERCURY

Code transmitted	*Orders*
Mercury	Servicio de Intervención [Intervention operation]
Venus	Estado de Prevención [Reinforcement and Vigilance]
Jupiter	Supresión de permisos [Cancellation of Leave]
Mars	Alerta [General Alert]
Saturn	Estado de Excepción [Maximum Alert]
Uranus	Movilización [General Mobilization]
Pluto	Operación [Action]

There followed detailed instructions for the implementation of each successive stage of the secret plan to foil any possible coup d'état. The orders, addressed to the captains general of each of the twelve military regions, instructed them at the moment of receipt of each codeword to ratify it at once by telephone and telex with the Chiefs of the General Staff before carrying out each order.

Bernal was impressed by the apparent efficiency of the plan, but was disturbed by a certain resemblance it had to something he had recently seen. 'Paco, would you get out the infra-red enlargements Varga took of the scrap of paper Brother Nicolás was clutching when we found him?'

Navarro extracted the photographs from the relevant file and brought them to Bernal's desk.

'Now compare the back of the fragmentary letter with this top secret plan.' Navarro placed the endings of the seven words: -ención, -nción, -isos, -ta, -ón, -ción, -n, against the key to the code used in Operation Mercury. 'You see? It matches exactly with the Government's secret instructions to military commanders for foiling coups d'état. Now this can't possibly be coincidental. How could a humble monk from the priory in Aranjuez get hold of the secret orders of the Ministry of Defence?'

'Could he have been spying, jefe?'

'It's possible, but it isn't likely. After all, to the best of our knowledge he was trying to send the information to the Interior Ministry. What would be the point of that? Any reasonable person would have assumed that all the cabinet ministers would be *au fait* with these secret counter-measures.'

'In any case, chief, the Ministry of Defence hasn't invoked any of the successive stages of the plan, has it?'

'Not according to the King's secretary. Officially there is no emergency and no counter-operation, yet he had a number of reports two days ago that extra guards were being posted at barracks in some of the military regions and that the troops who lived out had been told to stay in barracks.'

'That makes it look as though part of the plan is being put into effect, in certain sections of the land forces at any rate, without the JUJEM having ordered it,' commented Navarro.

'That's the worrying thing, Paco. I'd better ring the royal secretary to tell him about this at once, as well as to give him the news about the MAGOS meetings being planned for Sunday. After that I think I'll take Miranda and make a surprise call on the Marqués de la Estrella. We haven't interviewed him yet.'

'Don't forget that you're meeting Inspector Ibáñez for lunch, *jefe*. He suggested the Parrillón at one-thirty.'

There were flurries of snow when the official car deposited Bernal and Navarro at the door of the Marquis's house in the Calle de Zurbano just after twelve noon. They were admitted by the same butler, who today was dressed in more formal clothing.

'The Marquis is in the private chapel, Comisario. There is a special Mass for St Eulalia. The family has a particular regard for her feast day, since they own lands around Mérida, which was her birthplace.'

'We shall wait until he is free, if you don't mind,' replied Bernal politely.

The butler looked at them dubiously, as if they would steal the silver given half a chance.

Seeing his hesitation, Bernal grasped his opportunity. 'If you yourself intend going to Mass, would there be any objection to our accompanying you? We shall be quite happy to sit unobtrusively at the back.'

'I'm not sure if the Señor Marqués would be willing,' the butler hesitated once more. 'But there is the servants' gallery—'

'That will do splendidly,' said Bernal with determination. 'We're public servants, aren't we? Our presence probably won't be noticed.'

The servants' gallery was at the back of the small church and they reached it by climbing a narrow spiral staircase. A fretwork screen hid them from the small congregation in the pews below, while they had a perfect view of the proceedings.

The chapel was crammed with rich baroque ornamentation in the eighteenth-century French style, and had a most elaborate reredos, encrusted with precious stones.

The entire Lebrija family appeared to be present, together with some twenty high-ranking army officers in dress uniform, including a lieutenant-general, Bernal noticed. He could only see him from the rear and above, but could it be Lt – Gen. Baltasar? Bernal looked keenly down at the civilians who accompanied the *marqueses* and their children: were they just friends of the family, or did they have a more sinister role?

Bernal directed his gaze to the rich altar and recognized the red-robed celebrant as the same bishop he had seen on his previous visit to this house. He had just reached the collect, specially ordained to be said for St Eulalia: '*Omnipotens sempiterne Deus, qui infirma mundi eligis ut fortia quæque confundas*—Almighty and everlasting God, who choosest the weak in the world to confound the strong . . .'

Before the last gospel was read, Bernal and Miranda slipped out of the gallery and descended to wait in the library opposite. From there they would be able to observe the congregation as they emerged, without attracting attention to themselves.

'There are a lot of the top brass there, *jefe*,' commented Miranda.

'Including Lieutenant-General Baltasar,' said Bernal. 'I'm sure he's a key figure in all this.'

When at last the Marquis joined them, Bernal explained that he wished to complete the formalities concerning his son, the late Capt. Lebrija. 'I've obtained the highest authority, Señor Marqués, for you to have the body for burial without need of a hearing before the judge of instruction. So you will be able to proceed with the interment whenever you wish.'

'That is most thoughtful, Comisario. All of us are very grateful to you,' the nobleman said blandly.

'What is still not quite clear to me, sir, is what your son was doing up on the hills above La Granja early on a winter Sunday morning, in deep snow. Can you throw any light on his activities?'

The Marquis looked rattled and impatient at the same time. Bernal guessed that this was his usual temperament, which he had been trying to control.

'Oh, he was a keen huntsman, like myself, y'know. He often went out with guns at first light in all weathers. Nothing odd in that at all.'

'But would he have gone out alone?' persisted Bernal, who could see the Marquis growing ever more ill at ease.

'He sometimes went alone. Not a lot up there at this time of year, though.'

'No, indeed,' commented Bernal drily. 'The weather couldn't have been more atrocious.'

'José Antonio was absolutely fearless, Comisario, you must understand that. He had nerves of steel. Nothing was impossible as far as he was concerned.' Tears now welled in the old aristocrat's eyes. 'Spain needs men like that, or we'll be finished as a nation for good. Just look at our cities, Comisario. Sodom and Gomorrah had nothing on what we see today!' He grew red with fury, but managed to bring it under control remarkably quickly. 'I'm sorry I'll have to leave you now, Comisario,' he said more smoothly. 'Have to see to my guests, y'know. Thank you for coming.'

After they had emerged into the icy wind that was bearing quite large snowflakes down from the Sierra del Guadarrama, Bernal told Miranda to keep observation on the Marquis's house and to follow him if he left.

'You can keep the official car if you like, Carlos. I'm going to lunch with Ibáñez in the Parrillón, which is only round the corner up Eduardo Dato.'

'No, chief, this car's too conspicuous. I'll get in with you and we'll drive off to the corner. I'll radio for a K-car. I hope they'll have something available that's got a heater.' Miranda shivered and banged his arms across his chest. 'Last time they gave us a soft drinks lorry which in any case wasn't ideal for the task.'

'Ask them for something small and speedy. Remember he may go off to Andalusia at any moment. If he does, try to liaise with Ángel in Seville. You may find out more by shadowing the Marquis than I shall in Madrid. I wish we could put surveillance on the general, but military intelligence would be certain to spot it.'

After leaving Miranda at the corner of the Paseo de Eduardo Dato, from where he could observe the Marquis's house while waiting for his K-car, Bernal told the driver to take him up the street to the Plaza de Chamberí. In the elegant restaurant he found Ibáñez waiting for him at the small bar.

'I've booked a table for us upstairs, Luis, but have a drink first.'

'This is very posh, Esteban. Have you had a pay rise?'

'You insisted on paying at Lhardy last week, so I thought I'd reciprocate.'

After tackling a superbly grilled *mero* or jew-fish, Bernal felt too full to take any of the splendid *postres* that were offered.

'Can't you manage some fresh pineapple, Luis?'

'Not even that. I'll just sip this excellent Marqués de Murrieta, and watch you finish.' Bernal observed, with admiration for Ibáñez's still youthful digestive system, how he had demolished an enormous *cocido castellano*, the bean stew that was the plate of the day.

'It's that ulcer of yours, Luis. Why don't you go and have it seen to? I thought they'd invented a new wonder drug for it.'

'I've taken so many different pills, Esteban. I think they make it worse, apart from the Kolantyl tablets, which soothe it after meals.'

When the coffee came, Ibáñez took a sheet of paper from his inside pocket, and glanced around to make sure no one could overhear.

'At last I've got something for you, Luis, but it didn't come off the central police computer. I managed to get at recent Civil Guard reports. They owed me a favour. How about that for your MAGOS?'

The sheet was a Xerox copy of a brief official report:

8 December. Province of Cadiz: Trebujena.
Some field or training activity noted in past few days of a group called Movimiento Apostólico de Generales, Oficiales y Suboficiales, thought to be connected with the Casa Apostólica (religious house) with local address in Calle de la Feria, Seville. Some 130 members wearing distinctive red and blue uniform with cross-headed dagger emblem on epaulettes seen test-firing sub-machineguns and bazookas on banks of Guadalquivir during past week.

Bernal looked up in some excitement. 'You've got it Esteban. The Apostolic Movement of Generals, Commissioned Officers and NCOs. You've cracked MAGOS. It looks to be a group of ultras in the armed services encouraged by this religious order. I must ask Interpol for some information, because the order was founded in Cologne.'

When the two friends left the Parrillón, the snow flurries had ceased but the afternoon was unpleasantly cold and grey, so Bernal decided to take a taxi to his other apartment at Tribunal.

That night Bernal sat at the *mesa camilla* in his dining-room at Retiro, poring over the MAGOS messages once more, while Eugenia was preparing the usual supper of leftovers. He got out the rough table he had made of the first four published messages, and compared it with the feasts which the late Brother Nicolás had indicated with bookmarks in his missal. The first four matched exactly:

Purple A.1 stood for 29 November, *Blue A.1* for 8 December, *Pink A.1* for 13 December, and *Purple A.3* for Christmas Eve. So there were three more messages to come if the monk had been correct: the Feast of Circumcision, the Vigil of Epiphany and Epiphany itself, i.e. 1, 5 and 6 January, respectively; the last date was clearly to be the culmination of the secret plan. Bernal was sure it was meant to coincide with the Pascua Militar at the Oriente Palace in Madrid, over which the King and Queen would preside.

If his calculations were correct, he could expect *La Corneta* to publish the fifth message about a fortnight before the date of the proposed action, round about 15 December, the sixth message about the 22nd, and the last message a day later. The publication of that would give the final go-ahead to the plotters. But what did each stage of the plan involve and how did the names of the royal palaces come into it? Something had indeed happened at San Ildefonso (La Granja) and at Aranjuez (before its time), but nothing very important had occurred at El Pardo or Segovia.

A fresh idea suddenly came to him, and he searched in his briefcase for the secret Ministry of Defence operation for combating coups d'état. Operation Mercury had seven stages, just as it seemed the MAGOS plan might have. He wrote them out side by side:

OPERATION MERCURY		MAGOS CONSPIRACY
Mercury:	Servicio de Intervención	San Ildefonso
Venus:	Estado de Prevención	El Pardo
Jupiter:	Supresión de permisos	Segovia
Mars:	Alerta	Aranjuez
Saturn:	Estado de Excepción	not yet known
Uranus:	Movilización	not yet known
Pluto:	Operación	not yet known

He gazed at the list for a while and then it came to him. The names of the royal palaces were a blind! The code-words were acrologically based; only the initial letters mattered. Thus *S*an *I*ldefonso stood for *Servicio de Intervención*, *E*l *P*ardo for *Estado de Prevención*, and so on. How ironic, thought Bernal; the King's secretary had called him in only because of the mention of the royal palaces in the cryptic messages and the possible danger to the royal security, but the messages did not threaten that. The leaders of MAGOS had formulated a shadow-plan to the Government's own counter-plan, and they were using the same steps of increase in military activity as the Chiefs of the General Staff would use if an imminent coup d'état were suspected. By using the Ministry of Defence's own plan and modifying the code-words from the planets to the palaces, they must be trying to pre-empt the official counter-coup measures.

Bernal sat back and admired their ingenuity; if the JUJEM were to put Operation Mercury into action that very night and were to flash the word *Mercurio* around all the Captaincies General, the military regional commanders, after checking back to the Chiefs of Staff in Madrid, would order intervention of communications and power lines and soon find in some cases that the task had already been carried out. If that was followed by *Venus*, they would soon find that strict vigilance was being kept and that the guard had already been doubled, and so on. By ordering the official plan, the Government would in fact be forwarding what it was trying to prevent. The plan was diabolical, or divinely inspired, perhaps, given its apostolic origin? Its real ingenuity lay in the circumstance that, by closely shadowing the Ministry's operation, it rendered nugatory any official attempt to prevent its own fulfilment. The daring of it took one's breath away.

Bernal had heard the phone ring in the hallway and had

been aware that Eugenia had gone to answer it, but he had paid no attention, engrossed as he was in his calculations. Now she was calling him insistently:

'Stop dreaming in there, Luis! Come and talk to your son.'

Still half-absorbed, Bernal took the receiver from her. 'How are things, Diego? When are you coming home?'

'We've finished most of the test-borings around Trebujena, and we've come into Camas for the evening. It's no great shakes, I can tell you, but we're having a drink in the bar.'

'Tell me when you're planning to return, Diego.'

'On Sunday, on the TALGO that leaves at midday.'

'Have you got enough money?'

'Yes, I think so. I've still got half of what you gave me. By the way, Papi, we've seen more of those soldiers in the peculiar uniform.'

'Where was that, Diego?'

'Between here and Trebujena, and down by the river. They've set up a test-firing range, which has upset our seismic readings. There are ten of them out there drinking in the bar as I'm talking to you. They seem to be a kind of GEO, or special operations group, to judge by their big talk.'

'What exactly is the uniform like?'

'Blue, with a curious epaulette, which has a red flash shaped like a dagger on the edge and a three-headed cross higher up. They're drinking and boasting a lot, and say they're going to a special parade near Santiponce on Sunday.'

'At Santiponce? But it's a small village.'

'I know that, Papi, but the rally or parade is going to be held at Itálica nearby. They even had the cheek to ask to see our identity *carnets* when they came into the bar.'

'Did they see yours, Diego?'

'Yes. I had it with me, fortunately.'

Bernal thought it most unfortunate, since they would have seen Diego's father's name. 'I wish you'd come home at once, son. Can't you give some excuse and come back on the first plane from Jerez tomorrow morning?'

'But why, Papi? Is there any danger? I'd be letting down the others in the field-work party if I leave now, and I might lose a credit for the geology course.'

'Very well,' said Bernal reluctantly, 'but don't separate from the others in your party whatever you do, and don't talk about your father's job—not at all, do you hear?'

As soon as Bernal replaced the receiver, the phone rang again, and Elena Fernández came on the line.

'I've been trying your number for some time, *jefe*, from a call-box,' she said somewhat accusingly.

'I'm sorry, Elena, my errant son was on the line from Santiponce.'

'Santiponce? But that's an extraordinary coincidence! I've managed to see the correspondence on the Editor's desk at *La Corneta*'s office, and he's going to Seville on Saturday ready for a meeting on Sunday at Santiponce. He's going to stay with the Marqués de la Estrella at his country seat.'

'It's a most unfortunate coincidence that Diego happens to be in the area on a geological field-course, Elena. I've tried hard to urge him to return at once, but he insists on staying until the work's complete. They're coming back on Sunday morning. Have you seen any more copy for MAGOS messages to be inserted in the personal column?'

'Nothing yet, *jefe*, but I'm keeping a sharp look-out.'

'Watch for three more insertions, probably for publication on 15, 21 and 22 December.'

When he had rung off, Bernal decided he would have to arrange to go to the Zarzuela Palace first thing in the morning, and explain his findings in detail to the King's secretary.

Eugenia interrupted his thoughts and shouted to him from the kitchen: 'Unroll the oilcloth, will you, Luis, and get the Cebreros wine out from the cupboard. I'm warming up some squid's tentacles left over from lunch. They're really delicious, and will be light for your digestion.'

Bernal's stomach gave a lurch at this announcement, and he reeled slightly as he made his way back along the icy tiled corridor.

ADVENT: THIRD SUNDAY (13 December)

'Wake up, Luis! It's nearly seven-thirty.'

Bernal woke up with a start and looked at his watch.

'But it's Sunday, Geñita. Why are you up so early?'

'It's the Gaudete Mass, the pink vestments today, remember? You've got to help me take them down to Father Anselmo.'

He groaned, and reluctantly put his feet out on to the moth-eaten bearskin rug which offered the only protection from the cold tiles.

While he was shaving, the phone rang.

'It's one of your colleagues,' shouted Eugenia, 'the lady one, the builder's daughter. I still can't imagine why her father permitted her to take up such a sordid profession as yours.'

Bernal hoped that Elena hadn't caught this remark, as he hastily pulled the woollen dressing-gown round his shoulders and hurried to the phone.

'It's in this morning's issue, *jefe*, the fifth MAGOS message. I didn't have a chance to ring you last night.'

'What does it say, Elena?'

'MAGOS *White N.5. El Escorial.*'

'*N.5?* Are you sure?'

'Quite sure, chief. I saw the final proofs of the first edition yesterday evening.'

'Righto, Elena. Leave it with me. Have you heard from Angel?'

'No, chief, he hasn't come back from Seville, and the chief despatcher is pretty cross with him. He phoned in to tell them that the van had suffered a serious breakdown and the Seville garage couldn't yet find out what was wrong with it.'

'Do they suspect anything?'

'Oh no, I don't think so. Our cover's still intact, I'm sure.'

While Eugenia served him the coffee made of ground acorns, Bernal studied the liturgical calendar at the front of his mother-in-law's Roman missal, while his wife eyed him in suspicious astonishment, but refrained from commenting on his suddenly acquired piety.

White N.5: that was a difficulty. It should refer to 1 January, the Feast of Circumcision, according to the bookmarks left inside Brother Nicolás's missal. Then Bernal spotted the solution. He counted the days when white liturgical vestments were prescribed, running backwards from 1st January up the page, and the first would be Christmas Day. Of course. *N* stood for the season of Nativity. 25 December was *N.1*, the Feast of St John the apostle and evangelist on 27th was *N.2*, the Infra-octave of the Nativity on 30th was *N.3*, and the Feast of St Silvester, Pope and confessor, on 31st was *N.4*. All these days had white vestments. Thus Circumcision on 1 January, which was also white, was indeed *White N.5* in the MAGOS code. Once one knew the key, it was easy; any loyal son of the Church could work it out.

After leaving Eugenia at the sacristy door with the hamper of pink vestments which she and the portress had so carefully cleaned, Bernal took a taxi along the Calle de Alcalá to the Puerta del Sol, where he ordered a second and better breakfast in the Cafetería Manila, one of the few cafés open at that hour on a Sunday morning. As he dunked the hot *churros* one by one into the delicious coffee, he opened his copy of *La Corneta* and turned to the personal column. Yes, Elena had been right, there was the cryptic message: MAGOS *White N.5. El Escorial.* It meant that on 1 January the fifth stage of preparedness— 'the state of exception'—would be reached in those barracks controlled by the MAGOS conspirators.

Bernal turned to the editorial page, which sometimes carried mysterious oracular pronouncements underneath the editorial proper. '*This is a special day for preparation. Loyal Christians get ready during Advent and rejoice in the imminence of the Saviour. The day of the Three Kings of Orient will be particularly memorable this year.*' He thought it curious how they couldn't help dropping strong hints about their secret plots. The 'Saviour' could also be a secular figure; Lt-Gen. Baltasar, for instance. Bernal folded *La Corneta*, and turned to the saner and more intellectual presentation of the news in *El País*.

When he got to the office, he found Navarro already at work.

'Ángel phoned in late last night, *jefe*. The pamphlets and posters he had to take to Seville were to be delivered to a warehouse in the Calle de la Feria. He went afterwards to the Ayuntamiento records and found that it was rented by the Casa Apostólica, whose priory is near by. Miranda has now joined him, having followed the marquis from Madrid. Estrella took the bishop with him in the chauffeur-driven Mercedes.'

'Did you send Lista down there as I suggested?'

'Yes, *jefe*. He's gone to cover the village of Santiponce to see what is planned to take place there today.'

'My son said there was to be a rally at Itálica. It's a very odd place to choose, but I suppose the old Roman amphitheatre can hold a lot of people, and it's off the beaten track. A secret meeting wouldn't be easily noticed there. I hope Diego does catch the TALGO today. I'm uneasy about his getting involved in all this. You know how impulsive young people can be.'

'There's a report coming in on the teleprinter, chief. I'll just go and see what it is.'

Bernal puffed at a Kaiser cigarette as he waited. It was strange how nervous he still got in the face of an imminent action, even though he wasn't directly involved in it on the ground.

'It's from Interpol in Frankfurt, *jefe*,' called Navarro.

Bernal joined him at the machine and together they read the message that rattled on to the continuous green-striped sheet in rapid bursts, interrupted by quite long hiccoughs. The message read:

BERNAL DSE MADRID STOP RE YOUR INQUIRY 11 DEC APOSTOLIC MOVEMENT FOUNDED KÖLN 1932 STOP PROVISIONALLY REGISTERED AT VATICAN UNDER PIUS XII STOP FORMED CONNECTION WITH HITLER ORGANIZATIONS ESPECIALLY SA STOP VATICAN HAS NOT BESTOWED FULL RECOGNITION STOP PRESENT BRANCHES IN ITALY FRANCE SPAIN ARGENTINA AND CHILE STOP HEAD OF SPANISH BRANCH OF ORDER FR GASPAR STOP MAIN PURPOSE MORAL REARMAMENT OF POLITICAL AND MILITARY LEADERS STOP ORDER DEDICATED TO CULT OF MAGIC— The machine stopped again suddenly.

'Magic?' exclaimed Bernal incredulously.

The rattling resumed:—CORRECTION STOP CULT OF MAGI OR 3 KINGS OF ORIENT WHOSE RELICS PRESERVED IN KÖLN CATHEDRAL STOP NO RECORD OF CRIMINAL ACTIVITY BUT ORDER HAS COOPERATED WITH NEO-FASCIST ELEMENTS IN EACH COUNTRY WHERE IT OPERATES STOP MESSAGE ENDS

'That explains Father Gaspar's religious name, Paco,' said Bernal. 'The Order is dedicated to the Three Kings of Orient, and the Prior just took the name of one of them. It also accounts for the symbol they use: the triple-headed dagger, which is like three arms of an Iron Cross. I looked up the Espasa-Calpe Encyclopædia and technically it consists of the top and cross-piece of a patté cross. What Interpol haven't told us is where the money is coming from. If the Order is not fully recognized by the Vatican, the Church certainly won't be supporting it, yet the house at Aranjuez must have cost a lot to buy and enlarge, and they appear to live in some style.'

'What about the Marquis, chief? He might be financing them.'

'It's possible, but I shouldn't have thought that his fortune could permit that level of generosity. There must be someone or some organization richer and more powerful still. The army members of the Order can't possibly be raising sums of the size required; they are the targets of the Apostolic Movement, not its driving force.'

'What about the name of the Lebrija marquisate, *jefe*?'

' "The Marquis of the Star" you mean? The star that led the Magi to Bethlehem? It's too pat, I think. Just a humorous coincidence, but it may have led to their coining the name of this plot, and choosing 6 January for its implementation.'

'And there's Lieutenant-General Baltasar,' added Navarro.

'Yes. If we worked on the level of the literal meaning and took it to its logical conclusion, the second Magus, Gaspar, brought frankincense, which is proper for a monk like Father Gaspar, because that gift represented the spirituality of Christ. The third Magus, Balthazar, who is usually represented as black-skinned, brought myrrh or precious balsam, used for laying out the dead—an ominous gift from a military man like General Baltasar.'

'Do you think they were attracted to bringing him into the plot just because of the name, *jefe*?'

'Well, his record in the División Azul under Hitler

would have been well known to them, and perhaps the surname was just a bonus. Put together with the Marqués de la Estrella's name it may have satisfied someone with a piquant sense of humour. That's the person I want to find out about, Paco. Who is bringing the gold? Who is Melchior? He is masterminding this whole business.'

By the evening they had received a flood of reports from Seville. In a small hired Citroën Ángel had shadowed a plain black van into which the pamphlets and posters had been reloaded in the Calle de la Feria in the early afternoon, and it had left Seville by the Aracena road. By 4.0 p.m. Lista had noted great activity at Santiponce with the arrival of many military vehicles which brought officers wearing the distinctive blue uniform with red epaulettes. This rig-out was quite unknown to the General Staff or to the official tailors to the Army; Bernal had rung them to enquire. Then at 5.10 p.m. Miranda had called in from Trebujena to report that the Marquis and the bishop had left the nobleman's house in the Mercedes limousine, travelling northwards on the A.4 towards Seville. By 5.30 he phoned in again from Camas to say that they had taken the N.630 north-westwards from Seville, and that he had fallen well back on the assumption that they were making for Santiponce.

Bernal looked at the large wall-map of the Peninsula and could see that they were all converging on Itálica and its Roman remains. Lista would by now have taken up a vantage point there and would report in as and when he could.

During the lull, Navarro sent down for *bocadillos* of mountain ham and Manchegan cheese and four bottles of beer to sustain them through the waiting period. At 7.30 Bernal telephoned Eugenia to find out if his son had arrived on the TALGO that had left Seville at midday.

'Not yet, Luis, but he'll surely be here soon.'

'Ring me here at the Gobernación and let me know as soon as he comes, will you, Geñita?'

'You missed the beautiful Gaudete solemn Mass this morning, Luis. The pink vestments looked splendid.'

At 8.20 Lista at last broke the long silence and came on the line.

'I'm back in Seville now, *jefe*. It was an extraordinary business up there at Itálica. The Roman amphitheatre was the venue, and I managed to get up on to the higher terraces, which are in a pretty ruinous state, I can tell you. They used flares at dusk and handed out special badges, as well as the posters and pamphlets. A military helicopter arrived at seven p.m. and landed in the arena, raising a hell of a lot of dust, and General Baltasar got out and made a speech using an improvised public address system.'

'How many officers were present?'

'About four hundred or so. They were all wearing the special uniform.'

'Could you hear the speech, Juan?'

'Snatches of it, *jefe*, but I was very high up and had to keep out of sight in one of the stairways leading to the top terrace. It's an eerie spot in the dark, that's for sure.'

'What did you hear the General say?'

'He talked about the importance and solemnity of their mission on 5 January and how they would be bringing back the old Spanish values.'

'Are you sure he said the fifth?'

'Quite sure. He repeated it and then gave a long spiel about the disastrous moral state of the country. He spoke for about three-quarters of an hour, and then the bishop blessed them.'

'Did the Marquis take part?'

'He didn't speak but he was standing alongside Father Gaspar, the general and the bishop.'

'You are sure it was Father Gaspar?'

'Quite sure. He came in the helicopter with the General.'

'And was there no one else, no other leader with them, Juan?'

'No, just the four of them, and a fellow who looked like the General's aide-de-camp.'

'Thank you for all you've done. You should now liaise with Carlos and Ángel. You'd better tell Ángel to get that van belonging to *La Corneta* magically repaired and to bring it back to Madrid, or his cover will be blown.'

Bernal now got more and more concerned about his son's failure to return, and he rang Eugenia again at 9.0 p.m.

'No, Luis, Diego's not back yet, but he'll be here soon, I expect. Are you coming home for dinner?'

'I'll let you know later. Tell Diego to ring me here immediately he arrives.'

Bernal lit another Kaiser and looked out at the pavements below in the Calle de Carretas, packed with people taking the Sunday evening *paseo*, since the weather had temporarily turned much milder. Most of them were window-shopping, attracted by the commercial Christmas displays. After a while he called Navarro in.

'Would you look up the RENFE timetable and see when the midday TALGO from Seville was due at Atocha station, Paco?'

Navarro soon returned with the information. 'It should have got in at 19.34. I'll ring them to check, if you like.'

'Please do that. I'm concerned abut Diego. He was in Camas and Santiponce on Wednesday and he hasn't rung home since then.'

Finding the number engaged, Navarro rang the Station Comisaría. The inspector on duty informed him that the Seville TALGO had actually arrived at 19.52.

'Then he should have got home by now,' said Bernal, increasingly worried. 'Will you call the Faculty of Science

at the Universidad Complutense and see if they've got
any news of the geological field-work party that has been
in the lower Guadalquivir Valley for the past fortnight?
Unfortunately I don't know the name of the expedition
leader.'

After much telephoning, Navarro returned. 'They
can't contact the staff in charge at this time on a Sunday
night, chief. Only the security men and the caretakers are
there. They don't know the name of the group leader.'

'I'm uneasy about Diego, Paco. What if we try the
RENFE at Seville? The party had seat reservations and
there were thirty or more students in it. They must have
had half a carriage reserved for them.'

Navarro went back to the phone and Bernal found
himself unable to concentrate on the MAGOS reports; he
chain-smoked. Finally there was some news.

'The deputy chief of reservations at Seville says that
thirty-four seats were booked, but he can't be sure if they
were all taken when the train departed. The *jefe del tren*
would know if any failed to turn up, but they don't think
he will have checked the individual names.'

'Can he be contacted?' asked Bernal.

'They don't think he could be tonight. His home is in
Seville, and he'll be returning on the morning TALGO.
They expect he'll spend the night in an hotel or *pensión*
near Atocha station, but they don't know which.'

'And was the reservation in the name of the leader of
the party?'

'Unfortunately not; they had the booking down as
"Universidad Complutense". The tickets were originally
issued here in Madrid, in the RENFE office in the Calle
de Alcála.'

'Then they'll know who paid for them.'

'Yes, chief,' replied Navarro patiently, 'but they're
closed until tomorrow morning. The Seville Office tried
the computer terminal, but the group leader's name

hadn't been recorded. Shall I call the Policía Nacional in Seville?'

'Not yet. Let's see if there's any further news here first.'

By 11.0 p.m. Bernal had rung his wife a number of times, but their son still hadn't appeared. At 11.10, she called him back to say that a Dr Montalbán had telephoned. He was the leader of the geological survey group and he'd been concerned when Diego Bernal didn't turn up with the other students at Seville station to catch the TALGO. He had decided to bring the others back.

'Did he leave a telephone number, Geñita?'

She gave it to him.

'I won't be home for some time. Don't keep me any food.'

As soon as he'd rung off, he dialled Dr Montalbán's number. When the geologist answered, Bernal introduced himself. 'Did my son say why he was leaving the party? When did you last see him?'

'We went into Seville for the last night, Superintendent, and had to put up at two small hotels; there were too many of us to fit into one. After dinner the lads went out on a spree to the Triana quarter. I heard them get in after three a.m., but your son didn't happen to be among the students lodging in my hotel. I didn't realize he was missing until we were at the railway station, but his fellow students said he had told them he would see them there. They last saw him well after midnight, in a bar where there was a *tablao flamenco*. They claim he got bored watching the typical dancing and left, saying he'd see them on the train.'

'And he gave them no explanation?'

'They assumed he'd picked up a girl and had arranged to take her on to another nightclub.'

'Did they see the girl?'

'No, I don't think so, but when we were in Seville for

the evening a week ago he got to know a dark-haired girl. I saw her myself.'

'What about Diego's luggage, Doctor? Was that left at the hotel?'

'The student who shared a room with your son packed up all the things he had left an hour before we were due to leave, and deposited the case with the hotel receptionist, because we had to vacate the rooms by midday.'

'What's the name of that student?' enquired Bernal.

'Federico Payo. I'll look up his address if you'll hold on, Comisario.'

'I'll hold.'

Armed with the student's address, Bernal telephoned his home only to find that he had gone out after dinner.

Navarro now entered the inner office looking serious. 'The desk sergeant says that a boy handed this in a few minutes ago, wouldn't give his name when asked for it, and ran off. It's addressed to you personally *jefe*, but the address has been printed with a Letraset outfit by the look of it. You'd better prepare yourself for a shock, chief.'

The message read: COMISARIO BERNAL. IF YOU WANT TO HAVE YOUR SON DIEGO BACK IN GOOD HEALTH, LEAVE MAGOS IN PEACE. IF YOU DO NOTHING FURTHER, HE WILL BE RETURNED AT EPIPHANY. MELCHIOR.

Bernal slumped into his chair and lit a Kaiser.

'You've read it, of course, Paco?'

'Yes, chief.'

'I felt it in my bones, you know. Things were going too well.' He drew on his cigarette. 'We must get him back quickly. I'll leave for Seville on the night plane.'

'Would that be wise, *jefe*? Wouldn't it be better for someone not emotionally involved to search for your son? After all, we've got three inspectors there on the spot, Carlos, Juan and Ángel, and they're very experienced. Let's use them. The MAGOS organizers almost certainly aren't aware that they've been followed to Andalusia and shadowed to their rally at Itálica, nor have they got wise to Ángel's undercover role. But they'll be watching you here.'

'Ángel mustn't return with that van to *La Corneta*'s offices. They'll remember he used to work at the DSE. Perhaps we should pull Elena out too.'

'Don't be rash, chief. I agree that we should keep Ángel in Seville. That van he's got could prove very useful. But let me get on to Miranda and Lista at once. They'll start retracing Diego's movements in the Triana quarter last night. Shall we call in the Seville Police?'

'I happen to know the chief there, Paco; we used to be colleagues. But we mustn't have a massive search operation. They'd get wind of it and liquidate Diego. Remember they may have infiltrated the local police. I'll talk to the chief there and ask for discreet assistance.'

'You'd better tell the King's secretary, hadn't you, chief?'

'Not yet. Let's wait until tomorrow. He might pull me out of the whole case.'

ADVENT: EMBER WEDNESDAY
(16 December)

Bernal was awakened before dawn by Eugenia's movements in the kitchen. He sat up in bed to listen, and after a while called out to her: 'Why are you up so early, Geñita? Is there any news of Diego?'

She appeared at the bedroom door clutching a bundle of enormous church candles. 'No, there's no news yet. I've got to go out soon, Luis. I promised Father Anselmo I'd take these candles down. It's the Golden Mass of Ember Week early this morning, the *Rorate Cœli*. We light the candles to show that the world is in darkness before Christ.'

Bernal wondered if she had any natural feelings at all about her son's kidnapping, but he did not comment.

'It sounds as though it's raining hard, Geñita.' He could hear the rain beating on the plant-pots on the terrace. 'I hope it's not going to leak through the corridor ceiling again. The president of the *comunidad* really must send the contractor to see to the tiles.'

'Isn't the rain appropriate, Luis? Today's introit begins: "Drop down dew, ye heavens, from above, and let the clouds rain down the Just . . ." '

'It's doing that all right. Mind to take your umbrella, won't you?'

'Don't worry about Diego, now, God is watching over him. Father Anselmo will be including a special deliverance prayer for him.'

As he shaved, Bernal had to dodge about to see himself properly in the bathroom mirror, which had the silver peeling off the back. What had Eugenia said? It was Ember Week of Advent. Certainly it was their ember week. Since the news of Diego's kidnapping came on Sunday evening Bernal's feelings had assumed the grey fragility of coke.

Perhaps Paco was right: he should be pulled off the case. No policeman could work properly when the investigation involved a member of his own family. Yet he would feel worse than useless sitting about at home, never sure if his colleagues were doing all in their power to rescue his son. By going in to work he could at least look through the reports and files, and try to find out who this monstrous Melchior was, who intended to take over the country and had started with Bernal's son.

The phone rang as he was dressing.

'It's me, Luchi. Are you free to talk?'

'Yes, Consuelo. Eugenia has already gone to Mass.

There's no news yet. They won't let me go to Seville to direct the search operation on the spot.'

'Quite right, Luchi. Let the others do it. Perhaps these plotters are trying to draw you out and kidnap you as well. Stay where you are.'

'We've already got armed bodyguards, Conchi. Eugenia's not pleased to have a plainclothesman following her to church and everywhere else, but he'll be a better man for it, that's for sure. I insisted they wait downstairs. I couldn't bear to have them in the apartment.'

'I'll stay in touch, Luis. Keep your chin up, now.'

As soon as he replaced the receiver, the instrument rang again.

'Chief? It's Elena.' She sounded breathless. 'I got into the office early and had a look at the mail on the Editor's desk.'

'For God's sake, Elena, do be careful, or they'll take you too. Where are you speaking from?'

'I've slipped out to the café down the street. No one had arrived at the office, and the cleaning woman is friendly.'

'What did you find?'

'A letter postmarked Estrella del Marqués, addressed to the Editor personally and marked "Confidential", but I haven't got the means to steam it open.'

'H'm, the Marquis's country seat is near there, of course. I wonder if they're holding Diego there. It's a pity you couldn't risk opening the letter.'

'Rather than risk their spotting it had been opened, I've filched it, chief. If you or Varga will meet me, you can steam it open and reseal it, and then get *Correos* to take it back with the mid-morning delivery. The Editor will never know it arrived by the early post. His secretary hasn't come in yet.'

'I'll ring Varga immediately to come and meet you. Tell me the name of the café.' He wrote it down. 'I'm eternally grateful to you, Elena, but you've taken a dreadful risk. Perhaps it would be safer if you pulled out now.'

'But they don't suspect a thing, *jefe*, I'm sure they don't. Let me stay a bit longer,' she begged.

Bernal weighed up the odds. 'All right, but at the first sign of suspicion, go sick, will you?'

After calling Varga, Bernal placed his service pistol in his shoulder-holster and hurried to put on his commando-style raincoat and a trilby hat. He descended the eight floors in the elegant mahogany cabinet of the ancient lift, and met the plainclothes policeman at the porter's lodge.

'I've got the official car waiting outside, Comisario,' he said.

'Very well. Let's get to work,' answered Bernal briskly, feeling more exposed to an assassin's bullet as the car crawled through the mounting rush-hour traffic than if he'd taken Line 2 of the Metro from Retiro to Sol.

When at last they reached the Gobernación Building, Varga was already there, having collected the letter from Elena. Bernal and Navarro joined him in the technical lab as he set to work on the confidential missive.

'We don't steam them open these days, *jefe*, as people think. It's much less noticeable if we use one of these thin rods of toughened steel and insert it through the lower flap.'

Bernal admired his skill as he rolled up the folded sheet of the letter inside the envelope, without unsticking the flap, and carefully drew it out. He spread it out with a pair of tweezers.

'There'll be fingerprints, *jefe*. I'll use the electron autographic method.'

The letter was written in an old-fashioned, florid hand:

Dear Friend,
    The package has arrived safely, and we have it

stored in the cellar. Let us know by the usual means when Melchior thinks the time is ripe to dispose of the contents.

L.

'The envelope is postmarked Estrella del Marqués yesterday at midday, chief,' said Varga. 'There's no sender's name and address on the back.'

'The letter is surely from the Marquis, don't you think, Paco?' Bernal remarked. '*L* for Lebrija? The aristocracy usually sign with their family surname only, not with the name of their title.' Navarro nodded his agreement. 'The package must be my son,' Bernal went on, 'so there's a chance that he's still alive and held prisoner in the cellar of the Marquis's *finca*.'

'We must get on to Miranda at once,' said Navarro. 'The Seville police will help him to organize a raid on the place, if you will ring the police chief.'

'Shall I allow this letter to be delivered, *jefe*?' asked Varga.

'Yes, send it on. I don't think it will do any harm.'

'I'll reinsert it into the envelope, and no one will know it has been tampered with,' replied Varga. 'I'll take it straight over to Cibeles and get the post office to deliver it with the rest of the noon delivery.'

'I think we'll use our royal warrant to intercept all the mail going to the offices of *La Corneta*, to the Marquis's house here in Madrid and his estate in Seville province, and to Father Gaspar and the Casa Apostólica at Aranjuez. I'd like to do the same with General Baltasar's mail, but it may be more difficult to arrange.'

'What about their telephones, chief?' asked Navarro.

'Yes, we'll get an order to make the Compañía Telefónica listen in and record the conversations of the same gentlemen.'

In their upstairs office, Bernal and Navarro debated the

possibility of organizing an attempt to rescue Diego.

'Whether we are successful or not in getting him out alive, it will bring things to a head prematurely, Paco.'

'But that would be a good thing, *jefe*. It would pre-empt whatever action they're planning for 6 January.'

'I'm not convinced of the wisdom of it, Paco. They would disband without our knowing who they all are, and most of them would survive to plot another day. I'll talk it over with the royal secretary, while you telephone Miranda and discuss the possibilities. The man on the ground is almost always the best judge of the situation.'

The King's secretary, when called to the scrambler phone, was prepared to let Bernal and his colleagues take whatever course they thought best.

At midday they received a call from Miranda in Seville. 'I've traced your son's movements on Saturday night, *jefe*. He was picked up by a dancer called Elisa Moreno and led by her from the *tablao flamenco* where the other students were to a quiet bar called El Cisne further down the same street in the Triana quarter. I've interviewed the barman there, who says that Elisa is a seventeen-year-old failed dancer and drug addict, who has turned to street-walking. They had two drinks and then left around one-thirty a.m. The barman got the impression she was going to take Diego back to her place, to judge by the clinches they went into.'

'I see,' said Bernal grimly. 'Have you tracked her down?'

'I've been to the room she rents in the Plaza de Miguel de Carvajal, but the landlady, who looks like an ex-pro herself, claims she hasn't seen Elisa since Saturday evening.'

'Did you search the room, Carlos?'

'Yes, but it's clean metaphorically speaking, though literally it's pretty squalid.'

'I expect the Moreno girl was well paid to lure him into

a trap and then make herself scarce for a fortnight.'

'Here's the interesting bit, *jefe*. The Seville police have let me consult their vice squad files, and they show that Elisa Moreno was born in Estrella del Marqués. Her mother used to be a maid at the Marquis's *cortijo*.'

'So they knew where to get hold of the girl quite easily, Carlos. Perhaps she's being held with Diego, to stop her talking. She sounds pretty unreliable.'

'The Seville police are keeping watch for her and your friend the chief of police will have her quietly picked up if she reappears in her old haunts. He's agreed to help us organize a raid on the Marquis's country house.'

'But is that wise, Carlos? It could provoke them to kill Diego.'

'We've managed to obtain detailed plans of the sixteenth-century building from the Biblioteca Colombina here, and we've worked out a way to get into the extensive wine-cellars, assuming he's being held in them, where the Marquis stores his vast production of *manzanilla* wine, which he markets in Jerez from time to time.'

'What's the plan?' asked Bernal.

'We're going to use *La Corneta*'s own van, which Ángel has had put right, and he's going to drive it. The Seville police are providing their own special operations squad— a crack unit armed with shock grenades, nerve gas, the lot. We want you to get Elena to ring from *La Corneta*'s offices late tonight to the Marquis's *finca* here, and give them a phoney message that a special delivery will be made early on Friday morning.'

'Is that the earliest you can arrange?'

'I think so, chief, if we are to do it properly. The special squad wants to have a rehearsal at a similar *finca* on the other side of the city to coordinate the details of the action with Ángel.'

'Very well. A dry run is a good idea. Friday the eighteenth it is,' said Bernal, who was warming to the idea.

'We must do it at first light, when their defences will be weakest,' said Miranda. 'The false message should allow us to get the van through the gate, which is guarded by two men armed with sub-machine-guns, and get up to the servants' entrance, which fortunately is alongside the steps that lead down to the wine-cellars. The fourteen-strong squad will then jump out of the back of the van when Ángel opens the doors pretending to unload, and over-power any opposition. They'll then burst into the cellar through a row of small windows at ground level.'

'It's a hell of risk, Carlos, but it's better than letting him languish there. What's Ángel going to pretend to deliver to them?'

'He's still got on board some packages of old newspapers returned unsold from the kiosks. They'll do as cover for the specials to hide behind in the van.'

'What back-up will you have?'

'The chief of police will send three K-vehicles with armed uniformed police hidden inside. The problem is that any traffic approaching the *finca*, which is built like a fortress, on a hill, can be seen from a long way off. The police vehicles have to be unmarked and disguised as trucks that happen to be passing along the local road towards the A.4, but they'll keep in radio contact with us. Some cover is provided by a thick pine-wood near the village.'

'All right, Carlos,' Bernal said with some reluctance. 'Go ahead with it, but keep us informed as soon as you set out.'

FEAST OF THE EXPECTATION OF
THE B.V.M. (18 December)

Luis and Eugenia Bernal were awake before dawn, both of them too anxious in their varying ways to sleep at all while their younger son remained in illegal detention. Moreover they both knew that this was to be the day of the attempt to free him from the Marquis's estate at Estrella.

Bernal was eager to reach the office before 7.30, when the rescue operation would begin.

'I don't want any breakfast, Geñita,' he said wearily.

'All right, Luis, I'll leave it until later myself. I'm going to take communion at early Mass. It's Our Lady of Hope today, you remember? Mary of the O. Don't you recall how popular a feast it was when we were young? So many girls were christened María de la O after it, and didn't think it at all odd to be named after the old Mozarabic rite, in which the clerics in the choir used to utter a loud "Oh" after Vespers on this day to express their longing for the coming of the Redeemer. Come with me to Mass, Luis, and we'll pray for Diego's deliverance together. I've been keeping a vigil since he was taken, you know. I'm a firm believer in the efficacy of prayer.'

'And you know I think it needs to be helped along by a little action, Geñita. I'll walk with you as far as the church, but I must be at the Gobernación before the Seville police begin the rescue attempt, so as to keep in touch with Miranda and the other officers.'

To please her at this time of their trial, when she had shown more emotional involvement with her children than he ever remembered, he sat at the back of the almost empty church, while the two armed plainclothesmen hovered uncomfortably at the door. The white-robed celebrant began the first office, with its special liturgy, originally peculiar to the Spanish Church and dating from the seventh century. From the note in his mother-in-law's missal, Bernal had seen that some scholars had attributed the feast of Expectatio Partus to St Ildefonsus, crediting him with the moving of the Annunciation from 25 March, which usually fell in Lent and couldn't therefore be properly celebrated, to 18 December. The result was that Spain and a few other countries had come to celebrate the Annunciation twice during the liturgical year.

He listened to the introit, collect, and lesson from Isaiah 7, verse 15, and when the priest came to the gradual: '*Tollite portas, principes, vestras: et elevamini, portæ æternales*—Lift up your gates, O ye princes: and be ye lifted up, O eternal gates . . .', he muttered the words to himself and mentally applied them to the gates of the Marquis's *finca*. Soon he slipped out, followed by his bodyguard, and almost at once they found a taxi to take them to the Puerta del Sol.

There Bernal found the loyal Navarro already presiding over the permanent telephone link he had fixed up to Seville.

'The special squad has set out, *jefe*, a little after schedule.'

Bernal looked at his Bulova Accutron watch. 'Not bad for Andalusians, though. It's only seven forty-two. Get some coffee and croissants sent up, Paco. There'll be a long wait now.'

While they were breakfasting, Varga arrived in a state of some excitement.

'You remember Brother Nicolás's missal, chief, the one he posted to his sister? I've puzzled over it again and again to see whether he'd left us more information than just the seven dates he indicated by placing markers in the appropriate pages.' Varga paused for breath.

'Well, go on,' said Bernal eagerly.

'I reasoned that he probably wouldn't have had access to any synthetic invisible ink, so I ran the usual tests of iodine crystals, heat, and black light, expecting he would have used milk or fruit juice with the head of a pin. Some of the older priests knew all about secret inks and used them during the Civil War when they found themselves trapped in Republican territory.'

'So what did you find, Varga?' pressed Bernal.

'Well, the old fox had used urine. A very old trick, but still effective. I've made you photographs of the relevant pages, and this is what came out.'

Navarro and Bernal craned their necks over the enlargements, which read:

29 Nov:	Control of the power supplies and telephones at the Zarzuela and Oriente Palaces.
8 Dec:	Extra vigilance and doubling of guard at all MAGOS bases.
13 Dec:	Leave cancelled at all MAGOS bases.
24 Dec:	Initial Alert begins.
1 Jan:	State of Exception in all Military Regions
5 Jan:	Mobilization: main force to move into pre-arranged positions in Madrid.
6 Jan:	Takeover of Oriente Palace during Military Passover Ceremony and Pronunciamento by new Government.

'Phew! You've got it for us, Varga. Well done. I'll ring the King's secretary at once. Were there no names at all? No key to the identity of the MAGOS chiefs? Especially Melchior?'

'My assistant is still trying, *jefe*, but you realize that there are 1224 pages of very fine paper in that missal. It'll be a long business trying out the test on every page. It would help if you'd give us permission to disbind it.'

'Disbind it, pull it to bits, do anything necessary, but

make sure you check it all. How I admire that old monk, even if he did hit the bottle now and then. He was still *compos mentis* enough to try and denounce a neo-fascist attempt to take over the State. My one regret is that it's going to be difficult, if not impossible, to bring his murderer to book.'

When Varga had gone back to his lab, Bernal picked up the red scrambler phone and called the royal secretary. After listening to Bernal's long account of the details of the MAGOS plot, the official said: 'We're taking countermeasures, Comisario. We are sure of the loyalty of the National Police, and of most of the armed forces and Civil Guard. The King will telephone each captain general in each military region, and, of course, every military governor in the fifty provinces.'

'But you won't advise that the JUJEM invoke Operation Mercury, will you, Mr Secretary? As I explained to you before, the MAGOS Operation is a carbon copy of it, a shadow plan, probably supported only by a few wild spirits, but they are spread through many regiments and units. If you set Mercury in train, it will simply correspond to what they themselves are doing, and cause immense confusion. The generals loyal to the King might fall into the trap of aiding the conspirators unwittingly. I hope you appreciate how very cunning this plot is.'

'We do, Comisario, we do. The King is fully apprised. What has been decided is that His Majesty will give in person by telephone and telex message a general order to every commander and governor to do nothing, to take no emergency action of any kind, and above all, to prevent any kind of mobilization or movement of troops. In that way any units that move will be seen to be rebel units, disobeying the royal command. He will arrange locally, in Madrid, for certain units of the National Police and the GEOs to control the two palaces and various key-points.'

'You'll also see that the roads into Madrid are watched,

as well as the railway stations of Atocha and Chamartín, Barajas airport and the military airfields at Torrejón, Alcorcón and Getafe?'

'Yes, it is all arranged. The King hopes that you and your team will be on hand at the Oriente Palace on 6 January. He plans to go ahead with all his engagements, including the Pascua Militar at Epiphany, though discreet precautions will be taken at the palace and in the surrounding streets.'

'And they must be effective,' said Bernal. 'You realize that many, if not all, the plotters are on the guest list for the morning ceremony on 6 January?'

'Yes, we do. His Majesty says that will make it all the easier to cope with them.'

'Let's hope he's right,' said Bernal.

'What about your son, Comisario? We are anxious for news.'

'We have none yet. The Seville police units are just moving in.'

'Please keep me informed.'

As he put down the receiver, Bernal saw Navarro gesticulating to him from the outer office, and he rushed to join him.

'Ángel's van has reached the entrance to the Marquis's estate. It seems that Elena's message of last night has worked like a dream. They've let him through.'

Bernal relit one Kaiser from the previous one, which he left half-smoked. 'Then so far, so good.'

The loudspeaker Navarro had fixed to the telephone link crackled again. 'The support units are at the foot of the hill,' said the disembodied voice. 'The newspaper van has almost reached the *finca* building. It's turning to the right towards the outbuildings at the side.' There was a pause.

Then the voice broke in once more. 'Some packages are being unloaded from the rear of the van.' Now the growing note of incredulity in the unknown observer's voice could be distinguished even from 550 km. away. 'Inspector Gallardo is now closing the rear doors of the van. The special commando unit has not, repeat, has not got out. He's returning to the driver's cab. The van's in motion! It's returning down the main drive!'

'What on earth is happening, Paco?' exclaimed Bernal. 'Why haven't they gone into action?'

The loudspeaker crackled again. 'The van has stopped at the main gate,' continued the observer, in the same shocked tone. 'Inspector Gallardo is joking with the guards, and he's giving them a packet of cigarettes. They've opened the gate and he's driving out. The other K-units are being ordered to withdraw along the A.4 highway.'

Then there was absolute silence. 'What's gone wrong, Paco? Why did Ángel pull out without letting the special squad go in there and at least try to get Diego out?'

'Have some brandy in that coffee, *jefe*,' said Navarro, trying to soothe his chief's nerves. 'We've got no option but to wait on events.'

During the nerve-racking delay, Consuelo came on the phone and asked for Supt Bernal.

'It's for you, *jefe*. It's a lady from the Banco de Castilla.'

She had never rung him at the DSE before, but the emergency seemed to her to warrant it. Bernal took the call in the inner office.

'Is there any news?' she asked in a small voice.

'No, not yet. I'll ring you back in a few minutes, when we should have some.'

Suddenly the loudspeaker relay from Seville came alive once more in the outer office, and Bernal rushed out to Navarro's side.

'Hello, Madrid. We've got a radio link with Inspector Gallardo for you.'

Bernal took up the mouthpiece. 'Is that you, Ángel? What has happened? Why didn't the specials go in?'

'Don't be alarmed, *jefe*. I've got Diego here in the back of the van.'

'You've got him out?' exclaimed Bernal unbelievingly. 'Is he all right?'

'Quite all right, though he smells a bit, the others tell me. He's got a minor cut on his wrist, that's all. I'll get him to call you as soon as we get to Seville.'

'How did you manage it without breaking into the cellars?'

'We didn't have to, chief. He had already got out by his own efforts. The girl was in there tied up with him, and she managed to help him cut the cord tied round his wrists with a broken wine bottle. Since she knew the place from childhood, she showed him how to get out through a small chute alongside the cellar steps.'

'He must have thought you were sent from Above, Ángel.'

'He certainly did. He said it was like a Hollywood B-movie.'

'My wife will say it was through the efficacy of prayer. Did you get the girl out too?'

'No, chief. Diego says she absolutely refused to come. She was suffering badly from drug-withdrawal symptoms, and insisted on being left gagged and bound as the Marquis's guards had left them the night before. She wanted it to look as though he had escaped unaided.'

'But they might kill her if they suspect—'

'She told your son they'd find her wherever she went and torture her to death if she went with him. It's like Mafia-land down here, *jefe*. They've got very long memories.'

'What are you going to do now?'

'We're going straight to the airport and Miranda, Lista and I will bring Diego back to Barajas airport on the first available flight. We'll see if he can get a shave and a shower, as well as a change of clothes before departure.'

'I hope he's suitably chastened by his experiences of the last few days. He'll probably want to pick up his luggage at the hotel, but on no account allow it, Ángel. The Marquis will shortly discover he's missing, and he'll alert his contacts in Seville.'

'Don't worry, *jefe*, we'll guard him all the way to the airport.'

'I don't think you should bring him here to the Gobernación, Ángel.' Bernal racked his brains and then came up with a solution. 'Take him to his brother's apartment in the Plaza de Castilla for the moment. I'll warn Santiago that Diego's on the way, and I'll send over a squad of armed plainclothesmen to provide security.'

'OK, chief, will do.'

'Don't go back to the newspaper office, Ángel. Your cover will be completely blown by now. You could leave the van with the Seville police. From now until 6 January you will be in charge of Diego's security.'

Navarro now entered the office with a bottle of brandy. 'Shall we have a celebratory drink, *jefe*?'

'In a moment, Paco. We should first think of the safety arrangements. I think it would be best if Eugenia moved out to my married son's apartment near the Plaza de Castilla and spent Christmas there with Diego. They've got plenty of room, and the flat's on the tenth floor of a new block, so it's easy to guard.'

'We could use one of the safe houses on the outskirts of the city, chief, if you prefer.'

'No, I don't think that's a good idea. They'll be safer in Madrid, and we must take Christmas into account. None of them will want to be cut off in a remote spot. Now I must call my wife and tell her the good news. Then I'll phone the King's secretary. While I'm doing that you might like to slip out and buy me a bottle of champagne. We might as well celebrate in style.'

After he'd gone, Bernal dialled his home number.

'He's safe, Geñita, Ángel Gallardo has got him out. They're on their way to Seville airport now, and they'll be in Madrid some time this afternoon.'

'I was sure the Blessed Virgin would intervene for him, Luisito, especially on Her special day of hope for the coming of Our Lord. Shall I make some lunch for you both?'

'He won't be coming to the apartment, Eugenia, it would be much too dangerous.' When he explained what he had in mind, she adamantly refused to be shifted.

'I can't possibly spend Christmas up at the Plaza de Castilla, Luis. It's much too far from the church, where I have to help with all kinds of preparations.'

'But don't you realize these kidnappers may take you instead?'

'Me? What use would I be to them?' she said incredulously. 'As it is I've got this plainclothesman following me everywhere. Surely it would be worse if I was cooped up in Santiago's flat? In any case, I'm making a *belén* for our grandson as usual, for when he comes here to dine with the whole family on Christmas Eve, after which we will all go to the *misa del gallo* that Father Anselmo will sing at midnight. The portress and I are cleaning the golden vestments especially for it.'

'But don't you see that we can't do the usual things this year, Geñita? Because of this threat against us?'

'Rubbish!' she expostulated. 'I at least shall be doing the same as always, come what may. If it's God's will that we be sequestered, we must bear it as best we can; we can't avoid what He ordains for us.'

Bernal could see that she was determined not to begin to grasp the problem and was utterly fatalistic into the bargain. 'But, Geñita, common prudence dictates—'

'Cowardice, you mean!' she flashed back at him. 'I don't want to hear any more of this nonsense. I'll continue to make the usual preparations,' she declared with great firmness of purpose. 'But if you want Diego to stay at his brother's flat for the time being,' she conceded, 'that's all right by me, for I'll be staying here as I've always done.'

Bernal gave up, and saw he would have to arrange a more complicated security system to guard his family in two different houses until 6 January had come and gone. In the event of the MAGOS coup succeeding, he would have to get his children out of the country, now that he was in the conspirator's bad books.

He now remembered to telephone Consuelo, to tell her about Diego's rescue, and told her he'd try to slip away from his armed bodyguard at 3.0 p.m. and meet her at their secret apartment.

Just as he was going to the red scrambler phone to call the royal secretary, his ordinary phone rang and Inspector Ibáñez came on the line.

'Will you meet me for lunch, Luis?'

'That will be difficult, Esteban, there's a bit of a flap on. I could meet you for an apéritif at about one p.m.'

'Very well. In Lhardy, downstairs at the back of the shop.'

When Navarro returned bearing a bottle of Codorniu Black Label and two glasses, Bernal told him about the security problem.

'Señora de Bernal won't be shifted, then?'

'Absolutely not. So I'd better stay with her, while my two sons, my daughter-in-law and grandson are guarded in force up at the Plaza de Castilla. It's a mess, really.'

'Why don't we break up MAGOS now, chief, and arrest the Marquis and his henchmen and hold them on a kidnapping charge, and confine Father Gaspar to his priory, as an accomplice?'

'And what about Lieutenant-General Baltasar?' asked Bernal. 'Who will dare arrest him? And the editor of *La Corneta*? There'd be an outcry from the extreme right.

Nevertheless I'll consult the King's secretary. It would certainly be handy if we held one of them as a bargaining counter.'

Already aglow from the celebratory drink, Bernal left his office in the Calle de Carretas accompanied by his armed bodyguard. As they turned into the crowded Puerta del Sol and passed the Librería San Martín, Bernal couldn't help recalling that it was outside that very bookshop that the prime minister José Canalejas was gunned down by an anarchist in 1912 while he was innocently gazing at the books on display; such are the perils of literary curiosity, he thought.

The pavements of the Carrera de San Jerónimo were extremely thick with shoppers, and the bodyguard stuck close to Bernal's side. The crowd thinned as they made their way towards the prominent antique lanterns that hung outside the famous Swiss restaurant and pâtisserie. The armed plainclothesman decided to keep guard at the entrance, while Bernal sought out Inspector Ibáñez at the back of the shop.

After they had helped themselves to cups of consommé from the large heated urn, they asked the waiter, who looked more like an ancient retainer, for *barquillas* of devilled kidneys, a speciality of the house, which they washed down with white port.

'I won't need any lunch after this, Esteban. These are delicious but very filling.'

'They're really first-class.' Glancing round to make sure they weren't being overheard, Ibáñez passed Bernal a sealed envelope.

'I dug something out on Melchior from the old files, Luis. There was nothing at all on the central computer, but I noticed five years ago, when the automated system was introduced, how many of the political files from Franco's time quietly disappeared, especially those of his earlier associates. Some of them have managed to perform a marvellous transformation act, from being fascist henchmen in 1940 to liberal politicians in 1981, and some of them even receive the ultimate accolade—an invitation to write in *El País* on Spain's democratic future. Naturally you won't find their dossiers coming up on your computer terminal.'

'But I don't remember anyone called Melchior, Esteban.'

'You wouldn't, Luis. It wasn't a man, it was a firm. They had factories in Bilbao and Barcelona before the Civil War, and they supplied arms and munitions first to the Republic, and then to both sides after Bilbao, very conveniently, fell to Franco's forces on 19 June 1937.'

'Is Melchior S.A. still in the Register of Companies today?'

'No, Luis, but I dug out the old register for you from the Ministry of Justice's records in the Calle de San Bernardo, and here's the list of the directors in nineteen-thirty-four.'

Bernal, making sure they weren't being observed, opened the long buff envelope and drew out the contents. He looked down the list of names and whistled softly.

'Nearly all from the same family, and one of the richest in Spain!'

'In Europe, I'd say,' added Ibáñez. 'The Lebrija family is small fry compared with the Malthius clan.'

'Middle-European in origin, weren't they?'

'Probably. They settled in Germany in the nineteenth century, and the family home is in Cologne. They were powerful during the Third Reich and helped Hitler to power. The Spanish branch was started by the youngest son of the founder of the family, who had quarrelled with old Malthius. He began his career as a small-time smuggler through Tangiers and Gibraltar before the First World War, and even had a record in the old files of the Coast-guard Section of the Civil Guard, but it was expunged in

1923, under the Primo de Rivera dictatorship.'

'He became a millionaire out of the armaments business, didn't he?'

'That and many other things. Gottlieb Malthius even spied for England and Germany and got well paid by both sides. His fleet of small ships carrying contraband was well placed to spy on the navies of the belligerents. He even got a decoration from King George V in 1919.'

'So he gained respectability?'

'You might say he bought it. He married into a Spanish aristocratic family, became a philanthropist, and in his will he left a very large sum to create a Foundation in his memory. It's curious how most of history's brigands try to buy a place in heaven.'

'But he died a long time ago, so he can't be Melchior.'

'No, I realize that, but his heirs are active in our armaments industry, and there's the question of the ex-Nazi branch of the family. They took refuge here in 1943 when they could see that Hitler was going to lose the war. They now own two Spanish banks, many manufacturing companies, five construction firms, a chain of department stores, a large chunk of the Andalusian wine industry, and a multinational armaments firm. They've made the Marqués de la Estrella a member of the board of some of the companies they control.'

'But is one member of the family particularly involved in the MAGOS conspiracy, Esteban?'

'I should have thought the son of Gottlieb Malthius, Hermann, is too old to play an active part. He lives in retirement in Minorca, and only comes over to the Peninsula once a year for the annual meeting of the clan.'

'Probably all the active members of the family are involved, to protect or further their business interests. Obviously they're against the new Constitution and the liberties it has brought to the political parties, trade unions and workers' commissions. They must be fearful for their profits,' said Bernal. 'It's not surprising that they're using the MAGOS organization—especially if they had connections with the Apostolic Movement in Cologne in the 'thirties. We can check with the West German Police.'

'But why would they infiltrate the Church here, Luis? I don't understand that.'

'By financing the Casa Apostólica they appear to be using the Church to persuade the Army, or a sufficient part of it, to overthrow the shaky democracy and return to a dictatorship of the Right. Lieutenant-General Baltasar is just a convenient figurehead. If they succeed, they'll bring about an alliance of the *poderes fácticos*, those economic and social groups which have immense power when combined, and they'll bring back Francoism under a new guise.'

'I wonder if they've infiltrated the police, Luis. They will certainly have tried.'

'It's a pity we cannot obtain a detailed list of the plotters, but if the Government wants to forestall the conspiracy, it has enough information to arrest the leaders.'

'Only one man stands in their way, Luis.'

'The King, you mean. You're right, of course. But will he be able single-handed to resist such a combined onslaught?'

'It will depend on how he reacts. He has been sure-footed up until now, adhering strictly to the constitutional protocol, and keeping the armed forces within the new *Reales Ordenanzas* which govern their actions under the 1978 Constitution. And he can always appeal to the people direct.'

'If they let him, Esteban, if they let him.'

When they emerged from Lhardy, they found Bernal's bodyguard waiting for him at the door, and he took his leave of Inspector Ibáñez, whose vast knowledge of the police files had served him so often.

'We'll walk for a while,' Bernal said to the plainclothes-men, 'and then I'll take a taxi while you go and get some lunch.'

Further along the Carrera de San Jerónimo, they came to the Casa Mira. Bernal's eyes widened in delight at the window-display of old-fashioned sweetmeats in the famous *turronería*. The array seemed quite unchanged from his childhood memories of the days before Christmas, when he used to peep over the window-ledge of this old establishment at the large sepia photograph of Señor Mira, the founder of the shop, who still presided in spirit over the unattainable stands of crystallized plums, apricots, tangerines and pears, the huge slabs of *turrón*— the soft almond and honey paste from Jijona and the hard nougat from Alicante, not to mention the delicious burnt marzipan, the *praliné de chocolate* and the *turrón de yema* or egg-yolk paste—and the tiny mixed variety of bonbons wrapped in shiny frilled papers. In the 'twenties he didn't have enough *céntimos* in the much darned pocket of his schoolboy's short trousers to buy even the smallest of those delicacies; today, when his sweetness of tooth had been lost for ever, his wallet bulged with five-thousand peseta notes which could purchase anything he fancied there. But the *ilusión*, the excited anticipation, wasn't the same.

He decided to join the enormous queue in the doorway, and buy a modest selection as gifts for his five-year-old grandson and for Consuelo. The bodyguard waited dis-approvingly behind him, but did not comment. Bernal was really astonished by the huge orders being placed by the upper-middle-class housewives, who loosened their fur collars and dug into their capacious handbags for fifteen- or twenty-thousand pesetas to pay for the traditional confectionery usually eaten on Christmas Eve and Christmas Day. What a lot of friends and relatives they must have, he thought, or were they purchasing all this just to impress the neighbours when they dropped in for a seasonal drink?

Once the harassed shop-girl had cut his half-kilo slabs of the various kinds of *turrón* made on the premises, Bernal emerged once more into the chill wind, and thought how best to give the bodyguard the slip.

'Just find me a taxi, will you? Then you can go and have a spot of lunch and meet me back at the Gobernación at five.'

'But I should stay with you, Comisario. Those are my orders.'

Just then one of the new white taxis with a red diagonal stripe on its side—the most notable change wrought in the Madrid scene by the socialist mayor so far—stopped at Bernal's frantic waving, and he jumped in and slammed the door.

'Don't worry,' he said to the plainclothesman, 'I've got my service pistol, and I'm only going a few yards.'

In the Calle de Barceló, Bernal asked the taximan to leave him outside the theatre. He then made his way to his other apartment, where he found Consuelo, looking radiant, and welcoming him with a bottle of champagne in her hand.

'It's French, Luchi, and one of the best—Krug 1971. I've been keeping it for this special occasion.' She eyed the packages from the Casa Mira, and he handed her the larger of them and embraced her.

'Oh, you know how I adore *turrón*! Open the champagne, will you? I have chilled it.' She fell upon the package and untied it feverishly. 'Let's not wait until Christmas. We'll celebrate it in advance.'

He stripped off the silver-paper and removed the wire clamp, remembering the only useful practical trick his father-in-law had ever taught him, which was to open a champagne bottle by turning the bottle, never the cork.

Surprisingly it always worked.

'I'm so glad everything went off all right,' said Consuelo, who was already cutting herself a slice of chocolate praline. 'Isn't it marvellous that Diego got out by his own efforts? And just when your men got there.'

'It certainly saved us the scandal of a minor skirmish with the conspirators,' said Bernal.

'At long last I can tell you our news!' she said excitedly.

He noticed she had emphasized the possessive adjective. 'Our news, Conchi?'

'I've been dying to tell you for over a week, but I couldn't while you had the worry over your son.'

'What news are you talking about?' he asked, genuinely puzzled.

'Well, I told you I had asked for special leave from the bank, but the manager, who's an old sweetie, has come up with a better solution. He's succeeded in getting me a transfer to the Canaries from January for six months, and I'll be posted to the branch in Las Palmas on Gran Canaria. I've already managed to hire a small villa in the hills above the town, where it will be cooler.'

'You're going away?' Bernal felt lost and wondered what he would do without her. He realized with a shock how much he had come to rely on the daily comfort she offered him. It wasn't so much the sexual contact, though that had been the most important thing during their first years together, but now much more the love and companionship they shared. She represented everything he had failed to receive at home for the past forty-five years.

Consuelo burst out laughing at the look of dismay, even despair, on his face. 'I'm not deserting you, you silly boy, I'm going away to avoid any possible scandal.'

'But what scandal, for heaven's sake?'

'There won't be any, you'll see. I'm going to bear you a child, of course,' she said beaming with delight. 'Didn't you have even an inkling?'

Bernal looked stunned, and slumped into an armchair. 'I don't believe it,' he muttered.

'Don't look so shocked, love. It happens you know, it's perfectly normal.'

'But at the age of sixty-two, to be a father again?' he said, still dazed by the news.

'But I'm only thirty-three. It'll be quite safe, you'll see. Oh, Luchi, it's what I've always wanted! And I've got everything arranged. My brother and his wife will look after Mamá—she's failing a lot now, you know—and when I come back with the child, I'll bring a *canaria* as nursemaid, so that I can go back to work. I can always say the child's adopted, can't I? Or that it's a nephew or niece I'm bringing up? In any case, there are plenty of single parents about these days, and there'll be more with the new divorce law.'

She was so gloriously happy that Luis didn't dare ask what had gone wrong with 'the usual precautions' she had give him to understand she was using, let alone whether she had contemplated his arranging for an abortion—she would clearly be too shocked by such a suggestion. And not out of religious scruples, since he knew she was agnostic, but because she showed every sign of wanting to bear his child. Or was it the prospect of being a mother that was the underlying cause of her joy, despite all the social difficulties she would incur? He should get a divorce, he decided; the new legislation had been passed in the summer, though people said that the procedure was cumbersome and extremely slow. Nevertheless he should make the offer.

'I'll ask Eugenia for a divorce, so that we can get married.'

She kissed him. 'That's a lovely thought, but you'd never get it through in time, not by 18 July.'

'Is that the date the doctors have told you?'

'Yes, and they're pretty accurate in their estimate these days. But it's a horrid date for a child with a socialist mother, isn't it—the anniversary of Franco's rising against the Republic? Let's hope it will be premature by four days.'

ADVENT: FOURTH SUNDAY
(20 December)

All night Bernal had found it difficult to get to sleep: the supper of lentils and blood sausage which Eugenia had warmed up for him and then served with a dressing of wine vinegar still sat heavily in his duodenum, quite un-digested. He was also put out of sorts by the presence of the armed bodyguard dozing in a deckchair in the hall of their apartment, and the knowledge that a second man was posted in the downstairs vestibule.

At 6.30 like clockwork Eugenia stirred and put her feet out on to the cold tiled floor. Luis pretended to be asleep as the ancient double mattress, which many years ago had developed an uncomfortable, lumpy mound along its centre, rose and fell like a ship in moderate seas as she looked for her slippers. Soon he could hear her opening the door of the large cupboard in the dining-room, inside which she switched on the coloured lights that decorated the shrine of Nuestra Señora de los Dolores installed as a private oratory. He knew she would pray there for at least twenty minutes, so he decided to get up early and pay a surprise call on his elder son's apartment to check the security there.

He tried to move quietly into the kitchen to light the decrepit gas geyser, but the security man heard him and called out softly, 'Is that you, Comisario?'

'Yes, I'm going to get dressed and slip up to the Plaza

de Castilla in half an hour.'

'I'll order the car, sir. We'll be changing shifts at seven-thirty.'

'In that case we had better wait for your relief to arrive, and then we can drop my wife off at the church as we go. We'll have some breakfast in the bar down the street, if it's open.'

When Bernal had shaved and dressed, Eugenia emerged from her dawn devotions.

'I'll make some coffee for you and the police guard, Luis.'

'There's no time, Geñita,' said Bernal hastily, hoping to save the plainclothesman from savouring her ersatz coffee. 'We'll drop you off at the church.'

As they emerged on to the pavement, it began to rain heavily, and Bernal asked Eugenia jokingly, 'I bet it's the *Rorate Cæli* Mass this morning.'

'You're quite right, Luis. It's astonishing to find how much you've learnt. And the vestments will be purple,' she said firmly.

The official car arrived with the two relief bodyguards, and they all piled in to ride the short distance to the parish church, where one of the relief guards alighted with Eugenia.

As they sped up the completely deserted Paseo de la Castellana, Bernal puffed nervously at his third Kaiser of the day, which made his tongue feel like a rusty scrubbing-board.

He instructed the driver to stop as soon as he could see a *cafetería* open, and above the Nuevos Ministerios they found one, where they all took a breakfast of *café con churros*.

At the modern apartment block where Santiago lived, they found an unmarked K-car in position in front of the door, and in the hallway sat two plainclothesmen, who greeted their colleagues wearily.

Bernal and his personal guard went up in the fast lift, and found yet another guard outside the apartment door. 'No one's come out yet, Comisario.'

The door was opened by his daughter-in-law who was carrying her five-year-old son. At the sight of his grandfather, he clapped his hands with delight, and shouted '¡Yayo! ¡Yayo! What have you brought for Quico?'

Bernal kissed him and pulled Mercedes's leg. 'You're bringing up that child to talk like a *péon* from Albacete. *Yayo*, indeed.' He took little Enrique from her and felt in his pocket for a toy soldier he had brought specially, knowing very well that he was regarded by the child as a permanent source of toys and sweets.

'You spoil him, Papá,' said Mercedes chidingly. 'Now he'll want to play before he has his bath.'

'How are you managing? Is everything all right?'

'Not too bad, but it's a bit of a strain,' she said. 'I don't mean having Diego here; he's no trouble. I've never seen him do so much studying. But it's being guarded all the time, that's the real strain. Santiago's quite upset by it, and can't sleep.'

'It won't be for much longer, and we can relax a bit as Twelfth Night approaches.'

'I was going to ask you about that. I'll have to go and do some shopping for presents in the Corte Inglés, as well as getting the normal household goods in.'

'That's all right. A plainclothesman will go with you. You just inform him where you want to go.'

When he got to the Gobernación building, Bernal did not expect to find anyone in the office at eight on a Sunday morning, so he was surprised to discover Navarro and Varga the technician waiting for him.

'We've been trying your apartment, *jefe*, but there was no reply. We got quite worried.'

'My wife's already gone out to early Mass, and I've

been up to my son's apartment. Why are you both here so early?'

'Varga's got some important evidence for us, and he rang me at home.'

'It's Brother Nicolás's missal, *jefe*. We spent days and days testing every page for further signs of secret ink, but found nothing. Just when I'd given up, I suddenly thought of the bookmarks that he'd placed at certain points to indicate the seven stages of the MAGOS operation.'

'And you got something?'

'Yes, chief. On the back of each of the flimsy religious cards he left us long lists of names in the tiniest possible writing. I think he must have used the point of a pin, and it must have taken him many hours. I've made enlargements for you.'

'What an extraordinary man he was,' said Bernal admiringly. 'We should have had him on the force.' He examined the seven photographs with great care.

The first contained more than sixty-five names of army personnel, all of captain's rank or above, and they were arranged by military region and unit. The second contained names of members of the Civil Guard, the third of the Navy, and so on through the branches of the armed services. The sixth card interested him most: it dealt with MAGOS members in the various police forces, while the seventh concerned the mass media.

'Have you made copies of these?' Bernal asked Varga.

'Yes, chief, three of each.'

'Good. I'll ring the King's secretary at once and arrange to see him this morning. These names will be invaluable for his counter-coup plans.'

'Have you seen *La Corneta*, chief?' asked Navarro. 'The sixth MAGOS message still has not appeared.'

'I'm wondering if they've got cold feet, Paco. Elena rang me last night and told me that there would be nothing in today's issue. Yet it's due, I'm sure, if they maintain the usual fortnight's notice.'

'Perhaps our rescue of your son has given them pause.'

'Or it may be that they will give their followers less notice as the date approaches. That way they could abort the operation at the eleventh hour if they wished.'

Bernal took an unmarked police car to the Zarzuela Palace just before 9.0 a.m., and his bodyguard was asked to wait with the sentries at the main gate while the royal secretary drove the Superintendent up the palace drive.

'I want to show you the counter-coup plans, Comisario. We'll go over them together.'

'Is the King here at present?' asked Bernal.

'Actually, he isn't. He took the Queen and the royal prince and princesses down to Granada for the weekend, on a private visit. It won't be announced to the press.'

'You are sure they are well guarded there?'

'Quite sure. They're doing a spot of hunting.'

'You'd better see these lists first,' said Bernal. 'We've only just come across them. Brother Nicolás probably copied them from secret documents he came across in Father Gaspar's study. On that Saturday night, the Prior must have rumbled what he was up to.'

'These names are most vital for our plans, Comisario. Well done! This way we can avoid engaging the assistance of anyone who is implicated in the MAGOS plot, and keep surveillance on the units to which they belong. You couldn't have served us better. The King will be delighted.'

Bernal examined the detailed plans drawn up by the JUJEM for the control of the central military region, including the imposition of a cordon round Madrid on 5 January, to prevent any rebel units from entering. He was impressed by the foresight demonstrated in the proposed arrangements, and expressed himself reasonably satisfied.

'What about the protection of the Oriente Palace on the

morning of the sixth?' he asked.

'We're still working on that, Comisario. I'll show you the plan in a few days' time. We naturally want you and your team to be in close attendance at the ceremony.'

VIGIL OF THE NATIVITY OF OUR LORD (24 December)

Bernal was awakened on Christmas Eve by the insistent ring of the telephone, and the armed bodyguard got to it before him.

'It's Inspectora Fernández, Comisario.'

'Hello, Elena? What news?'

'I'm sorry to ring you so very early, but I simply couldn't find the opportunity late last night. The sixth message will be in today's issue of *La Corneta*. It reads: 'MAGOS *White N.7. Moncloa.*' Does that mean they're going to attack the President of the Government in the Moncloa Palace, *jefe*?'

'No, I don't think so, Elena. *Moncloa* stands for "Mobilization". They're going ahead with the plan after all. Is there any sign of activity in the office?'

'There was a lot of drinking going on late last night in the Editor's office, chief. A group of high-ranking officers called in, including Lieutenant-General Baltasar.'

'I see. There won't be an edition published tomorrow, will there?'

'No, chief, not until Saturday.'

'Watch your step, now, Elena. Pull out at once if you think they suspect you.'

'I'm sure they don't, *jefe*. The production manager, who's an ardent admirer of mine, has hinted that there will be an extra special edition in colour on 6 January, but it won't be published until noon.'

'If you see any copy for that edition lying about, try to

get it for us.'

'Will do, chief. They've already asked for a lot of photographs from the archives.'

'Of whom?' asked Bernal.

'Mainly of famous generals of the past. Narváez and Martínez Campos and other *fachas* of the late nineteenth century.'

'Keep a check on which ones they ask for, if you can.'

After she had rung off, Bernal consulted the old missal in the dining-room, and turned to the liturgical calendar. He soon worked it out. Starting at Christmas Day itself, the seventh day for which white vestments were prescribed was 5 January, Vigil of the Epiphany, that was *White N.7*. There could only be one more message: for Action on Epiphany itself. Once that was published, there would be no going back.

Eugenia now brought him some fried stale bread and lukewarm coffee.

'I hope all the family will come this evening as usual, Luis. I'm preparing the special *paella* of spider crabs, and you'll have to get the wine in. This marzipan serpent you bought in Toledo is enough for ten Christmases, so we shan't need to buy any more *turrón*. In any case I think I've got some *polvorones* that my sister brought from Seville last year put by in the cupboard.'

'But I've told you again and again, Geñita, that it won't be safe for them all to come here. It would be much better if you would agree to go up to Santiago's.'

'And risk missing the beautiful Midnight Mass that Father Anselmo will celebrate in the golden vestments? Never!' she exclaimed. 'The gradual of the Mass is so lovely, Luis: "With Thee is the principality in the day of Thy strength: in the brightness of the Saints, from the womb before the day star I begot Thee." ' She appeared to go into a mystical trance.

'But you'll be back in plenty of time for it, Geñita. Why

don't you honour your daughter-in-law by dining with her for once.'

'I'll think about it,' she said grimly. 'But only if you swear you'll bring me back by eleven p.m. to help the portress in the sacristy.'

'I swear.'

When Bernal got to the office at 8.30 a.m., Navarro had a pile of typewritten transcripts piled on his desk.

'These are the telephone intercepts for the past three days, chief. It will take us all day to read them.'

'Has the Telefónica put an intercept on Hermann Malthius's line, Paco?'

'Yes, chief, and on those of all the Malthius family. The transcripts should be in this bundle.'

'Have a look at those first.'

Bernal helped Navarro to sort out the immense amount of material, and they sorted it into separate piles for each group of known conspirators.

'Here they are, chief. We've got them for the three days up to yesterday.'

They took a wad each, and started to skim through the boring mass of material dealing with the domestic affairs of Mr Malthius's residence, and the many calls made by his secretary on financial matters.

'Here's something, chief. The secretary has ordered Malthius's private jet to be made ready to bring him to Madrid on 28 December.'

'The Day of the Holy Innocents,' said Bernal, 'when people play practical jokes on one another. So the old man is going to pay us a rare visit. He wants to be in at the kill. Where will he be staying?'

'His majordomo has made a call to the Madrid house— it's an old mansion the family has on the Castellana—to instruct the servants to prepare for Mr Malthius's forthcoming stay for an indefinite period. He's also told them he will come himself to arrange a banquet to be given there on New Year's Eve.'

'We must try to get microphones into the house, Paco.'

'I'll call Varga back to see what he can do.'

Bernal smoked another Kaiser and flicked through Father Gaspar's transcripts. The monks weren't great users of the telephone, and the calls all seemed to be innocuous.

When Varga came, Bernal asked him about the feasibility of bugging the Malthius mansion.

'We could try and get in there, *jefe*, but it isn't strictly necessary because we've got one of these new long-range laser listening devices. So long as they haven't got metal shutters across the windows, we can direct an invisible laser beam from the street on to some object in the room where the banquet is being held—a mirror or picture on the further wall would do—then we pick up the vibrations of any sound made within the room and receive it along the laser beam with hypersensitive equipment. I could then amplify it for you to hear everything that was said.'

'But that's fabulous, Varga. Why haven't you told me about it before? It means no one is safe from eavesdropping anywhere.'

'We've only just taken delivery of it, chief. It's Japanese, as you might guess. But as I say, thick metal shutters would neutralize it.'

'I doubt if those old nineteenth-century houses up there have got metal shutters,' said Navarro. 'You could try it out in advance. The servants will be getting the rooms ready in the next few days.'

The red scrambler phone rang, and Bernal went to answer it.

'Could you meet me in half an hour at the Palacio de Oriente, Comisario?' asked the King's secretary.

'Yes, of course.'

'I want to go over with you the detailed plans for the ceremony on 6 January.'

Bernal took a coffee with his bodyguard in the small bar at the corner of the Calle de Carretas before taking a taxi to the royal palace. The cab-driver left them at the Puerta del Príncipe, and they showed their credentials to the palace door-keeper and to the officer on duty.

In the Secretaría, the King's secretary had a large plan of the Oriente Palace spread out on the table.

'I propose that we confine the Pascua Militar ceremony to the rooms on the first floor facing the Plaza de la Armería. The King and Queen will begin the day by attending a private Mass in the royal chapel at the north end of the palace, but this year we won't permit anybody else to worship with Their Majesties. While the solemn Mass lasts from nine until ten a.m., the ceremonial guard will line up in the Plaza on the south side, and the four hundred guests will start arriving and be shown up the Grand Staircase to the Salón de Alabarderos. The main ceremony of the Military Passover will be held in the ad-joining room, the Salón de Columnas, which is the largest in the palace. We won't use the Salón de Embajadores or throne room this year. After the ceremony ends, at about one p.m., the guests will proceed along the Tranvía de Carlos III to the Gala Dining Room, where luncheon will be served. That room faces west over the Campo del Moro.'

'How will the King and Queen be brought here?' asked Bernal.

'By royal helicopter from the Zarzuela Palace. You know the King likes to pilot it himself.'

'I take it the Air Force will provide covering protection.'

'Oh yes. He normally lands it in the Campo del Moro Gardens.'

'What about radio and television coverage? Will that be provided?'

'Yes, as usual. Radio Televisión Española will have cameras in the Plaza de la Armería to cover the King reviewing the guard, on the Grand Staircase to show the guests arriving, and in the Room of the Columns itself. Radio Nacional will also have reporters here, and Cadena SER, which will be broadcasting the proceedings live in their entirety. They're setting up their equipment now, if you'd like to come and see.'

Bernal accompanied the official through the large inner courtyard to the Grand Staircase with its superb, light vaulted ceiling of Colmenar stone with a fine Neapolitan painting representing the 'The Triumph of Religion and the Church'.

'I forgot it was all so magnificent,' muttered Bernal to the secretary. 'This is the staircase on which Napoleon Buonaparte said to his brother Joseph "*Vous serez mieux logé que moi*", isn't it?'

'That's right, Comisario, and it's reputed that he grasped hold of one of these finely carved marble lions and exclaimed: "*Je la tiens enfin, cette Espagne si désirée!*" '

'But he didn't hold Spain for long, thanks to the *madrileños*,' commented Bernal.

'With the help of the Duke of Wellington and the English,' added the royal secretary with a smile. 'They ought to be given some credit.'

One of the palace lackeys now approached them with that very special gait, between a walk and a trot on tiptoes, that Bernal supposed to be a very ancient way of ambulation, confined nowadays to royal servants; perhaps they learned it unconsciously from each preceding generation of lackeys, he thought.

'What is it, Fernando?' asked the secretary, who obviously knew them all by name.

'There's a very urgent telephone call for Comisario Bernal, sir. The Superintendent could take it here in the office at the Visitors' entrance.'

Bernal took the phone, and found a breathless police bodyguard on the line.

'I'm in a café in the Plaza Mayor, Comisario. Your daughter-in-law decided to bring your grandson to the Christmas fair here this morning, and I accompanied them, but now I've lost them in the immense crowd.'

'I'll come at once,' said Bernal. 'Have you rung for reinforcements?'

'Yes, chief. I've rung the guards at the Plaza de Castilla to get men to relieve them there and then to come down here. At least they know what your daughter-in-law looks like.'

Bernal explained what had occurred to the King's secretary.

'You'd better go there immediately, Comisario. Keep me informed.'

Together with his bodyguard, Bernal took a taxi from the Calle de Bailén through the narrow streets leading to the Calle Mayor. At the western corner of the Plaza Mayor, they paid off the taxi and ran to the square, which was filled with market stalls offering piles of holly, ivy and mistletoe, figures of the Holy Family and the animals in all sizes for making Christmas cribs, and a noisy array of trumpets, tambourines and drums which thousands of tiny prospective purchasers were enthusiastically trying out.

Bernal fell back in dismay, and said to the plainclothesman, 'It'll be well nigh impossible to find them in that crowd. It would be much better to cover all the exits from the square. No vehicles are allowed to enter nowadays, and there are only eight exits. See if you can find your colleagues and dispose them to cover all the gates.'

By now they had made contact with Mercedes's own bodyguard, who came up shamefacedly to Bernal.

'The child slipped away, chief, like greased lightning he is. Señora de Bernal went to look for him, and then I lost sight of her too.'

'If we can keep command of all the exits, we're bound to find them in time,' said Bernal.

When finally this had been arranged, Bernal decided to walk through the middle of the extremely busy fair to the famous equestrian statue of Philip III, cast in Florence by Pietro Tacca in 1613, the base of which had in recent years become a meeting-place for hippies, out-of-work musicians and drug-addicts. Perhaps he would find Mercedes here, where she could stand on the pedestal to get a better view.

Could the MAGOS conspirators have taken their chance to kidnap his grandson, he wondered? They were certainly capable of it, but the point of doing so was beginning to escape him, if not them. He had passed all the information he had to date to the King; there was very little left to uncover. Yet they wouldn't be fully aware of that, he reasoned. They still thought of him as a danger to their plans.

He resisted the natural temptation to search along each alley of the hundreds of covered stalls packed with shoppers in festive mood. It would be pointless, and lead to confusion.

He looked about him in more and more desperation, his ears assailed by the cacophony of different carols coming from the loudspeakers, though the predominant one was the old German tune *O Tannenbaum*, sung with Spanish words. He remembered reading that in some countries it had become a revolutionary song, and in England the socialists somewhat incongruously sang the words of *The Red Flag* to it.

Suddenly a tiny head appeared from under the tarpaulin of the stall nearest to him, and a child's voice cried: '¡*Yayo!* ¡*Yayo!*' and a silver-paper trumpet was blown at him.

'Enrique! Where have you been? And where's your Mamá?'

He picked up the child and hugged him to his chest.

'Buy this for me, *Yayo*,' begged the little boy, kissing his grandfather affectionately.

Just then Mercedes appeared looking harassed, and began to berate Enrique, who paid no attention to her reproaches.

'And can I have these kings to put in *abuelita*'s crib, *Yayo*?' He leaned down to touch three polychromed figures of Melchior, Gaspar and Balthazar.

FEAST OF ST SILVESTER, POPE AND CONFESSOR (31 December)

Nochebuena and Christmas Day had passed without further incident, and Bernal and his team waited each day to see if *La Corneta* would publish the last order that would put the MAGOS plot into operation. The national festivities were now entering into the second of the three stages: the first had been Christmas Eve, when the office parties took place, the National Lottery for El Gordo or 'The Fat One' was drawn, which this year had enriched most of the inhabitants of a small village called Navalmoral de la Mata, and the more traditional and religious families went together to the *Misa del gallo* or Cockcrow Mass.

Now the second, much more secular stage of *Nochevieja* was upon them, when the livelier inhabitants of the city would gather at midnight in the Puerta del Sol, each clutching twelve grapes, or, if they were too poor to pay the inflated prices on that day, then segments of a tangerine, which they would swallow one by one at great speed as the Normal Clock on the Gobernación building struck in the New Year, and make twelve wishes. After that a carnival spirit would take over, and they would roam the streets wearing party hats, false noses and eye-masks, and beat drums, blow trumpets, throw coloured streamers and thrust *matasuegras* or mothers'-in-law-tongue blowers at unsuspecting passers-by, while emitting a rude raspberry noise.

In the office with Navarro, Miranda and Lista, Bernal reviewed the plans for protecting the Pascua Militar ceremony on 6 January.

'I think we ought to be present on the eve of *Reyes*, too,' he said. 'I had a look at the balcony of the Panadería in the Plaza Mayor this morning, and the King's secretary may be right in supposing that an assassination attempt on the Queen and the royal children would be very difficult; nevertheless I should be happier if we were there and took up useful vantage points in the square.'

'Should we be armed with more than service pistols, chief?'

'I don't think it would be sensible to take rifles, if that's what you are thinking. The King's own security men might take a pot-shot at you if they mistook you for an assassin.'

The phone rang and Elena came on the line.

'I've slipped out to a bar to call you, *jefe*. The Editor of *La Corneta* has just handed the advertising department an insertion for tomorrow's paper. I managed to memorize it. It reads: "MAGOS *White E.1. Oriente*".'

'That's it, Elena. That's the final go-ahead. Well done. You could pull out now, you know.'

'But I want to try and get you a copy of the draft of the special issue they're planning for 6 January. I've heard the production manager say it will be an extra edition to be run off at midday.'

'Very well, but be careful.'

Bernal turned back to his team. 'It's on, then. Once this message is published, they won't be able to cancel the plan.'

'It certainly looks as though they're going ahead to judge from this transcript of the speeches made at Hermann Malthius's banquet, *jefe*,' said Navarro, 'but they didn't refer to any details.'

'No, but General Baltasar's speech makes it clear he expects to be President of a new Council of Ministers from 6 January,' commented Bernal.

'Why does this last message say "*White E.1.*", chief?' asked Lista, looking at Bernal's scribbled copy of the contents.

'You'll have to consult your missal, Juan,' said Bernal jokingly. '*E* is for "Epiphany" and the Day of the Three Kings is, of course, the first day in that religious season when white vestments are worn.'

'And "*Oriente*"?' asked Miranda. 'Does that refer to the royal palace where the ceremony will take place?'

'That's the most cunning part of the whole business, Carlos,' said Bernal, 'You have to admire them for it. In the acrological code, *Oriente* stands for "*Operación*", the day of action, but of course it's also the name of the main royal palace, and, by a third coincidence, it recalls the Three Kings of Orient, the Magi who will be coming on that day. Clever, isn't it? But not very intelligent of them, since the code is too easy to understand, once you've grasped its liturgical basis.'

That evening, Consuelo rang Bernal to tell him she had managed to secure two tickets for the theatre.

'I got them at the bank, Luchi, and they're for Buero Vallejo's *Caimán* in the Reina Victoria. The New Year's Eve *cotillón* is included in the price.'

'But that's the play about the little girl falling down a hole and never being found, isn't it? Wouldn't you find it too depressing?'

'There weren't any other tickets left, Luchi. I expect it'll be quite interesting. And we can take the champagne and eat the twelve grapes in the theatre. You know they stop the performance at midnight and the actors come down into the auditorium to see the New Year in with the public. Perhaps they'll even serve *chocolate con churros* at the end of the performance.'

'All right, then. Shall I collect you at nine? We could dine up at Curro's in the Calle de Coslada. It's very discreet and the food is good. I'll try to shake off my bodyguard.'

In the event they found the Buero play much too depressing for such a festive night, and after hearing the ghostly voice of the dead child haunting the bereft mother for the third time, it was more than Consuelo could stand, more especially since she herself had entered the expectant state.

'Let's take our little bag of grapes and run to the Puerta del Sol,' she urged.

They crept out of the Reina Victoria theatre and hurried along the Carrera de San Jerónimo, reaching Sol just in time to hear the famous old clock begin to strike, and they swallowed their grapes, pips and all, at each stroke, the wishes they secretly made being a single, identical one.

'I wonder how many cases of appendicitis they treat at La Paz Clinic on New Year's day, Conchi?' said Luis, burping a little. 'There must be far more than on any other day of the year.'

VIGIL OF THE EPIPHANY (5 January)

At 7.30 p.m. on Twelfth Night, all the shops were packed with people buying last-minute presents, which would be put at the foot of their children's beds, assuming they ever got them off to sleep, while adults would exchange gifts at midnight. The *pastelerías* were doing a roaring trade in *roscones de reyes*, large bun-rings decorated with chopped nuts, glacé cherries and angelica, each of which contained a *sorpresa*—usually a ceramic or plastic trinket nowadays, rather than one of gold or silver—so that those who partook of the traditional fare in the early hours with a cup of chocolate had to watch out not to break a tooth on one of the 'surprises'.

Bernal and his men walked from the Gobernación building, where the municipal police had already closed the square to traffic in readiness for the *Cabalgata de los Reyes*, the annual Epiphany procession, and made their way to the Plaza Mayor. He had checked with the King's secretary that no unusual activity had been noted on the roads leading into the city, or at the railway stations or airports. Bernal wondered exactly how MAGOS planned to get their men into position for the operation the next day. Perhaps they would try during the night, under cover of the festivities.

He positioned his small team in a number of vantage-points around the Plaza Mayor, he himself choosing the pedestal of the Philip III statue, whence he could see the balcony of the Panadería, and the main entrances to the square. They kept in touch with two-way radios, and he could speak directly to the Zarzuela on a different frequency.

The National Police kept the large space in front of the balcony free of sightseers, and metal barricades had been placed to allow the lorries and floats of the procession to have room to manœuvre into the square from the east and leave it by the west gate.

The night was dry but very cold, and Bernal was glad he had put on his dogstooth tweed overcoat and a hat. He knew from the programme provided by the Ayuntamiento that the procession would form out at the Retiro park, though many of the floats were being prepared in the outer suburbs, and would join the column at the corner of Alcalá and O'Donnell streets. They were due to start out at 8.0 p.m. and would take approximately twenty minutes to reach the Puerta del Sol.

The road surfaces had already been sprinkled with sand to prevent the horses' hooves from slipping, and the municipal dustcart made a last inspection for refuse, the lorry receiving a cheer from the waiting crowd, who consisted mostly, he noticed, of parents with children.

At 8.0 p.m. a small van swept into the square, and two men descended from it and began to let off rockets, which whizzed above the square into the night sky, and descended slowly, releasing balls of green, red and silver lights. One of the still burning tubes landed near him, and he jumped to avoid the sparks.

There was a long delay, during which the crowd became restless. The Queen and the royal children, who had emerged to watch the fireworks, had returned to the warmth and safety of the Casa de la Panadería.

At 8.30, three heralds rode into the square, and blew trumpets. Queen Sofía and the Infantes emerged once more to greet them. These ceremonially dressed harbingers now departed, to be succeeded by troops of police, dressed in the various historical uniforms of the service through the ages. The crowd cheered each new wave of riders, and the children kept asking, 'Are the *Reyes* coming soon?'

A series of floats mounted on modern lorries now entered the square, including a cage of live peacocks lent by the Parque Zoológico, who must be feeling the cold, Bernal thought, and one representing a goal-mouth with a man dressed as a large orange—the *Naranjito* symbol of the *Mundiales* or World Cup matches to be held in Spain in 1982—dodging about with a football.

There followed a troop of girl pipers, three live camels loaded with gifts, and finally the floats of each of the Three Wise Men mounted on lorries. The first was Melchior, who sat under a golden canopy and held a large urn studded with precious stones; as he passed he threw coins and wrapped sweets to the children in the crowd, who all cheered him. Bernal could see that the man dressed up as the first Magus really was old, but he knew that the senior *concejales* or city councillors fought jealously each year for the privilege of assuming one of these benign roles.

He checked on his radio with the rest of his team positioned in the square, and all reported that things were going normally. He then tried the frequency of the Zarzuela Palace, and heard from the King's secretary that the surveillance teams on the approaches to the capital had reported no unusual activity, other than was normal at the festive season.

The second float now came towards him, and he could see that it represented Gaspar, who sat under a silver canopy and held an incense boat; he waved graciously to the crowd from time to time. Alongside each of the first two Magi's floats were thick files of soldiers in blue uniform. As the second Magus passed the statue in the middle of the square, Bernal had a sudden close-up view of the councillor's face, half-hidden by the false beard and the silver crown. My God, it was Father Gaspar! What on earth was he doing in that rig-out, and where was the *concejal* originally chosen to play the part?

Now Bernal wondered abut the first Magus: could it have been Hermann Malthius dressed up as Melchior? He got on to the Zarzuela Palace to tell the King's secretary of his suspicions, and asked him to have the starting-point of the procession checked out to see where the substitution had been effected. Then he altered the frequency on his portable transmitter to speak to his team in the square and warned them to watch out for any suspect activity from the Magi's floats. But Gaspar's, he saw, continued to sway gently to and fro as the disguised Prior waved to the Queen and the royal children in most benign fashion, and then proceeded normally out of the Plaza Mayor by the gate that led down to the Plaza de la

Villa and the city hall.

The third and final float was now moving into Bernal's line of vision: Balthazar, with blackened face and rubied crown, was raising a pot of myrrh between his gloved hands and beaming at the crowd. Could it be, was it possible that MAGOS had taken things so absurdly far? Bernal craned his neck to get a better view of the face. Yes, he was sure, it was Lt-Gen. Baltasar, made up as his namesake. He too began to throw presents to the children in the square, and waved graciously to the royal family looking down from the balcony, which was draped with the royal arms.

But what was the point of it? Bernal asked himself. No threat was being offered to the royal family. It was just a silly charade, nothing more. Then a thought struck him and he looked closely at the three or four hundred troops who had protected the Magi in the procession. They were supposed to be dressed in the various historical uniforms of the police, many of which would be unfamiliar to the people in the crowd. Earlier, in the first part of the parade, Bernal had noticed the sequence of the various Civil Guard uniforms from the eighteenth century to the present day, which had been followed by the Count of Romanones's *guindillas* or 'cherries', the assault guards of the Second Republic, the Francoist *grises* or 'greys' and the present-day beige and brown uniforms of the Policía Nacional. At first he had taken these blue-clad troops to be wearing something appropriate for the Magi's personal guard, but now he could see that they were dressed in the special blue uniform with the red epaulettes in the shape of the patté cross and dagger—the Apostolic Movement's symbol. Of course, he realized, that was the purpose of this elaborate substitution: to get the rebel troops into the city without the authorities spotting them. What a fool he had been!

He radioed immediately to the Zarzuela Palace: 'The MAGOS are here. The rebel troops are in the city. Now they're proceeding to the Casa de la Villa and the barracks nearby. They will be well placed for an assault on the Palacio de Oriente tomorrow.'

Later that night, when Bernal and his team had returned wearily to their office in the Gobernación building, Navarro gave them the news that the three city councillors, who had thought that they would be enjoying the honour of representing the Three Kings of Orient, had been discovered bound and gagged in their underclothes in a deserted birdcage in the old zoo in the Retiro Park. Fortunately only their civic dignity had suffered any damage.

FEAST OF THE EPIPHANY OF OUR LORD (6 January)

The Day of Christ's Manifestation to the Magi and the Gentiles, thought Bernal, that's what it meant. He paced anxiously up and down the corridor on the east side of the Oriente Palace, hoping that all the further precautions he and the King's secretary had talked over with the JUJEM would prevent a coup. He knew that a special squad of fifty GEOs and a three-hundred strong detachment of the National Police were concealed on the mezzanine floor immediately above the state rooms where the ceremony of the Pascua Militar was to be held.

The secretary had assured him that the King was determined to proceed as usual, and now at 9.0 a.m. he and the Queen were already in the royal chapel attending the special Mass for the day.

From the hallway Bernal could hear the royal chaplain singing the words of the introit: '*Ecce advenit Dominator Dominus: et regnum in manu ejus, et potestas, et im-*

perium—Behold the Lord the Ruler is come: and the Kingdom is in His Hand, and power, and domination.' Very ominous, Bernal considered them, if one applied them to the temporal context.

He checked again that all his team were in position on the Grand Staircase and in the Hall of Columns, and he saw that the guests had begun to ascend. He had insisted with the royal secretary that all the military men, who formed the majority of those invited, should be asked to leave their weapons in the vestibule, on the grounds that the old Spanish custom did not permit anyone to enter the royal presence armed in any way. He had also installed a discreet metal-detecting device near the door, and any civilians who entered and caused a positive reading were taken politely away by Miranda and Lista and asked to turn out their pockets.

Their Majesties now emerged from the chapel, the Queen wearing white gala dress with a striking necklace of large emeralds set in white diamonds, while the King wore the uniform of a captain-general, with the collar of the Toisón de Oro and the sash and star of a knight commander of the Order of Charles III.

Bernal inclined his head as they passed, and Doña Sofía stopped and came to talk to him.

'Superintendent Bernal? We want to thank you for everything you've done. It will not be forgotten. I gather that your son and all your family are safe. We're very glad about that.'

'Yes, thank you, Majesty.'

The King now descended the Grand Staircase to inspect a guard of honour drawn up in the Plaza de la Armería, while Doña Sofía waited in the Halberdiers' Room, chatting amicably with the guests. Bernal could hear the distant strains of the *Marcha Real* performed by the military band as the King appeared on the parade ground.

Miranda now came to look for him. 'What about the guard of honour, *jefe*? The majordomo tells me that they usually line the Grand Staircase and the Salón de Alabarderos presenting arms as the King enters to begin the ceremony.'

'Well, today they mustn't have weapons, or at least not loaded ones.'

'But there'll be no time to empty them, chief. There are more than three hundred troops involved.'

'It's vital that they leave their arms at the entrance, then, like everyone else. I'll talk to the King's secretary and the Head of Security about it at once.'

After an animated discussion, Bernal's wishes prevailed, and he and Miranda supervised the handing in of the weapons when the brief parade was over. As the troops filed in, Bernal noticed with alarm that the platoon detached to line up inside the Hall of Columns was commanded by the artillery colonel from the college at Ocaña.

'Please ask your men to leave their rifles and pistols here,' Bernal ordered him.

The officer began to protest, but the King's secretary reassured him.

'It's the custom, Colonel. No one is to bear arms in the King's presence inside the throne room.'

After much muttering and half-raised complaints by the artillery officers, all the arms were safely lodged at the lower entrance lodge. When all of them had gone up the staircase, Bernal called Miranda over.

'It's a very long shot, Carlos, but let's take a quick look at the butts of these rifles belonging to the Ocaña contingent.'

'OK, chief. There's not a lot of time, but I take it we're looking for minute bloodstains or hairs in the crevices of the weapons?'

'Yes, especially the stocks, just in case we can spot the

weapon that was used to bludgeon Brother Nicolás to death. A few of these military types, who still seem to believe that Spain is their personal domain, regard themselves as unreachable by the arm of the law, but I hate to see injustice thrive and serious crime go unpunished. It's our duty to try, at any rate.'

When they were less than half way through their inspection of the rifles, Bernal exclaimed suddenly and called Miranda to his side.

'Have a look at this one,' he said excitedly. 'Do you see those irregular indentations on the edge of the stock and this rust-coloured staining on the underside? Do you happen to have a glass with you?'

Miranda produced a small jeweller's glass and, taking the rifle by the barrel, examined the butt with care. 'There are three tiny hairs lodged in this groove, *jefe*. This could be the murder weapon.'

'Keep holding it by the barrel, Carlos, and don't wrap it in anything in case the friction of the packaging removes the evidence. Run it up to Varga, will you, for him to test it in the technical lab? Is the serial number legible?'

'Yes it is, chief.'

'Then get it checked out with the army records. I want to know to whom it was issued.'

While they had been carrying out their hasty inspection, the ceremony had begun in the Salón de Columnas, under the harsh arc-lamps placed there by the television crew. Bernal chose a vantage point near a small staircase leading to the mezzanine floor, whence he viewed the imposing scene.

The first to go to the microphone was the civilian Minister of Defence, who made an hour-long speech in which he reviewed the previous year in the armed forces, talked at length about Spain's forthcoming entry into NATO and the increased opportunities that would give for the armed forces' new role in the defence of the West, and generally managed to say little in many words as is the custom of politicians. The serried rows of high-ranking officers and the members of the Cabinet swayed in boredom, while the King and Queen stood at the royal dais with impassive faces and backs as stiff as ramrods.

When the Minister had finished, there was a momentary shuffling of feet and clearing of throats, and then Lt-Gen. Baltasar came to the microphone. As commander-in-chief of the central region it fell to him to make a loyal address. Bernal felt the atmosphere become much more tense, as the general drew a thick wad of notes from his inside pocket.

'Majesties,' he began solemnly, 'Mr President of the Council of Ministers, Chiefs of the General Staff, and brother officers: in the past few years we have seen our country reach the edge of an abyss. The Fatherland is breaking up into tiny fragments, lawlessness is uncontrolled, the economy is in a disastrous state. This cannot be allowed to continue. We need a Government of National Salvation, composed of all the political parties with a strong man at its head.'

A thrill of expectation went round the hall. Was there to be a military pronunciamiento? The King and Queen remained stiffly impassive. The director of the television crew came up to Bernal and whispered urgently: 'Should we continue broadcasting this?'

'Yes, don't cut him off. But mind you broadcast the King's speech too. They may attempt to pull out the plugs when Baltasar has finished speaking.'

'It is with a heavy heart, Majesties,' the General went on, 'that I have to tell you that some of us must act to prevent the total collapse of the Spanish State, which is not months, not days, but hours away.' The audience stirred uneasily again, and the Prime Minister conferred in a whisper with the Minister of Defence. 'Let me reassure you all that we are not aiming for a military coup d'état, nor yet for a military dictatorship—after all, that would be *lèse-majesté* without Your Majesty's consent—but we demand the immediate installation of a government of concentration, which most of the political parties, even the Communist Party, have called for again and again. Only in that way can we hope to begin to tackle the problems that are bringing our country to its knees, that are causing it to wallow in the mud of immorality and the dust of dishonour.'

Another ripple went through the still orderly standing ranks.

'I call upon you all to support the King's action today, and, if he will do me the honour, to recognize in me, not a military dictator, not a new *caudillo*, but the firm head of a cabinet of lay ministers chosen for their quality from all the political parties represented in the Cortes—a true government of all the talents.'

There was a stunned silence as he finished the short speech, and Bernal glanced out of the window into the Plaza de Oriente. There he could see people starting to gather at the gates of the palace in the Calle de Bailén. He wondered whether they were MAGOS supporters come to witness the coup.

The rebellious general now resumed his former position in the front row of the assembled military, some of whom congratulated him on his speech and shook him by the hand.

What a strangely cut-off caste they were, thought Bernal. They lived and worked quite apart from the rest of the nation in their own barracks and training-grounds, with whole villages and towns for their wives and children specially built alongside, even with their own schools and colleges; they really constituted a small, privileged élite within the nation, not very different from the Bolsheviks in Soviet Russia. Nor was it a very small élite: with more than 1,300 generals and 25,000 commissioned officers commanding hundreds of thousands of conscripts in the three main services, the officer corps was larger than those of the NATO countries put together. This *flor y nata* or choice part of Spanish society had its own shops and *economatos*, its own holiday places at the seaside and in the hills, its own transport. And all of it was paid for by the State, by the ordinary tax-payers. The members of it were no different, Bernal reasoned to himself, than their medieval forebears, who had been given all those privileges in order to defend society, to form the first estate of the realm. But the last shot they had fired in anger against a foreign enemy was in North Africa in the 'twenties, and the last international war they had fought was against the United States of America in 1898, when Spain had lost Cuba. Since that time they had waged war only on about half the population of their own country, who had helped to pay for their upkeep.

Now as the King moved gravely towards the rostrum, Bernal could see and feel the tension growing. Would Don Juan Carlos approve of this pronunciamiento, the latest in a long line of such declarations that stretched back into the eighteenth century and beyond? Bernal remembered the story about Cardinal Cisneros in the early sixteenth century, who took over the government with a handful of troops. When the frightened grandees asked him by what authority he assumed power, he pointed from the balcony to the squad of soldiers below: 'There is my authority, until the prince should come!' A clear precedent for the *23-F* last year.

As the King took his place before the microphone, Bernal could see that the crowd outside was reaching large proportions, and was already spreading across the gardens in the square, and he could see many more streaming in from the Plaza de la Ópera.

Don Juan Carlos opened the text of his prepared speech, while Doña Sofía stood imperiously by his side.

'Señores: the Minister of Defence has reviewed for us the progress of the armed forces during the current year. Soon you will be entering the North Atlantic Treaty Organization and will have new opportunities to practise your arms in Europe at large in defence of the free world. The *Reales Ordenanzas* which I promulgated under the 1978 Constitution have worked well in general terms, though there have been minor local difficulties in their interpretation.' This veiled reference to the temporary takeover of the parliament building in February 1981 caused a mild titter.

The King went on: 'Our country, like all the other countries of Europe and the free world, is facing a recession, which brings many problems in its train. None of the difficulties we are suffering is unique to Spain; they all exist in greater or lesser measure in the rest of Europe.'

The television director came up to Bernal and whispered, 'We have lost power from the mains supply, but we've switched to the emergency generator in the van.'

'Continue transmitting at all costs. Resist any attempt to cut you off.'

The King went on to review the political changes that had taken place in the country since General Franco's death, and the many sacrifices made by the armed forces and the police, especially in the Basque country. Bernal watched the crowd outside grow to immense proportions. Were they all Falangists and right-wing extremists who had come at MAGOS's bidding to enforce a change of government? It already looked like the scene familiar to everyone from the annual gathering in that square on 20 November, the anniversary of Franco's death. Would they shortly produce little national flags, and yell '¡*Viva Franco! ¡Arriba España!*' and demand that General Baltasar come to the balcony?

The King now closed his morocco-leather folder, and looked round at the assembled company. 'One of you this morning, on this religious feast when we commemorate Christ's being made manifest to the Magi and the Gentiles, and reaffirm our faith in our high constitutional mission, one of you, I repeat, has called for stronger government, for a government of concentration. Let me tell you all that I took a solemn oath to serve the sovereign people of Spain and to respect their wishes. By a referendum and two general elections properly conducted they have voted for the 1978 Constitution and all that flows from it. Let me assure you now, so that there should be no doubt in your minds, that no attempt to carry out a coup d'état will be able to shield itself behind the King. It is against the King! Now perhaps you would all join us for luncheon.'

Through the first-floor window, Bernal could see that the immense crowd, perhaps 400,000 strong, had started cheering, and the front ranks had begun to unfold a long banner, which, as he soon saw, read '¡VIVA EL REY! ¡VIVA LA CONSTITUCIÓN!'

The assembled guests became aware of the noise from the square, and went to the large windows to see what was happening.

Bernal approached the royal couple. 'It would be best if you made an appearance on the balcony, Majesties, the crowd are calling for you.'

'I'll take the Prime Minister too,' said the King, 'as well as the Chiefs of Staff.'

'It would be better if you went out alone at first,' opined Bernal.

'Very well. But tell your colleagues I don't want any arrests to be made here today, do you understand? No arrests, and they'll soon calm down.'

Bernal watched as the erect and handsome figure of Don Juan Carlos strode to the now opened windows that led to the balcony overlooking the solid press of *madrileños*, who had been drawn there by the direct radio and television broadcasts of the ceremony to demonstrate their sovereign will to their sovereign. The very panes of the tall windows reverberated to the enormous cheers as the monarch appeared on the balcony, and wave upon wave of democratic chanting reached the discomforted ears of the more extreme right-wing generals inside the palace.

After the official luncheon had begun and the huge crowd had begun to disperse, Bernal conferred with the Head of Security and the King's secretary, who considered that the danger had now passed and that the JUJEM would meet later to decide what action to take against the MAGOS conspirators. Bernal sought out Lista and they made their way back to the office in the Calle de Carretas, where they found an excited Elena Fernández awaiting them.

'The Editor of *La Corneta* ordered the whole of the special issue run off at midday to be burnt, *jefe*,' she told him in a rush. 'But I managed to get three copies.'

She held up the front-page headlines for them to see. 'GENERAL BALTASAR ASSUMES POWER!' it screamed. 'KING APPROVES GOVERNMENT OF CONCENTRATION!' Below an archive photograph of the King pinning a medal on Lt-Gen. Baltasar's broad chest, were smaller pictures of a number of nineteenth-century generals who had seized power by pronunci-amiento, and a prominent one of General Franco.

'We'll send one copy to the King's secretary as a mem-ento,' said Bernal. 'Where is the Editor now?'

'He left in a hurry, after getting his secretary to shred the contents of his private filing cabinet. The Marqués de la Estrella came at 2.0 p.m. in his chauffeur-driven Mercedes limousine to pick him up and they drove away at high speed.'

'Is there any news of Hermann Malthius, Paco?' Bernal asked.

'His private plane left Barajas airport half an hour ago,' Navarro reported. 'The flight plan notified to the authorities was for Paris.'

'And Father Gaspar, is there any word?'

'He took the Europa Express from Chamartín station; the plainclothesman who followed him to the booking-office says that he took a first-class single to Cologne, via Paris.'

'It's all collapsed, then; the King knew them better than we realized.'

Varga now came in with a preliminary report on the rifle Bernal and Miranda had found at the Palacio de Oriente.

'It's definitely human blood, *jefe*; I've done the leuco-malachite test as a preliminary check. The hæmatologist will run more sophisticated tests to see if it matches Brother Nicolás's blood-print. The hairs lodged on the stock of the rifle are certainly similar to those of the late monk, and they are definitely head-hair, but hair-matching is not as conclusive as a blood-print, as you know. Otherwise there are only some blurred glove-prints, and Miranda's dabs on the barrel, of course.'

'And whose rifle was it, do we know, Paco?' asked Bernal. 'I'd give a lot to bring the good brother's killer to judgement.'

'The artillery regiment's supplies depôt informs us that it was issued to Captain Lebrija Russell for training purposes, seven years ago.'

'But Lebrija died, presumably by accident when trying to dynamite the power cable, almost a week before Brother Nicolás was murdered!' exclaimed Bernal. 'So who wielded it? It must have been the soldier who took it to this morning's ceremony at the palace. Almost certainly it was someone who was under Lebrija's command, perhaps the person who accompanied him on the fateful mission to San Ildefonso. Our only chance is to ask the palace authorities if any of the troops complained that his rifle was missing when the guard left at lunch-time. I don't for a moment suppose that the guilty man did so. They'll have tricked us at the last.'

*

When Bernal got home, disgruntled at having discovered that no one had asked the palace lackeys for a missing rifle, and upset that he could not placate Brother Nicolas's ghost by bringing to justice the perpetrator of the crime that the missal included among those that cried out to Heaven for vengeance, he was surprised to find his entire family *en fiesta*.

Eugenia and his daughter-in-law were busy in the kitchen preparing the spider-crab *paella*, while his two sons were opening bottles of Codorniu Black label.

'I decided that we should have the usual Christmas lunch at Epiphany, Luis,' said Eugenia, 'since we were prevented from having it at the right time. I hope you've got a good appetite.'

'¡ *Yayo!* ¡*yayo!*' yelled his grandson excitedly. 'Come and help Quico finish making the *belén*. Where do I put the Three Kings of Orient? Among the animals?'

'That's rather a good place for them, Quico. They'll be quite happy there.'

As he was dragged off by the highly contented child to the dining-room to see all the presents that the *reyes* had brought, Bernal saw the beginning of the *telediario* on the old black-and-white television set. The cameras were panning the dense crowds in the Plaza de Oriente three hours earlier and showing Don Juan Carlos de Borbón y Borbón on the main balcony waving to his loyal subjects. Old republican that he was, Bernal could not help recalling what Talleyrand was reputed to have said about the Bourbons: '*Ils n'ont rien appris, ni rien oublié.*' Now he had to admit that the only reigning Bourbon in the modern world had learned something important in a very short time: that no internal political or military faction could easily defeat a firm alliance between a constitutional monarchy and the people.

THE END

DEC 2 2 2001	DATE DUE		
JUL 2 8 2003			